Holymoly

by Heide Goody and Iain Grant

Pigeon Park Press

Published by Pigeon Park Press
www.pigeonparkpress.com

A long, long time ago

A kick in the shins and suddenly he had legs.

A stomp on the belly and, at once, he had a body, a torso, arms.

A bigger hoof-strike to the head and he had a face. He had a mouth and eyes. He had a brain.

He opened his eyes.

Satan looked down at him like something he had just scraped from the bottom of his hoofs. He *was* something Satan had just scraped from the bottom of his hoofs.

"Get up, Rutspud. You've got work to do," said Satan and moved on.

Rutspud got up, brushing rock and crud from his newly-formed body. His arms were spindly, weedy things, but Satan had given him one hell of a kick to the head. He had a nice big head, big eyes, big ears, a big brain. Rutspud had come into existence a clever demon.

One hell of a kick...

Ninety percent of Hell could be divided into three parts: things that were on fire, things that were screaming and things that were both on fire and screaming. The other ten percent was made up of demons and rocks. Rutspud guessed the rocks were just there to provide some landmarks among all the fire and screaming.

To his left, Satan kicked another demon from the earth. To his right, a row of fresh demons looked at each other with the expressions of conscripts who had definitely not signed up for *this*.

A purple demon came down the row, pushing himself along in a wheeled contraption. He handed spiky implements to each demon in turn. Belphegor, thought Rutspud. The demon's name was Belphegor. Knowledge was expanding unbidden in Rutspud's brain, boxes of knowledge, boxes containing other boxes –

unfolding and unpacking in the vacant space of Rutspud's brain like new tenants moving into surprisingly-roomy accommodation.

"This is your pitchfork," recited Belphegor, loud and clear for all to hear. "There are many like it but this one is yours. Your pitchfork is your best friend. Without you, your pitchfork is useless. Without your pitchfork, you are useless. What counts is not the jabs you make, the sound of the screams or the blood you spill. It is the suffering that counts..."

Belphegor shoved a pitchfork into Rutspud's hands. It was short, weighty and covered in a black crust that might have been rust, might have been dried blood.

"What do I do with this?" said Rutspud.

Belphegor's squat vehicle wheeled round to face him. The demon lord's nostrils flared, great grey whiskers quivering.

"If you can't work that out, I don't think I have much use for you."

Rutspud looked at the pitchfork, looked at Belphegor, looked at the writhing sea of torment that was Hell. He raised his pitchfork and, with a battle yell, charged into the flames with no plan but making Hell a worse place than he'd found it.

Twenty-something years ago

"I'm just saying, I don't think Hell's like that," said Lennox.

"Oh, and you'd know, would you?" said Stephen.

There were four bikes on the grass just outside the Short Heath Park playground: two mountain bikes, a racing bike and a strange pink thing with a wide basket on the front. Most of the bikes were too small for their owners. The owners were in their mid-teens and bikes were a childhood thing; there wouldn't be any more bikes.

Ed held up a card. "*Shandor, the Mind Flayer*. Extremely rare."

"How much do you want for it?" said Darren.

"Ten quid," said Ed.

"Sounds like a bargain. Not," said Lennox.

"Take a chill pill, Len," said Ed. "I'm not selling to you."

Stephen nudged Darren. "You're not seriously thinking about it."

"I'm thinking, I'm thinking," said Darren.

The four boys sat in a row on the swings. The swings were definitely too small for them, but it was gone nine at night, it was dark, and the playground was theirs. This was their kingdom and they were kings unless a local resident told them to piss off or Nigel Herring's gang scared them away.

Nigel Herring was the current bane of their lives. He had been a schoolyard irritant until the summer just gone. Just before school broke up for the summer, Nigel had been kicked out of St Michael's scouts by old scout master Chivers – allegedly for doing something unspecified and unspeakable to a hamster. Because the unholy offence was unspecified, the teenage rumour-mill went into overdrive and Nigel became in quick succession the laughing stock of the school and the most capriciously violent thug in the area.

While Ed tried to sell Darren cards from the *Mana Clash* collectible card game for five times their true value, Stephen and Lennox pored over the *Infernal Adventures* roleplaying expansion book in the orange light of the nearest streetlamp.

"It just doesn't sound very... hellish," said Lennox. "What did it say about the demon lord Asmondius?"

Stephen read from the roleplaying manual. "Asmondius (level 30 fiend) is lord of the Dread Castle of P'tang, which he won from the Celestial gods as part of the Ancient Accord. He is commander of the Baantu demon army. He rules with his consort, the demoness Benzadine, and their daughter, Glyphanda. Unbeknownst to Asmondius, Glyphanda is betrothed to the demigod Kelemvor, to whom she gave the Crystal Shard to use in the battle of Baylon's Gate."

Lennox shrugged dismissively. "See, man? It's all just so petty."

"Petty bourgeois?" said Stephen.

Ed sniggered. Lennox had spent the previous school term describing everything he disagreed with as petty bourgeois. Stephen didn't really know what the phrase meant. He suspected Lennox didn't either.

"Just petty," said Lennox. "Change the names, it could be a storyline from Eastenders."

"He's right," said Darren.

"*You* bought this book!" said Stephen. "This is twelve ninety-nine of *your* cash."

"We need it for the campaign," said Darren. "Mirrorglim and his band of acolytes are on a quest to the sixth circle of Hell."

"Twelve ninety-nine on this and – How many cards are you buying off him?"

Darren had a dozen cards or more resting against his chubby belly.

"They're all really good ones," he said.

"You know, he steals them from his uncle," said Stephen.

"You have no evidence," said Ed. "Let's say twenty quid the lot, Daz."

Darren nodded reluctantly, as though buying *Mana Clash* cards was an addiction he was forced to feed (which it was) and reached into his pocket. Stephen stared.

"You have twenty pounds?"

Lennox leaned to look round Stephen to witness the appearance of the cash. Stephen wondered if it would be an actual twenty pound note. He'd rarely seen them before, never owned one. Money, in Stephen's life, meant coins. He got paid for his weekly paper round in coins. Paper money was something that appeared at birthdays and Christmases, grubby grey-and-red fivers tucked into cards, the blank stare of the Duke of Wellington promising a bag of Woolies pick'n'mix, a horror novel from WH Smiths, a bag of gaming dice and change for the bus home.

"Frig me!"

They watched in wonder as the twenty pound note emerged. Darren unfolded it nonchalantly.

"I will remember this moment forever," said Stephen.

"Who's it got on it?" said Lennox.

"William Shakespeare," said Darren.

Stephen peered. "Leaning against a pillar or something. He looks like he's wondering something."

"Wondering how the hell Darren Pottersmore got hold of a twenty," said Lennox.

They all knew that Darren got a ton of pocket money. That's why Darren was a constant supplier of roleplaying supplements, comic books and sweets. There were a lot of sweets in Darren's life – sweets and cakes and cones of chips from the chippy – and he didn't share them all. The evidence was mounting up around his midriff. There was only his mum at home and Stephen had no idea why Darren was so lucky in the pocket money stakes. Maybe that's what happened when your dad abandoned you and shacked up with a strumpet from Kingstanding. Stephen had always wanted to ask but wasn't sure how you phrased such a question.

Lennox received two quid a week pocket money, but Ed was like Stephen; neither of them got pocket money but had to take on part-time jobs if they wanted cash. Stephen had his paper round. Ed had his Saturday job in his uncle's shop.

"Thank you," said Ed, snatching the twenty from Darren's hand. "A pleasure doing business with you, sir."

Ed folded the note up and it vanished inside his army surplus jacket. Stephen wondered what else was concealed in that coat. It was common knowledge among the group that Ed stole from his uncle's shop. It was one of those shops that had started out as an ironmonger's decades ago and, as the bottom fell out of each market, shifted partially into a succession of equally-precarious niches. Ed's uncle currently sold football stickers, card games, Airfix plane models, sewing machines, metal detectors and pet fish. He even rented out videos.

Ed was a distilled, walking version of that shop, pockets stuffed with all manner of crap that you might just want but probably didn't. Stephen's mum had called Ed a spiv. Stephen had gone to the library to look the word up and she was right.

It was funny really. Their one common interest was fantasy roleplaying games, a hobby built entirely on the premise that you could pretend to be someone other than yourself for a few hours. And yet, Ed was always the thief of the group.

Tall, broad-shouldered Lennox was the fighter of the group, though they'd never seen him raise his fists in real life – maybe because he never had to.

Pale, indoorsy Darren was the magic user. He definitely had an interest in the occult. His reading tastes were sliding more and more towards the Denis Wheatleys and the HP Lovecrafts. Darren had even come into school with a 'tattoo pentagram' drawn on his arm in biro until someone told him pentagrams have five points and he was actually sporting a Star of David.

Stephen wasn't so sure if the same ironies applied to him. Did he always play characters who were secretly him? Mostly he was the Games Master, guiding Mr E Thief, Nox the Destroyer, and Mirrorglim the Mage through their fantasy campaigns. His own character was a cleric. They were tougher than mages; they were absolute tanks against demons and the undead; and they were healers, the glue that bound the group together. He supposed he did have a certain monkish bookishness about him. He certainly liked reading and had been complimented on his fine penmanship...

Stephen flicked back through the *Infernal Adventures* book.

"So, we're playing this Friday," he said. "At yours, Darren?"

They always played at Darren's. He had a big attic bedroom and his mum kept them supplied with squash, biscuits and the occasional plate of Findus crispy pancakes.

"Um," said Lennox heavily. "I might not be able to make it."

"Why not?" said Darren.

"I'm off out."

Lennox's parents ran a pub. They never went out, with or without their son.

"Out?" said Stephen. "Out where? It's Friday night. It's roleplaying night."

"I'm off to the cinema. Going to see that *Hunt for Red October*."

Stephen frowned, uncomprehending. They'd all seen that film the week before.

"With Bianca Turney," said Lennox.

Stephen was gobsmacked.

"You're fobbing us off to go out with a *girl*?" said Darren.

"Er, yeah."

Stephen was aware of a yawning gulf of unspoken conversations opening in front of them. As a group, they were definitely 'late developers' and girls were not yet part of their world. Stephen was aware of the general mechanics of, you know, *that*. There'd been a very helpful TV programme shown in a science lesson once and some even more instructive peeks behind the curtain in the specialist section of Ed's uncle's video rental. By and large though, the world of girls was a mystery to him – and a mostly uninteresting mystery. But Lennox had always been taller, more confident and indefinably more mature-looking than the rest of them (and that foul fiend, acne, had completely ignored him, which was simply unfair). If anyone was going to betray the group to chase girls, it would be Lennox.

"Bianca?" said Ed.

"Yeah," said Lennox.

"She's got that blonde friend, Tina."

"The one who'll snog any boy who'll give her a packet of Frazzles," nodded Lennox.

9

"You think you could put a good word in for me? Maybe make it a double date."

"You too!" cried Darren in despair.

Across the dark park, a light came on in a nearby house.

"You wouldn't understand," said Ed.

"Wouldn't I?" said Darren.

"I mean, you ride a girl's bike for one."

"It's not!"

"It's got a basket on the front."

"It's a post bike. Used to be my dad's."

"It's pink!"

"It faded!"

"I think it's all just disappointing," said Stephen, closing the book sniffily. "I expected better of you two."

"One day, when your balls drop, you might understand," said Ed.

"My balls have dropped!"

"Do you want to say that again but louder?" smiled Lennox.

Stephen pushed himself off the swing, partly because he was angry and partly because it was hard to argue about your maturity whilst squashed into a child's swing.

"My... equipment is perfectly as it should be, thank you, Edward. I could get a girlfriend if I wanted to, but I don't. Do you know why? I'll tell you. It's because there are more important things than girls – things like friendship, like commitment, and rolling a d20 critical against a level six troll."

"There speaks the eternal virgin," said Ed.

Lennox gave a neutral shrug that wasn't quite neutral enough for Stephen's liking.

"That's why you're always the priest of the party," said Ed. "Because you're gonna spend the rest of your life with your nose in a book, spouting high and mighty principles and only using your todger to write your name in the snow."

Stephen turned his back rather than say something he'd regret. His breath misted in the night air, turning orange in the street light. It was getting late. It was getting cold.

"I can never write my name in the snow," said Darren. "It's the 'r's. They're too fiddly."

Five years ago

These weren't normal stairs, thought Rutspud. None of the other spiral staircases in Hell circled clockwise and anti-clockwise *at the same time*. He looked up and found himself staring *down* into an infinite abyss of concentric spirals. He tried backing down the stairs and found himself climbing higher and higher.

He gasped, he swore, and he cursed the infernal designer he suspected was responsible, but still he climbed.

And he found himself in a tunnel. Not the normal, mostly molten-red type of tunnel he was used to, but a simple tunnel of grey stone which led onto a smooth-walled corridor which was brightly lit and garishly painted. There was carpet. Rutspud didn't like carpet.

"Satan's balls!" he moaned. This was not right.

He was turning to run back to the stairs when his attention was drawn to a large book open on the table next to him. It was written in Latin, the language of the priesthood and, thus, of many of Hell's residents. Rutspud looked at the open page and gave a small gasp of surprise as he read what was written there.

The demon, Rutspud, is seen as a soldier, all in red with the horns of a young goat. He is a cruel demon, a torturer who delights in the work of his hands...

Intrigued, Rutspud climbed onto the chair to read. There was a crumpled paper bag next to the book. He peered inside and saw a mass of tiny human effigies, red and green and yellow and black. They were covered in a fine white powder. Rutspud took one of the little effigies out of the bag. He'd never smelled anything like it before. He licked it then bit off its head. It tasted of jellified skin and bones with an only mildly off-putting hint of fruit. He chomped down the rest of it.

He took out another and gave its simple face a stern glare.

"Tremble little mortal, I am Rutspud, devourer of souls, scourger of sins," he said and popped it in his mouth. The unpleasant fruitiness was stronger in this one, but the overall experience was still worthwhile. He chewed and continued reading.

As he turned a page, he became aware that he was being watched. He looked up. There was a human in the doorway. Male or female? He couldn't tell (it was a weakness of his). Possibly a female, judging by its long dress. Rutspud ate another chewy person while he thought about it.

"No!" yelled the human. "How dare you! Those were for Brother Bernard! You can't just eat them now he's dead."

"Who's dead?" said Rutspud.

"Brother Bernard."

Rutspud shrugged. "Show me someone round here who isn't."

The human was nonplussed. "Am I dead?"

"Well, you're in Hell, so –"

"No, I'm not."

"What?" said Rutspud

"We're in St Cadfan's and you're trespassing!"

"This is earth?" Rutspud stood in surprise.

"Oh, God," said the human. "You can stand. You're real."

"Of course, I'm real."

"And, you... You're a demon! Are you a demon?"

"I'm in your book, madam," he said, pointing at the page.

"I'm not a madam. I'm a man."

"But the dress?"

"I'm a monk and you, you..."

The man ran to a shelf and searched frantically. "Dammit!" he said, clearly unable to find what he was looking for. "Right. Here goes, demon. I command you, unclean spirit, by the mysteries of the incarnation, passion, resurrection and ascension of our Lord Jesus Christ, by the descent of the Holy Spirit, by the coming of ... something or other. I command you to obey me to the letter. You shall not be emboldened to harm in any way this creature of God or –"

"What creature of God?"

"Bugger! You're not possessing anyone, are you? You're just ... there."

The man made the sign of the cross. There was a sudden twinge of pain in Rutspud's stomach.

"I cast you out, unclean spirit," the man shouted, "along with every Satanic power of the enemy, every spectre from Hell and all your fell companions, in the name of our Lord Jesus Christ. Begone! Go on now, go! Walk out the door! Just turn around now, 'cause you're not welcome anymore."

The pain in Rutspud's belly grew and grew. He curled up on the floor.

"That really hurts!" he grunted.

"Really?"

There was an unexpected trumpet of wind from Rutspud's anus. "Beelzebub's beard! Did you do that?"

"I might have done," said the man, wafting the smell away.

"Well, don't! You've given me a really bad tummy ache. What did you do that for?"

The man was unsure.

"To be honest, I don't really know. Instinct." He plonked himself down in a chair, bemused and defeated. "So, what are you going to do to me?"

Rutspud shrugged and farted again. It was a good question.

A few weeks ago

"Another jelly baby?" offered Brother Stephen.

"Do I ever say no?" replied Rutspud.

Stephen thought about it. "I don't believe you do."

Rutspud rootled around in the bag noisily while Stephen flipped through the book he'd bought that morning on the mainland.

"You've always got your nose in a book," said Rutspud.

"This is a library," Stephen pointed out.

This room, this space, was Stephen's home. Yes, the windblown and rainswept Welsh island of Bardsey was his home and, yes, the monastery of St Cadfan's was his home, but within the monastery itself – actually, slightly underneath it too as he was now in the cellars – the library was his real home. This was where the hermit-like snail of a man could curl up in the protective shell of the ancient holy house and be at one with himself. And his books.

"I'm trying to find something," said Stephen.

"Ah, studying the mysteries of the universe, divining the truth in some esoteric text."

"Sort of," said Stephen and showed him the cover.

"*Infernal Adventures* roleplaying expansion," said Rutspud.

"I found it in the charity shop in Aberdaron. Fifty pee. I couldn't believe it."

"Expensive, huh?"

Stephen gave the demon a look. Rutspud was an intelligent demon, whip smart, but there were many nuances of life and language that he failed to grasp.

"My friend, Darren Pottersmore, used to have a copy of this book when we were kids. We were big into roleplaying, the ol' *Dungeons and Dragons* thing, except we were more into *GURPS*, *MERP*, *Searchers of the Unknown*, a little *AD&D* on the side (second edition, of course)."

15

"Am I meant to be able to understand any of these words?" said Rutspud.

Stephen shook his head, feeling the warmth of personal nostalgia.

"My mates always said I'd turn out to be a monk. Ha! Well, a cleric. Had an eighth-level cleric character, Clarence Bodkin. Great times. Great adventures. Last I heard, Darren had become a Satanist or something equally ludicrous. Parting of the ways, I guess. Anyway, I saw this in the charity shop and I thought, why not? Also, I remembered there's an illustration in here of a demon lord that looks just like your friend Belphegor..."

He continued to flick through the pages, revelling in a memory brought back to life, the look of the book, the very smell of the thing.

"Stephen," said Rutspud.

"Yes, yes. Have another. Finish the packet."

"It's not that. There's this thing that's come up –"

"But, just saying, when the jelly babies are gone, they're gone. Colin the boatman isn't bringing fresh supplies for another two weeks." He paused and looked up from the book. "You were only up here two days ago. I wasn't expecting you until the weekend."

"Yeah, that's the thing," said Rutspud. "I've got to go away for a bit."

That sounded ominous. "Are you in trouble with Hell?"

"No more than usual. No, it's a mission."

"Oh?"

"To earth."

"Oh. As in...?"

"Earth. Yeah. I'm being partnered up with Joan of Arc."

"*The* Joan of Arc?"

"Teenager. Funky haircut. Likes to wave a sword about. I think there's only one."

"But she's one of the good gu– I mean, one of the other lot."

Rutspud's eyes twinkled. "Yeah, it's a 'wunza' thing. Clichéd, I know."

"Wunza?" said Stephen.

"Yeah." Rutspud put on a deep, cinema trailer voice. "Wunza teenage saint from the Celestial City. Wunza demon from the sixth

16

circle of Hell. Together, they fight crime and learn some heart-warming lesson or other along the way."

"You're fighting crime?"

"No," tutted Rutspud. "I was pretending that..." He sighed. "I just came to say goodbye."

Stephen felt an odd sensation, one he rarely got the opportunity to experience. It was jealousy.

"I thought we had a 'wunza' thing going on."

"Huh?"

"Wunza mild-mannered monk. Wunza cunning demon. Together they..." He mentally scrabbled around for something.

"Read old books and eat jelly babies?" said Rutspud.

"We do more than that. We... we're watching *Breaking Bad* together, aren't we?"

"We play darts," added Rutspud.

"We did it once. You put your back out," said Stephen.

"I've not got the upper body strength for sports."

"But we'll find something else."

"We could be meth cooks," said Rutspud.

"We're not being meth cooks."

"Spoilsport."

"We should never have started watching that TV show."

"I tell you, a monastery is perfect cover. No one will suspect us," grinned Rutspud.

Stephen couldn't help smiling, even as he shook his head.

"I'm going to miss you."

Rutspud pointed a finger at him. "Don't you dare try to hug me."

When he'd first lain eyes on Rutspud, all those years ago, Stephen thought the demon looked like a muppet – a muppet constructed by someone who wanted to give kids nightmares and didn't expect to stay long in the muppet-making business, but a muppet nonetheless. Rutspud wasn't the most huggable-looking of creatures, but he was Stephen's best friend.

"It's a dangerous world out there," said Stephen.

"It won't be my first time on earth," said Rutspud, waggling his eyebrows (or at least the nubs of flesh where eyebrows would have been) to indicate the world about them.

17

"The rest of the world is not like Bardsey," said Stephen. "Trust me."

Rutspud snorted. "What's the worst that can happen? I'm a demon. I'm immortal."

"There's worse things than death," said Stephen.

"Yeah, that's right," said Rutspud. "Say something cheery before I go."

Sunday

Rutspud sat with Joan of Arc in the Boldmere Oak, sipping his white wine spritzer. It tasted like fizzy urine. He liked it a lot. His recent adventures with Joan had opened their eyes to a great many new experiences, not all of them typical here on earth. Heaven had given the human participants a memory makeover and now Joan and Rutspud were among the very few witnesses who remembered the rise and fall of a breakaway nation centred on this very pub. Hooflandia had been the scene of the famous (and now forgotten) nun battle, and only a short way down the road he and Joan had dressed as schoolchildren for reasons they still didn't fully understand. Rutspud's favourite memory was the bizarre experience of seeing (and hearing) a sex party get interrupted by a computer hacker who played a tune by taking control of the couples' (and thruples') Bluetooth buttplugs. He would mention this new form of torture to Belphegor, when he was back in the office.

"We make quite a team," Joan said.

"Indeed, we do," said Rutspud.

"But..."

"It will be good to get back home," he said, firmly. "I've had enough of earth for now."

"Amen to that," she replied and clinked her pint against his smaller glass.

A sharp wind sprung up.

"Someone shut the door," said Rutspud, a half smile on his face as he turned to look round.

The pub door was shut.

"That's odd," said Joan.

Rutspud realised that this sudden gale had him at its very centre. Joan stared as she reached the same conclusion.

"Is this Hell's doing?" she said.

The tornado closed in around him, snatching his spritzer from his hand and smashing it loudly against the wall. Everything lost focus. He thought he saw Joan reach forward to grab him. Was that her voice?

"Rutspud!"

"Satan help me!" he shouted.

He could see nothing now. An indistinct and very unpleasant blur filled his vision.

"God, even!" his fading voice cried. "I'm not picky..."

The winds tore at Rutspud's body, forcing rude noises from the folds of skin around his saggier bits. If he wasn't being so discombobulated by the experience, he might have taken a moment to enjoy the flatulence of his bingo wings and thigh flaps. As it was, he was struggling to cope with up and down swapping directions (not to mention near and far, inside and outside, and me and not-me). The human world was still there, beyond the walls of the tornado, but it was smearing like a wet painting in a centrifuge. He battled against the wind that circled him but stormy ribbons of pink, blue and grey held him in.

At his feet, he saw the walls of the cyclone funnel down to a tiny pinpoint of light. Rutspud wasn't much of an academic but he knew a singularity when he saw one. They had one in the Pit of Puffed Up Egomaniacs. The demon lads who manned it called it 'the sausage machine'. Puffed up egomaniacs went in one end, monomolecular strands of human meat came out the other. It was fascinating to watch, but Rutspud had very little desire to experience it first-hand.

He twisted, trying to pivot away, but the singularity pulled at him with irresistible gravity. His feet became lead weights, stretching his legs like pulled elastic. He looked down – or up? – at them. They'd become as thin and taut as garrotting wire. As his head bent forward, gravity caught the tips of his huge ears and dragged them in.

"Oooergh," he moaned. "I do not feel good."

Then the crushing pull snagged his lips and tongue, and he was unable to make any sound except incoherent and increasingly-surprised wails.

Rutspud saw a bright light, retina-burning bright. And then it vanished – or burned his retinas out (it was impossible to know).

Rutspud screamed again.

Brother Stephen sat bolt upright with a gasp.

On television programmes, people waking from terrible dreams sat bolt upright and gasped, perhaps with sweat on their brow and a wide-eyed terror on their face. In real life, people woke up from nightmares as quietly and slowly as from any other dream. They might stare, blinking for a while. Some might instantly forget their nightmares and wonder what on earth they were doing awake at three in the morning. Others might remember the feeling of terror and question if it was the result of too many cheesy snacks or late-night horror movies. Yet others might remember an image from their dream, find something truly horrible or disturbing in it, and seek solace in cheesy snacks and late-night horror movies.

In real life, people did not wake from a nightmare and sit bolt upright. Stephen knew at once that his had been no normal dream. It had had an undeniable verisimilitude. Also, there was now a demon in a steam-powered wheelchair at the end of his bed.

"Belphegor?" whispered Stephen.

Silently, the demon backed his chair through the open door of the dormitory and sped away down the corridor.

Stephen glanced about to see if any of his fellow monks had also seen the demon, but they all lay still in their beds, silent but for the gentle grunts, snores and other nocturnal noises any group of sleeping men will produce. Stephen slipped out of bed, picked up his habit, and tiptoed into the corridor.

He found Belphegor in the locutory – a room which, in times gone by, had been the only place the monks were allowed to speak with each other. These days, it was where the monastery computers were housed and it also hosted, on a weekly rota, Brother Manfred's hot yoga sessions, Brother Henry's mime practice, Father Eustace's banjo recitals and anything else their tiny community decided needed containing and confining. Monks were a tolerant and forgiving lot, but even they had limits.

Belphegor held up a novelty toadstool from Bavaria that Manfred said was the gaze point for his *drishti*. Nobody had ever dared question what that was. "What is the purpose of this thing?"

"I had a dream," said Stephen, tying his rope belt.

Belphegor put the toadstool down and rotated in his chair. Stephen knew that Belphegor was a prince or duke of Hell or some such. He had the appearance of a giant, liver-spotted, glasses-wearing prune with limbs barely long enough to manage the controls of his motorised commode. He wouldn't have looked out of place among the lords and dukes in the British parliament.

"Rutspud is gone," said Belphegor.

"Gone where?" said Stephen. He tried to recall his dream. "There was darkness and he was falling. And he cried out to me."

Belphegor mulched his lips in cogitation. "Some theorise that a demon summoned through a Mephistophelean Bridge momentarily enters an aleph-like state and is, in that instant, able to reach out to any place and time."

"He spoke to me in my dreams?" said Stephen and then realised he was missing a bigger point. "Sorry? You said, summoned?"

"I did," said Belphegor. "Guess why."

"Rutspud has been summoned? As in... *summoned*? As in black candles and pentagrams and people in robes chanting badly-translated Latin?"

Belphegor nodded. His round, purple head sat necklessly on his round, purple body; nodding was the wobbling of one blob atop another.

Stephen blinked rapidly to wake himself. It wasn't enough, so he slapped his cheeks.

There was a *demon* in the locutory of St Cadfan's. There was a *demon* in the monastery.

This was less surprising than it perhaps should have been. Stephen's best friend was a demon. He'd also previously discovered that there'd been far more traffic between Hell and St Cadfan's than the church would approve of. Demons in the monastery were not a new thing.

Nonetheless, there was a *lord of Hell* in St Cadfan's, one of the most powerful beings in creation (and a notionally evil one, at that). And yet... Belphegor was on enemy territory, he was dangerous but out of his realm – like a tiger in a ball pool.

Questions shoved and jostled in Stephen's brain. Once he had them in order, he knew the answers. But he asked anyway.

"What's going to happen to him?"

"Nothing good," said Belphegor.

"What's Hell going to do about it?"

"Nothing."

"So, why tell me?" asked Stephen.

"Because you might want to do something about it."

Belphegor's motorised chair puttered back. He touched a pair of white gloves and a beret on a desk.

"You have mimes in this place?"

"Brother Henry," said Stephen.

"Ah. Then we look forward to welcoming him to the Theatre of Tedious Arts when it's his time. We have a large performing company – bagpipers, morris men, ballet dancers. They all perform at the same time. We call it fusion theatre. Its main advantage is that everyone hates all of it equally."

Stephen shook with impatience. "You have to explain to me what's going on."

"Have to?" Belphegor smiled. It was a frightening smile. Stephen knew his own emotions were composed mostly of fear, but now he felt fear for his friend, a feeling that was next-door-neighbours with anger.

"Explain," he said.

"Very well. In a moment of infernal uncertainty, as he returned to Hell from a recent mission to earth, Rutspud was summoned by the Rite of Ukahdo. We lose lesser demons to ritual summonings on a regular basis and, like cheap fairground goldfish, they are usually destroyed or returned to us in short order. But Rutspud is, unfortunately, too clever."

"Too clever?"

"Knowledge is power, monk. Power is useful. Anyone capable of the Rite of Ukahdo is no novice and will recognise what they have caught. They will keep Rutspud until he is utterly spent. It's a tragic loss to Hell's Infernal Innovation team. He recently invented this marvellous thing called a mankini. We insist that fashion bullies put one on as soon as they arrive."

"I think that was invented by Borat," said Stephen.

"You see? A great adaptor. A wonderful thief of ideas."

"But Hell won't send a rescue mission," said Stephen coldly.

"Of course not. It's an embarrassment. He's a soldier behind enemy lines. And, before you even suggest it, we're not going to ask the Upstairs lot for help either. That would be even more embarrassing. The powers that be refuse to acknowledge that this incident has happened."

"But you're one of those powers."

"I'm not the *right* power."

"But you can do something, surely."

"I am," said Belphegor pointedly. "I'm telling you."

Stephen huffed, tried to find a still centre and nodded.

"Okay, Lord Belphegor. Then what do I do?"

"Find him. Free him. Bring him home."

"But where is he?"

Belphegor made to shrug but didn't really have the shoulders for it.

"In theory, he could be anywhere, but the rite would have had an exponentially greater chance of success the closer the summoning circle was to Rutspud's last location on earth."

"Which was?"

"The city of Birmingham. A place called Sutton Coldfield. Heard of it?"

"My old hometown," sighed Stephen.

"Excellent," said Belphegor. "Then you should get onto it at once."

"But what do I do when I get there?" said Stephen. "How do I find him?"

Belphegor's nostrils flared, great grey whiskers quivering.

"If you can't work that out," he said as he wheeled past Stephen and towards the door, "I don't think I have much use for you."

Monday

Rutspud woke.

This was an unusual event in itself, as demons did not sleep. Sleep was a human thing, the brain's way of trying to put the chaos and madness of the day into some sort of order and file it neatly away. Demons, on the other hand, knew there was no order to the chaos and madness, and they were just peachy about that.

Rutspud groaned. Now he knew: being fed through a singularity felt like being beaten head to toe with a tenderising mallet. Or a one-hour Zumba class (an experience for which he had yet to forgive Stephen).

He sat up.

He was on a rough stone floor. No, not stone, he realised. It was too flat. Concrete. By the light of the naked bulb directly above him, he could see that the nearest walls were made of red brick and mortar. The furthest walls were hidden in darkness. There was concrete in Hell – management liked it for its business-like quality, its modern brutalist aesthetic and because it was handy for entombing the damned – but Hell really didn't go in for red brick. Despite its hellish colour, it was too darn folksy and nice.

"Earth then," he said.

He stood and went to look for an exit. He had not got more than a stride and a half before he stopped. He hadn't meant to stop. He tried again. He stopped again. There was a white circle on the floor around him, surrounded by letters, symbols, hierograms and other assorted squiggles.

"Aw, crap," he muttered and instinctively tried to step out of it again. He couldn't.

He didn't hit an invisible barrier. It wasn't like trying to wade into treacle. It didn't give him an electric shock, perhaps accompanied by some cheap, sparky special effect. It was simply that as his legs attempted to cross the circle, they seemed to forget what they had been told to do and went back to a default 'stand' setting.

"Nice circle that one," said a voice. "S'got a good girth to it. You don't get a decent girth with a lot of circles these days."

Two red eyes looked at Rutspud out of the darkness.

"Where am I?" said Rutspud.

"In a circle," said the voice. "Last time I was in a circle like that must've been in, oooh, seventy-six. Bunch of Swiss diabolists. Say what you like about the Swiss, they can engineer a precision circle. Course they went for the traditional chalk. Hand-crafted. Natural craftsman your actual Swiss, i'n' he? You got yourself a stencil and paint job there. No individualism but what you've got there is durability. Rite of Ukahdo. Quality. That's a circle as'll last a hundred years."

"Where am I?" Rutspud repeated.

A light came on at the far end of the room. There was another circle, similar to Rutspud's but not the same. At the centre was a demon, just a mite smaller than Rutspud. It had a shock of yellow hair and a set of over-sized teeth that wouldn't have looked out of place on a rodent.

"Reckon you've got a good foot more diameter than me," said the demon. "You'll feel the benefit of those extra inches, trust me."

Whatever difference in diameter there was between their two circles, Rutspud couldn't help but notice that the other demon's circle contained a reclining armchair, a short table, a little reading lamp, a coffee mug, a stack of what appeared to be *Heat* magazines and an ashtray. The demon looked very much at home.

With the lamp on, Rutspud could now see they were in a room without doors or windows. Solid brick walls all the way round. There was a flight of stairs in the corner leading up into darkness.

"A cellar," said Rutspud.

"Yeah, you get to spend a lot of time in cellars if you're a seasoned summonee," said the demon. "Still, I reckon if you want a break, get away from it all, a little holiday in a cellar's just the ticket."

Rutspud gave him a funny look. "Holiday?"

"So, where you from?" said the demon.

"Eh?"

"Name's Shafttoe. Third circle. Work mostly with gluttons. Not easy work but at least they're easy to catch."

Rutspud nodded warily. "Rutspud. Sixth circle. Infernal Innovation team."

"Ah, mucking about, making stuff," said Shafttoe. "S'a living, I suppose. Not proper work like donut-shovelling or fat-poking but I guess someone's got to do it, eh?"

Rutspud walked to the edge of his circle.

"You said this was a holiday."

"Yes, my friend," said Shafttoe, stretching out on his recliner. "Do it regular, me. They've had to go for the full Ukahdo to get you. Poor old Shafttoe, I'll turn up for a simple Abramelin ritual. Not fussy. This has got to be my twenty-second – no, twenty-third – summoning."

"I don't understand," said Rutspud, irritated because understanding stuff was very much his thing. "You chose to be here?"

"Not chose as such. You gotta take these things as they come. All I'm saying is I don't put up a fight when it happens. I reach out, feel the tug and let it take me." The demon grinned contentedly, teeth like a row of gleaming fridge-freezers. "What I'm really saying, Rutspud, is you're gonna be here for a while, so kick back and relax. You're on holiday."

Brother Manfred seemed concerned by Stephen's request. Manfred was the prior of St Cadfan's and, notionally, second in command. The abbot, Father Eustace, spent his days in contemplation of matters beyond the mundane and was, to put it mildly, several wafers short of a communion. Manfred was the mother hen of the monastery and the closest thing Stephen had to a boss. Stephen put his request to Manfred when he judged the prior to be at his most receptive – when he was up to his elbows in soap suds doing the washing-up after breakfast.

"You are wanting to leave?" said Manfred, a note of worry in his soft German accent.

"Just for a bit," said Stephen. "Call it a holiday."

"A holiday?" Manfred took his hands out of the water, shook the worst of the bubbles from his Marigolds, and turned to Stephen. "We had a holiday last year."

"We did?"

"We took a day trip to Llandudno, remember?"

Stephen did remember. He'd nearly got frostbite standing on that beach, Brother Gillespie had come to blows with an ice-cream vendor and, due to a miscalculation by the penny-pinching Brother Sebastian, their bus had run out of fuel outside Caernarfon on the way home and the monks had pushed it two miles to the nearest petrol station. Stephen remembered Llandudno. He didn't remember any holiday.

"I know what this is really about," said Manfred.

"You do?"

Manfred stripped off his rubber gloves and removed his cooking apron (which had the words 'Hot Stuff' handsewn on it in sequins for what Manfred assured everyone was health and safety reasons). He folded the apron neatly and set it aside.

"We all have doubts, brother. We all have... desires." There was a sparkle in Manfred's eyes that Stephen was entirely unsure about. "You are still a young man."

Whilst Stephen considered himself to be far from old, it was a good decade since he had thought of himself as young. But then again, age was relative and, among the octogenarians and nonagenarians that predominated at St Cadfan's, Stephen was barely more than a boy.

"In the spring, the sap rises in the young trees," said Manfred.

"Does it?" said Stephen.

"The sap is rising within you."

"Um. Really?"

"You feel it," said Manfred. "It is a good thing, nothing to be ashamed of."

Stephen patted himself down bashfully as though his sappiness was somehow showing.

"I'm not sure..."

"Oh, it is true," said the prior, shaking his grey locks. "When I was a young lad, I had desires. Strong, ruling passions. My sap was up."

"Right," said Stephen weakly.

"And I followed those passions. I went down into the depths. I put aside every moral code. I pummelled and pounded, and I did not stop even when I was sore and broken. I let temptation take me."

"Gosh."

Manfred shrugged. "Yes, in the end, I became the Westphalian Bake-Off Champion –"

"Oh. I see. When you said passion, I thought..."

"But it did not change my ultimate calling."

"God?" suggested Stephen.

"Service to God," Manfred nodded. He breathed with deep satisfaction. "Of course, you must go, Stephen."

"Thank you. I'll only be a few days, I'm sure."

"No," said Manfred and placed a hand on Stephen's. "Do not put a limit on desires. Go. Explore your passions. Let your sap run free."

"Um. Okay."

Manfred went over to the pantry and brought down a metal biscuit tin. "And now, our itinerant brother, I think you will be needing these."

"Biscuits?" said Stephen.

Manfred opened the tin and took out a key on a tatty piece of twine.

"What's this?" said Stephen.

"The key to the shed behind the Ship Hotel in Aberdaron."

"Oh."

"And take this." Manfred put a small roll of banknotes in Stephen's hand. "Passions need funding, these days more than ever. And this." He held out a chunky car key.

"For me?" said Stephen. "That's too much."

"You haven't seen the car yet."

31

"But I can't really drive."

"The car probably won't start so I shouldn't worry."

Rutspud paced the bare confines of the summoning circle. There wasn't much else to do. Across the way, Shafttoe was stretched out in his recliner, leafing through a magazine and muttering contentedly to himself.

"Gor, look at that, eh," he said, holding up the magazine so Rutspud could see the photograph of a human emerging from the sea. The human was wearing a bikini, so Rutspud was ninety percent confident it was a woman. His gender-recognition skills were improving all the time, but humans were tricksy creatures and he could never be sure.

"Totally let herself go," said Shafttoe.

"Let herself go where?" said Rutspud.

"She used to be in *Call the Midwife*. Call the fat police more like."

Rutspud waved at the magazine, the chair and Shafttoe's other items. "How come you have all that stuff?"

"This sweet haul?" Shafttoe's tone was nonchalant but there was an air of pride. "Earned it. Grafting, yeah. Poor old Shafttoe ain't no stranger to work."

"I thought this was a holiday."

"Working holiday," explained Shafttoe. "It's like on the cruises."

"The what?"

Shafttoe made a half-hearted search of his magazine stack. "There's an interview with Jane McDonald in one of these. Got a lot of time for Jane. Stand up girl. No nonsense. She talks about the cruises in the interview. She's doing nightly shows for the punters. Real crowd-pleasers, but the rest of the time she can use the facilities, the pool, the sun deck. S'like that."

Rutspud was none the wiser.

"But you gotta put the effort in." Shafttoe pulled the lever on the side of his recliner to bring him upright. "This gig, it's about showmanship. You're in the wish-granting business now."

"Am I?" said Rutspud, who had never granted wishes for anyone in his long existence.

"You are, my friend. You are a conduit for the powers of Hell. But you can't just stand there like a lemon, granting wishes to occultists with no razzamatazz. The razzamatazz is the shine on the apple. It's the hint of the exotic what gets you the bonuses and perks."

A light came on at the top of the stairs.

"'Ere comes Mo now," said Shafttoe. "An absolute sucker for my blend of razzamatazz. You just watch."

Feet in thick sandals and then the hem of a dark robe descended the stairs. This 'Mo' was a slim figure, with a turkey neck of saggy flesh beneath a much-lined face and ash-blonde hair tied up in a bun. Damned robes made it impossible to tell the men from the women, thought Rutspud. It was a nice robe, though: midnight black embroidered with golden thread. Brother Stephen and his mates would get more respect if they wore bad-ass robes like that.

Mo the occultist carried a heavy brass platter. It was too high up for Rutspud to see, but something red and congealed clung to its edges. That'll be the goat's blood, he thought. He knew very little about occultists or Satanists, but he'd heard they were all about the blood of goats. He wasn't sure how goats had earned the honour, but when blood was needed it was always goats that got the chop.

Shafttoe gave Rutspud a little 'watch this' look and settled into a claw-handed pose that might be entitled 'pantomime goblin' or perhaps 'ooh, what have I trodden in? I daren't look.'

"Puny mortal, you come into my presence once more," he groaned eldritchly, throwing in dramatic hand gestures like he was trying to communicate via semaphore. "What dark purpose brings you to my demesne?"

"Prince Shafttoe..." began Mo.

"Prince?" coughed Rutspud, trying not to laugh.

Shafttoe threw him a warning look, but Mo had turned.

"And I see our new guest is up. Greetings to you, mighty demon."

Rutspud had been poised to give this fool an earful about the inconvenience he was being subjected to, but the words 'mighty demon' – words he had never been addressed with before – threw him off balance.

"Um. Hi."

"I bring you a humble offering before we begin our mystical work, to give you strength in the trials to come."

Mo bent down with the brass platter. Satan's balls, thought Rutspud, looking at the smudge of glistening red slime, it's meant for me. Am I expected to eat it?

He looked at the plate and then at the occultist's face.

"That's, um...."

"A sandwich," said Mo. "But if you don't like jam, I can do marmalade. Or I might have half a jar of fish paste somewhere."

In the early afternoon, the wind whipped the Irish Sea into a treacherous meringue of froth. Colin the boatman piloted his craft from Bardsey toward a cove on the Welsh mainland. Stephen stood beside him in the wheelhouse and watched the spray against the window. He had lived on a tiny island for more than six years, had become accustomed to the salty seaweed-stink that pervaded almost every breath, and realised only now that he was going to miss it.

"Course, it's a different language now," said Colin, prompted by nothing at all.

"Is it?" said Stephen.

"For certain. Kids down in the village, I don't know what they're saying half the time. It's all 'talk to the hand' and 'as if' and 'don't go there, girlfriend'," he said, adding an unnervingly-sassy finger click.

"Ah, I see," said Stephen. "I'll do my best to pick up the lingo."

"You'll be out there long?"

"I don't know. I've got things to do."

"Brother Manfred was saying."

Stephen gave him a look. "I'm not sure what Manfred told you."

"It's okay. Bright lights, big city. I did it once."

"Did it once...?"

Colin nodded. "Wild weekend in Oswestry. The Vegas of mid-Wales."

"Think I might be going a little further than that."

The boatman looked at him askance.

"You're not going to England, are you?"

Stephen nodded.

"Out among the English?"

"It's where they live."

Colin gave a mighty and unhappy sigh. "You can't trust 'em. Dishonest. Bloody imperialist conquerors to boot."

"That's sort of in the past, isn't it?"

"You tell that to my sister, Gwen. Bloody retired English couples have bought up half the houses in her village."

Stephen nodded silently, thinking it best not to argue.

"You do know," he said eventually, "that I'm English. You do, don't you?"

"You, yes. But you're a monk. It's not like you're a proper person."

"Oh, that's all right then," said Stephen and went out on deck to get slapped in the face by good honest Welsh sea spray.

Rutspud munched on the jam sandwich while Mo's attentions turned to Shafttoe. The occultist plumped up his cushions, passed one at a time over the outer edge of the magic circle.

"So, you got no rest at all, Prince Shafttoe?"

"Rest?" he said incredulously, persisting in his hammy acting routine. "No, mortal. I am a beast of the deepest pit. Depravity is my cloak. Perversion is the trews I wear. Sin is... is..."

"Your shoes?" suggested the occultist.

"Yes. Yes! My shoes! In this world of light and love, every moment is exquisite agony to me. There is no rest for my kind!"

"Oh, shame. I thought that inflatable neck pillow might have helped. And you drank the Horlicks I made?"

Shafttoe picked up the empty mug from his little table. "It was very malty. Thank you."

"It's those cigarettes that are keeping you awake, my prince," said Mo.

"Tobacco is one of my vices," he drawled. "One of many. You have perhaps brought some as an offering...?"

Mo gave the demon an admonishing look then pulled a pack of ten Benson & Hedges out of one robe pocket, a cheap plastic lighter out of the other and tossed them into the circle.

"Your offering is acceptable," said Shafttoe and then ripped open the pack and lit up.

Mo sighed.

"I'll give the place a good spray with Febreze before the others come. You know Merilyn doesn't approve of smoking."

"Who's Merilyn?" said Rutspud, licking a smear of jam off the inside of his thumb.

"The most wonderful and clever person," said Mo but Shafttoe's face told another story. "Isn't that right, Prince Shafttoe?"

"As you say, mortal," said the demon. "I know you and Winnie have nothing but praise for her."

Mo seemed pleased with this utterly non-committal answer.

"So much to do, my lords. I must prepare," said the occultist and departed with a swish of black and gold skirts.

Once Mo had disappeared up the stairs, Rutspud put down his plate.

"Who are Merilyn and Winnie?"

"You don't wanna know, mate," said Shafttoe, leaning back in his recliner and puffing merrily on his cigarette.

"I do," said Rutspud. "That's why I asked."

"Curiosity killed the cat, you know."

"Good. I hate cats. I assume Merilyn and Winnie are two more demon-fiddlers, poking the unknown and meddling in things man was not meant to wot of."

"What?"

"Exactly."

"Listen," said Shafttoe, pointing at Rutspud with his cigarette hand and waving smoke tendrils through the air. "And listen well, chum. This is a good gig – fine food and creature comforts – and, with a little razzamatazz, these could be yours too. Mo is a proper diamond. Knows how to treat a demon with respect. Winnie, well, yeah, that one's a right lemon."

"Yellow and bitter?"

"Ain't got no brains or no spine."

Putting aside the thought that such a description could apply to any fruit, citrus or otherwise, Rutspud saw Shafttoe was leading up to a point.

"And Merilyn?" he said, prepared for the worst.

"She's... efficient."

Rutspud thought about this. "Efficient?"

"Yeah," said Shafttoe grimly.

"Not the worst adjective you can use to describe something."

"Efficient like a mouse trap. Like a bacon slicer. Like an atom bomb. You'll have to work hard to stay on the right side of that one or you'll end up..."

Shafttoe flicked away a crumb of tobacco that had gotten caught in his huge teeth and waved his hand toward the corner of the cellar. A heavy, stained sheet covered a large box of some sort.

"What's under there?" said Rutspud.

"Not what," said Shafttoe. "Who."

The Ship Hotel stood on the sea wall of Aberdaron, facing south. Directly in front of it was the Welsh coast. Somewhere in the murk and mists beyond lay the Pembrokeshire peninsula, the Bristol Channel, the tip of Cornwall... and, much further away: Spain, Africa and other such places where a trip to the beach didn't come with a wind chill warning. Directly behind the Ship Hotel was a rotten old lean-to garage that St Cadfan's had rented off the publican until such time as it fell down, which for years everyone had assumed would be tomorrow.

Stephen fought briefly with the padlock then shouldered open the door and walked inside, sucking a blood blister in the fleshy bit of his right hand. The garage was lined with slatted shelving units which had providentially extended the monastery's lease by bracing the walls from the inside. They housed the suitcases, travel chests, steamer trunks, duffels, rucksacks, bags and cardboard boxes of worldly belongings the Bardsey monks had set aside when they joined the monastery. Somewhere in here was a rucksack with a little tag tied to it with his name on.

The centre of the room was taken up by a stack of plastic crates, several unlabelled barrels and a thing Stephen was forced to accept was Manfred's car.

It looked like a car. It definitely looked like a car. If he had asked a five-year-old to draw a car the picture would have looked something like this: a sort of porkpie hat on wheels. It had a plastic body. (He rapped on it to check.) It had two doors and a back seat that was either for decorative purposes only or for passengers lacking both lower legs and knees.

Stephen got in, realised it was European left-hand drive, got out, went round and got in again. He tried to adjust the seat, but it put up a strong resistance and eventually won. After considerable searching, he found an unlabelled gear stick on the side of the steering column. He put the car in what he hoped was neutral, inserted the key and turned over the engine. The car made a noise like a sleeping dog that had just been kicked, a very angry dog at that. The engine settled into a misanthropic growl, but after a few moments it screamed and died.

"Great," said Stephen.

A large note had been sellotaped to the underside of the sun visor. Stephen recognised Manfred's writing.

This car is a Trabant, the finest car ever produced in East Germany. This is not just a car. It is a history lesson. Drive this car for even a minute and you will understand everything you need to know about East Germany.In the event that:

- *The fuel gauge reads as empty when the tank is not*
- *None of the gears make the car go forward*
- *The engine produces a mysterious smell*
- *The car refuses to climb a hill*
- *The steering wheel sticks at high speed*

or any other 'feature' becomes apparent, please consult the reverse of this sign.

Stephen flipped the sun visor and found another note.

Remember: This car beat the Mercedes A-Class in the 'moose test'.

If this is not enough, please consult the glove compartment.

Stephen opened the glove compartment.

Taped to the inside of the door was a photograph of a shaggy, round-nosed moose standing in a forest road. A speech bubble was drawn in blue biro next to the moose's head. *I believe in you*, said the moose.

"Thank you," said Stephen to the moose. And, oddly, he felt better.

Stephen got out, found the grime-covered rucksack with his name on it and slung it on the back seat. He got back in the car and started the engine again. The car shouted and growled but did not die this time. He gave the moose one final glance for luck.

"Hang on, Rutspud. We're coming for you."

The pack of cigarettes was finished.

The ashtray and Rutspud's plate were cleared away.

Febreze was sprayed. It made Rutspud's eyes sting and made the cellar smell revoltingly pleasant.

Tall brass candlesticks were placed in the corners and thick candles were lit. The candles were black. *Obviously*, thought Rutspud.

In his summoning circle, Shafttoe limbered up with some stretching exercises and lunges. Rutspud tried to dispel the air freshener smell with some concentrated farting.

Finally, someone struck a gong upstairs.

"Action stations," whispered Shafttoe. He ran his fingers through his hair and squatted in a hunched, dried-up pose – as though all his demonic wickedness had given him a fatal bout of constipation.

Rutspud wasn't sure what was expected of him, so he sat on the concrete floor with his arms and legs crossed in the pose of a sulky, pissed-off demon – which was easy because that was what he was.

The three occultists filed down the stairs, feet moving in solemn synchrony. They entered the cellar in descending order of height, so for a few moments on the stairs all three hooded heads were at the same level. The middle one – Rutspud reckoned it was Mo under that hood – held a heavy and important-looking book open in two hands and chanted heavy and important-sounding words. The short, dumpy one at the back was chanting along, although the short one's chanting sounded very much like "Mmmbop, ba duba dop, ba du bop, ba duba dop", which was no earthly or hellish language Rutspud knew. The tall one carried nothing and said nothing and had a general bearing that said the carrying and speaking of things was entirely beneath them. This would be Merilyn then.

At the base of the stairs, the three of them stood in a loose triangle, like sinister bowling pins. Mo closed the book reverently and fell silent. The short one gave a final "mmmbop". As one, the three occultists lowered their hoods.

Merilyn stared at Shafttoe and then at Rutspud, blue eyes glinting with menace like arctic ice in a dark fjord. It was a good stare, he thought. A demon would be proud of that stare. On a human it was something entirely other and Rutspud couldn't help but think a few centuries in a pit in the sixth circle would do something about that stare. Merilyn licked lips as dry and puckered as raisins.

"I'm missing *Strictly Come Dancing* for this, so it better be worth it."

"I'm sure it will be," said Mo, eagerly.

"I asked my Sky box to record *Strictly*," said the squat Winnie. "So, you can watch it round mine later if you like. Although last week it somehow managed to record the second half of the FA Cup football match instead. Scunthorpe United v Arsenal."

"How on earth did that happen?" said Mo.

"I just think Scunthorpe have been lucky this year and really pulled together as a team."

Merilyn ignored them. She approached the edge of Rutspud's circle and gazed down at him.

"And who are you?" she said.

"Rutspud," he said.

"Just Rutspud? Not Lord Rutspud? Not the Archdemon Rutspud? Not..." Merilyn sneered at Shafttoe, who still looked like he was trying to poop out a brick of pure demony demonness. "Not Prince Rutspud?"

"Just Rutspud," he said.

"And do you know why you're here, Rutspud?"

"I know I shouldn't be."

"You have been summoned to this dimension to serve our needs. Do as I command, and you will be released and returned to your original abode."

"Yes?"

41

"Yes."

"You implied there's a choice."

"Did I?" Icy eyes sparkled. "That was entirely accidental."

Behind Merilyn, Shafttoe was giving him frantic little looks. Comply, submit, play along.

"Nah. Screw it," said Rutspud. "I think I'll sit this one out. I'm not going to play ball with some pathetic, suburban Satanists. Do your damnedest, granddad. I'm unkillable. You want to threaten me, just remember that I have an excellent memory and I'll be waiting for you on the other side one day."

Merilyn was smiling. It was only a smile in the sense that the edges of that wrinkled mouth were slightly higher than the middle. There was no warmth in that smile, no humour.

"Who said we're Satanists, little imp? Do we look like devil worshippers?"

Rutspud made vague and mocking gestures towards their robes, the candles...

"We are upstanding and virtuous members of the public. We have summoned you here. We haven't invited you. You are fruit, plucked from the tree and we are going to squeeze you for all you have."

Merilyn's eyes flicked to the covered box in the corner. Nice touch, thought Rutspud. A nicely ominous touch.

"Right," he said, unconvinced. "So, I've been brought here to do good works? Uh-huh. You're not looking for – ooh, let me think – youth, beauty, uncountable wealth, the secret to immortality?"

The three occultists looked at each other.

"Oh, no," Mo reassured him. "We're not into that sort of thing."

"I wouldn't mind a little bit of youth and wossname," said Winnie quietly, but no one paid any notice.

"You will assist us in righting a few wrongs, demon," said Merilyn, "setting a few things straight. We do this not for personal gain but for the betterment of society. We want very little. We simply want a society where people treat each other with decency and respect."

"Good manners," said Mo.

"A little bit of pride in one's appearance," said Merilyn.

"Reasonable prices on the high street."

"A return to traditional family values."

"An end to public littering."

"An end to coarse language."

"And shoddy workmanship."

"Graffiti."

"Cold callers."

"Foxes!"

The other two stopped in their tag-team rant to look at Winnie.

"Foxes?" said Mo.

"We are nature lovers, Winnie," said Merilyn. "All of us. We like foxes."

"They tipped over my wheelie bin and ate the chicken leftovers," said Winnie. "Made a terrible mess of my back passage."

"Oh, *urban* foxes," said Merilyn with pronounced disgust. "No. That's not right. Never used to happen in our day, did it?"

"We are nature lovers though," said Mo.

"*Traditional* nature lovers," said Merilyn. "Starlings at dawn. Tits pecking at the milk bottle lids. Foxes in the countryside. Hedgehogs in the hedgerow. Squirrels in the trees."

"Red squirrels," said Winnie.

"Yes, none of this grey squirrel nonsense," agreed Merilyn. "Coming over here, taking over, not contributing to society..."

"Yes," said Mo. "We don't mind newcomers if they contribute. It's like that lovely Dr Venkataramana at the medical centre. Foreign chappy, but ever so friendly. He sent me a Christmas card last year which just goes to show, doesn't it?"

Rutspud had no idea what it went to show.

"It's quite clear that you're a bunch of nutters," he said, "dealing with forces well beyond your comprehension. I'll give you this one fucking opportunity to –"

He was cut off by a spray of liquid to the face.

"My daddy didn't fight in the Second World War so his girl could be subjected to those kinds of profanities," said Merilyn.

Rutspud blinked and shook his large ears. There was a spray bottle in Merilyn's hand. For a moment, he thought it was the Febreze again, but he licked his lips...

"Is that holy water?"

Merilyn stared at him, not surprised as such. Merilyn wasn't the kind of human who'd let surprise spoil the superior look on their face.

"What?" said Rutspud. "You want me to steam and melt, crying, 'What a world! What a world!'? Yeah, that's right. I do contemporary cultural references, biatch. Holy sodding water doesn't hurt me. I've built up a tolerance over the years."

"Is that so?" said Merilyn. "Stage two punishment then."

"Please don't, oh mighty one," said Shafttoe, dropping to his knees. "He's new to this game. Wet behind the ears, yeah? Give him a chance to apologise. He'll soon fall in line."

"Silence," said Merilyn and Shafttoe obeyed. "It seems our new servant needs to be taught a lesson."

"There's nothing you can do to hurt me," said Rutspud. "So, you might as well send me back to Hell."

Merilyn took the important-looking book from Mo's hands. It was weighty, bound in cracked but highly-polished leather with not one, not two, but three clasps to hold it shut. Of course, it could just be a book of cake recipes or knock-knock jokes, but people placed a lot of importance in the look of books. When they looked at a book they expected to see what its contents were. And when they were reading a book they wanted outside observers to see what kind of a person they were (or not, which was why sex-starved housewives liked Kindles). The book Merilyn held looked exactly how a demon-summoner's book should look: like it contained every mystical secret and spell in existence, even the one the Almighty used to create this pitiful universe.

"Hell is an entirely alien dimension to ours, Rutspud, and to give you a physical form in our three-dimensional world took a lot of effort," said Merilyn. "The hours of concentration, the physical exertion –"

"I put my back right out," said Winnie.

"And you've shown us no gratitude at all." Merilyn traced down the open page with a long finger. "We're hurt."

"Aw, *diddums*..." Rutspud cooed.

"We're offended."

"Bugger off."

"And I don't think you deserve three."

"Three what?" said Rutspud.

"Dimensions."

"Eh?"

"*Baalzai!*"

The cellar ceiling instantly flew away. Rutspud felt the disconcerting sensation of plummeting downwards and standing perfectly still at the same time. The occultists and Shafttoe ballooned in size and smeared like images in a rusting mirror. At the same time, origami was being performed on Rutspud's internal organs. They folded into neat little packages that then folded into each other.

Rutspud felt... wrong. His body didn't hurt. That would require him to know where his body was. The world was dark and flat and not half as fun as it had previously been.

"Urk," said Rutspud, which was all he could manage.

A black and pink and icy blue line moved in the nothingness.

"I hope that was an apology," said Merilyn's voice, coming to him as though through an echoing tube.

"Urk."

"Did we have to?" said Mo's voice as a black and grey line flared to the side.

"Transgressions must be punished," said Merilyn. "Punishments serve as illustrative moral lessons to others, don't they, Shafttoe?"

A white and yellow and entirely servile line flickered. "That they do, mighty one. That they do."

"Good," said Merilyn. "Now, to tonight's business. I think it's clear we must do something about your back passage, Winnie."

"I beg your pardon?" said a dark and utterly inconsequential line.

"The foxes. The *urban* foxes."

"I thought we were going to sort out the grey squirrels," said Mo.

"We can do both, can't we, Shafttoe?"

"Me, your powerfulnesses? I thought the new feller was gonna be doing it. As you know, I is more of a facilitator than –"

"You will be our conduit today," said Merilyn.

45

"Well, then I'd need specifics," said the demon. "Even great demons such as myself need –"

Merilyn's laughter span through Rutspud's squished and shadowy world like a flock of knives.

"We have seen little evidence of your greatness, imp. Do not disappoint us."

"Sure, but –"

"We want the foxes removed. We want everything tidied up. And the squirrels, they either need to shape up or ship out."

"Yes, so what you're saying is –"

"It's not difficult to understand, Shafttoe! We're not asking you to reorder the natural world! We're doing the ritual. We're doing it now."

Merilyn began a chant. Mo and Winnie soon fell into time. Lines of colour circled Shafttoe. In the immeasurable emptiness, Shafttoe grunted and gasped. A searing blue line flashed, a blast of lightning and all went quiet.

The dark lines moved off. Footsteps on stairs.

"We might catch the end of *Strictly* if we're lucky," said Winnie.

"I'll put the kettle on," said Mo. "I think I've got some fruit cake in the cupboard."

"No, thank you, Mo," said Merilyn. "I've eaten your fruit cake before."

Rutspud tried to move. This would be easier if he had a grasp of direction or of what had happened to his limbs.

"Urk," he said unhappily.

A pinpoint of light appeared. The click, crackle and sigh of a cigarette being lit.

"You should have done as I said," grunted Shafttoe. He sounded like he was in considerable pain. "Life is easier if you play the game, mate."

"Urk," said Rutspud, not yet ready to commit one way or the other.

Powered by a tank and a half of petrol (a helpful hand-written label inside the fuel cap door read, *Fill with two-stroke petrol only*, which meant nothing to Stephen when he filled up in Telford), the Trabant had crossed mid-Wales, passed over the English border into Shropshire and continued down the M54 towards Birmingham. Stephen possessed a driving licence, which meant he was legally entitled to drive but didn't mean he was capable of driving. He wasn't sure if it was his generally poor ability, his years of living on a carless and indeed roadless island, the perverse and truculent behaviour of the little Trabant or – and this was an outside possibility – someone had changed the rules of the road while he wasn't looking but, whatever the case, Stephen's journey was accompanied by a soundtrack of angry car horn pips and lorry horn blasts and, after a complicated roundabout near Welshpool, a thirty-second rant from the open window of the BMW in the lane next to him. However, on the plus side, after five hours of horrible and anxious motoring, Stephen reached Birmingham and the satellite town-slash-suburb of Sutton Coldfield and he hadn't crashed the car.

At least, not until he saw the squirrels.

He had just navigated the notorious Spaghetti Junction interchange and, more by chance than skill, had found himself on an exit for Sutton Coldfield, rather than one for Birmingham or Lichfield or one of the more hellish boroughs of the city. Night was falling but had not yet fully fallen, he was but a stone's throw from his childhood home and was pootling along what he was sure was the Chester Road or possibly Kingsbury Road but definitely some road that instinctively felt *right*, when he saw the squirrels...

There were at least five of them arranged across the pavement and gutter outside a residential house and they were giving a fox a good ticking off. Two squirrels, positioned in the road, waved admonishing little claws at a deeply confused fox and made general shooing motions. Over by the house wall, a bin bag of rubbish had been ripped open, presumably by the fox, and while one squirrel tried to close the rip with some artful tying, other squirrels were gathering up squashed tins, chip papers and the remains of a fried chicken takeaway and shoving them back in the bag.

Quite naturally, Stephen gawped, momentarily forgot he was driving, mounted the pavement and crashed into a post box. The fox gave a start and bounded off across the street. The squirrels looked up and then carried on with their work. Stephen shook his head and got out to inspect the damage, spilling a small quantity of papers and car rubbish as he stumbled out.

One of the superior safety features of the Trabant was its inability to travel at high speeds, so the crash had been little more than a forceful nudge. There was a hairline crack in the plastic bonnet but no other apparent damage.

A squirrel had come over to see what was going on. It looked at the car and at the dark scratch it had left in the post box's paintwork. It stuck out a tiny pink tongue, licked its claw and rubbed at the damaged post box. The scratch didn't clean up.

"Kwekwekwek!" the squirrel chirruped angrily at Stephen. The cry had a wet and kissy quality to it, but any notion that the squirrel meant it affectionately was crushed by the aggressive body language.

"Er. Sorry?" said Stephen, now wondering if he had concussion or some sort of whiplash-induced psychosis.

The squirrel gave him a look that clearly said an apology would not be enough and ran off.

Stephen got back in the car and tried to start it. The engine turned over, screamed and died. He tried again with the same result. He opened the glove compartment and, feeling only a little sacrilegious, implored the moose to offer its help. The engine screamed, died and something large went 'ka-doing!' under the bonnet.

"Bugger," he said softly and got out again.

The team of squirrels had tidied away the rubbish and skilfully resealed the bag. Stephen was unaware of this being normal squirrel behaviour, but he had been away from the city for a long time and urban animals were famously adaptable.

"You guys wouldn't know anything about car repairs, would you?" he said.

Five pairs of shiny eyes stared at him as though he was mad, which was probably an accurate assessment.

Sighing, Stephen took out his dusty rucksack of belongings and considered which way to go. Sutton Coldfield was north of the ring of motorway that bounded most of Birmingham like a fortified wall (not that the Brummies were overly protective of their city and culture; what they did have they weren't precious about and were historically happy to let invading cultures come in and mix things up a bit). The urban landscape north of the motorway was composed of Victorian and inter-war housing, mixed with a smattering of high-rises, outlined by brick-walls, canals and railway lines and served by a mish-mash of shops and workplaces that had ignored any kind of zoning or sense of town planning. Stephen didn't know where he was, exactly, but with the certainty of an Egyptian seeing a pyramid, he knew he was home.

The squirrel that had admonished him for damaging the post box returned, struggling to carry a tin of modelmaker's paint in its claws. It held an artist's brush in its mouth. It put the tin down and considered the black scratch on the post box and then levered the lid off the tin with the end of the brush. It was red paint.

Stephen decided to ignore this delusion, shouldered his rucksack and set off.

He walked with purpose but no aim. He had no clear idea of how to find Rutspud apart from an awful mental image of himself wandering the streets with a hand-drawn wanted poster, asking people, "Have you seen this demon?"

Stephen's plan did not extend beyond getting here, finding somewhere to stay and having a good old think and a bit of a cry. Finding somewhere to stay wasn't straightforward. Sutton Coldfield was his home town, but he had no home here. His parents had retired to North Yorkshire some years ago, swapping their perfectly safe suburban semi-detached for a storm-battered clifftop cottage somewhere near Scarborough. He had no other family in the area, no connections apart from those few friends he'd kept in touch with and the landmarks of his youth: the pubs, the takeaways and –

"I know this bridge."

49

Stephen looked out across the canal. In the deepening dusk, the water was a shimmering reflection of nearby streetlamps. The towpath was invisible in the gloom but the memory of this spot slammed into him. Stephen and his friends used to cycle up and down this section of canal all the time – him and Lennox and Darren and Ed. They'd cut through this way if they were heading to the Cascades Swimming Pool in Stechford or cycling between Darren's home in Erdington and Lennox's family's pub in Boldmere where, if they were lucky, Lennox could get them free cans of Fanta orange (Lennox was apparently happy to steal Fanta from his parents' pub because it was "hypocritical and petty bourgeois for working class publicans to serve a drink invented by Nazis.") This bridge was also the very spot where, more than twenty years ago, he had thrown a suitcase into the canal, compounding a rift with Ed that had never been mended. Of course, it wasn't the dumping of the suitcase that had destroyed their friendship; it was what Stephen had done minutes before, in Large Mike's fish and chip shop.

"Now," he said to himself, "if this bridge is here, then..." He held out an arm to align himself with the map in his memory. "Large Mike's is that way, Boldmere is *that* way, and that road is..."

He set off with renewed confidence in his sense of direction. He'd find a cheap hotel for the night and call a garage in the morning.

He slapped his pocket. He stuffed his hand in his pocket and felt around frantically.

"No, no, no, no, no..."

The money. The money Manfred had given him, tightly wrapped and held together with an elastic band. He'd used some of it to pay for petrol and he'd definitely put it back in his pocket and it had stayed there as he drove back to Birmingham and then he'd crashed the car and he'd staggered out, bewildered, scattering rubbish and then there was a squirrel and... and...

Stephen turned his eyes to the dark skies.

"For fuck's sake, God. You do have to make things difficult sometimes."

Then he immediately bowed his head and apologised to God and offered up a prayer of thanks that missing money and possibly imaginary squirrels were the worst of his worries.

He could picture the roll of money lying unattended in the road beside the abandoned Trabant. It wouldn't be there for long. It had probably already been found and pocketed by someone who subscribed to the 'finders keepers' philosophy of street salvage. It was the only funds Stephen had, the only means of paying for accommodation, food, car repairs or fuel. He felt frustration rise within him again.

"But, Lord, you are fucking kidding, right?" he said and immediately bowed his head again in genuine repentance.

He looked back the way he had come. It was dark and he had taken several turnings on unfamiliar roads. No, he didn't stand a chance of finding the street, the car, or the cash.

Alternating between bursts of swearing and fervent prayer, Stephen trudged along with no plan in his head and very little hope in his heart. He was so wound up in his own self-pity that he didn't notice the woman until she and her little flat-nosed pug dog were stood right in front of him, blocking his path.

"Sorry," said Stephen automatically and made to move round her.

The woman, an older lady who nonetheless held her slim frame erect, inspected him coldly. "So, you'll be one of those homeless people then?"

"Sorry?"

The woman nodded as though she understood everything. The dog sniffed the hem of Stephen's habit and yipped.

"Poor life choices," she said. "Not willing to give things a second try or a decent first try. Run away from home. Burnt your bridges but can't be bothered to rebuild them. There but for the grace of God go us all, eh? Would you recommend it?"

"Sorry?" said Stephen. "Recommend what?"

"The lifestyle. Can't say it appeals. I prefer my creature comforts. Home and garden. Englishman's home is his castle. Or Englishwoman's. Simple pleasures. You lot, you all smoke, don't you? Funny that, how you can't afford anywhere to stay but can afford your cigs and a little dog. You don't have one."

"Little dog?"

The pug barked again.

"Yes." The woman took a deep breath as though the conversation had touched upon something profound and now needed to come up for air. "You took a wrong turn."

"In life?"

"No, back there," she said, pointing. "It's left at the last T junction, not right."

"It...?"

The woman's face darkened a shade and she gestured to the suburban streets behind her. "There's nothing for you down there, young man. Be told. You need to go back to the T junction and it's straight on."

Confused and sapped of all willpower, Stephen backed away and took the turning as directed. He looked back once and saw the woman nodding approvingly and making shooing motions as though Stephen was an unwelcome pigeon that had landed on her lawn. Stephen moved on.

He almost immediately came upon a municipal building with its front doors open wide, lights on within and a temporary sign that read 'St Michael's Sharepoint Project – Food and Overnight Shelter.'

"Ah," said Stephen, enlightened. How nice that the locals were quick to identify him as homeless and tell him where he was and wasn't allowed to go.

He was loathe to go inside. He was hardly homeless. It was just that his home was a couple of hundred miles away. He even had a car he could sleep in, if he could find it.

"Don't just stand there, love," said a woman, coming out and placing an encouraging hand at his elbow. "Come in. It's all right."

In the vestibule, another woman, this one with a clipboard, took Stephen's name and asked him where he was from. Stephen told her, only out of politeness. He didn't want to make a fuss. The women looked at his monk's habit but neither made comment, again out of politeness. How very British we are, Stephen thought, as they ushered him into the main hall.

"Another one for you, Daz," the clipboard woman called over.

A man whose huge belly was covered by a home-knitted jumper adorned with a smiley, bearded man in the cockpit of a biplane and the legend *Jesus is my Co-Pilot* came over. The smiley Jesus on the jumper had golden tassels for beard and hair. It was quite an arresting sight.

"Okay," said the Lord's co-pilot. "You're new, aren't you? Let's give you the tour and then a cuppa. Or is it a cuppa first?"

Stephen turned round to view this main room. There was a dining area that was about half full, mostly men but some women and children too. Another corner was set out with shelving units stocked with dry goods and foodstuffs. Elsewhere, a team of people sat at desks, going through paperwork and making phone calls on behalf of individuals with painfully expectant looks on their faces. He instantly felt like a fraud and interloper.

"I don't need... anything," said Stephen. "I'm sorry. I've got to go. I've got to find my friend."

"It's okay," said fat jumper man. "Let me get you something. Maybe we can help you find your friend. A lot of people come through here."

Stephen laughed.

"Not this guy. He's kind of unique looking."

"Oh, we specialise in unique characters here."

Stephen considered the jumper.

"Yes. Yes, I can see."

"Says the man in the monk's robes." The fat guy smiled and put his hands together across his stomach in a gesture that Stephen found familiar. "I had a friend who, last I heard, went off to become a monk. Although I suppose your outfit probably came from a fancy-dress shop or –"

"Darren?"

"Yes?"

Stephen stared at the man. Fill in the bald spot. Shave of the bumfluff of a beard. Take away (and preferably burn) that hideous jumper and dress him in an XXL Megadeth T-shirt and some occult jewellery...

"Darren?"

Darren's quizzical look transformed into delighted disbelief.

"Stephen?"

Stephen grinned. Darren grinned. Stephen attempted to throw his arms around the man and was two-thirds successful. Darren returned the gesture and nearly crushed Stephen's spine.

"Mate!"

"Man!"

"It must be..."

"Twenty years?"

"Twenty-one. That summer when we tried to summon..."

"Meridiana."

"The succubus!"

Stephen laughed at the recollection. "What idiots we were."

"Complete losers," agreed Darren.

Stephen shook his head. "I thought you took up the Satanism stuff full-time. Changed your name to... what was it? Scumspawn?"

Darren put a shushing finger to his lips and drew Stephen to one side. "Pitspawn," he whispered. "Yeah, but that's part of my old life. Left that behind now. Not all the people here know so, you know..."

Stephen smiled.

"I get it. Ha! Maybe I will have that cup of tea now."

Stephen sat at one of the tables and watched as Darren poured two cups of tea from the electric urn at the food counter. Stephen was still smiling. He hadn't stopped smiling. He hadn't realised how much he had missed his old school friend.

Stephen tried to work out if the years had been unkind to Darren. He was certainly fatter and was going bald on top, but he still had the innocent boyish look to his face because all that subcutaneous fat was holding his skin in tension and keeping wrinkles at bay. In many ways, he looked like the same overindulged man-boy he had known all those years ago. He wondered if he'd ever moved out of his mum's attic, if she came round on a daily basis to do his washing and feed him oven-baked ready meals.

The one thing that had changed was Darren's dress sense. It was impossible to reconcile his Heavy Metal devil-worshipper aesthetic of yesteryear with the knitted, Jesusified monstrosity he currently wore.

"Your mum knit you that jumper?" Stephen asked as Darren brought the teas over.

"Yes, she did," said Darren. His tone wasn't defensive, but it had a certain hard finality to it. "Digestive?"

Stephen took a biscuit and dunked it in his tea. "She was always a big knitter, your mum. She knitted you that wizard's cloak for when we went LARPing as teenagers."

"And it stretched in the rain and nearly strangled me."

"And, how is she? See her much?"

"Too much," said Darren, taking a slurp of tea. "She's retired now so she hangs around the house all day."

"Oh, so you two, you're still...?" He remembered his biscuit and pulled it out of the tea before the soggy end fell off.

"Together? Yep," said Darren. "Still got my attic room, my man cave. Mum and I sometimes chat about the idea of moving out."

"Right."

"But she says she's too young to go in a care home."

"Right."

"And you?" said Darren.

Stephen made a sweeping gesture over his habit.

"I'm a monk."

"Wow. A real monk. When I heard, I thought it was just a phase. Like some people get tattoos. Some people go vegan."

"And some people join a religious order." Stephen considered this. "You're probably right. It was a phase. It wasn't a sensible or wise decision but, bizarrely, it's one of the best things that ever happened to me. I live on a tiny Welsh island with a bunch of mostly geriatric oddballs."

"Oddballs?"

"We once spent three days solid debating whether we should have custard creams or bourbons during tea breaks. Brother Clement was very strongly against the custard cream as he felt the swirly patterns were reminiscent of the pagan image of the Green Man, whereas Brother Sebastian felt the custard creams had the advantage of being less indulgent and more suited to the humble monastic lifestyle."

"I see."

"But Brother Henry said that by eschewing the darker bourbon we were perhaps complicit in the white-washing of the biscuit world and that we should welcome all biscuits."

"He thinks custard creams are racist."

"Not really, he just likes lots of biscuits but, yes, that was his argument and yet Brother Manfred was concerned that eating the darker, chocolate-filled bourbon might involve some unspecified form of cultural appropriation."

Darren thought about this.

"Three days?"

"Three days. I suspect it's not a normal monastery."

"But you're happy," said Darren.

"I am."

"And yet you're back in Sutton."

Tea, biscuits and nostalgia had distracted Stephen from the reason for his visit.

"I came back to... to find someone. It's a mission of sorts, I guess."

Darren's eyebrows rose.

"A mission? As in a quest?"

"I... suppose."

"You here for long?"

"I don't know," said Stephen.

"Got anywhere to stay?"

"No."

"Well, that's settled then," said Darren, downing the rest of his cup. "I'm on shift here until eight but then you'll stay at mine."

Stephen automatically opened his mouth to politely protest but then common sense cut him off before he could turn down the offer.

"That's very kind, mate." He looked about. "You need any help here?"

"Always," said Darren.

A quarter past nine, a cold breeze forcing Stephen to pull his cowl tightly around his neck, two men idled their way towards a house in Erdington.

"And there was that time you pretty much caused a party wipe with that Hand of Glory magic item," said Darren.

"Hand of Glory?" said Stephen.

"Yeah, yeah. You'd set up this fake dungeon for our PCs and that level twenty mage had cast an enchantment on the villagers so they'd all go on about this fabled Hand of Glory treasure, a fake hand that if you wore it gave you unlimited powers or something."

"Oh, yeah," said Stephen. "But it was just a metal hand. And you all fell for it. You had Lennox's character – what was he called?"

"Nox the Destroyer."

"Right. Nox the Destroyer cut off Mirrorglim's hand so he could attach the Hand of Glory. And when that didn't work, you had him cut off the other hand."

"Worth a shot. Then he cut off Ed's character's hands... and then I seem to recall Nox trying to cut off his own hands with that two-handed sword."

"I remember." Stephen laughed and then said, "I've missed this."

"Fantasy roleplaying?"

"Yes. But, no, I mean I've missed this. Walking and talking with old friends. Talking crap, talking about nothing. We used to..." Stephen looked round and tried to orientate himself. "Where's Short Heath Park from here? We used to sit on those swings, stare up at the stars and talk about TV shows and movies – so many bloody awful horror movies we rented from Ed's uncle's shop – and science fiction novels, board games, *Mana Clash*. You were mad for *Mana Clash* cards. The amount of money you wasted."

"I wouldn't say wasted."

"No? You'd pay any amount for them. And Ed was your dealer."

A darker memory stole over Stephen: a fight, a canal bridge, a suitcase thrown into the water.

"You see Ed at all these days?"

"Animal Ed?"

"*Animal* Ed?" said Stephen.

"That's what everyone calls him these days," said Darren. "Actually, ever since he came out of the young offenders' institute. You know he went to prison, yeah?"

"The thing with the policeman, yeah."

Stephen's heart sank. No one got a prison nickname like 'Animal' without reason. What had happened to him? Had mixing with the criminal fraternity turned him into an institutionalised monster? Had he become a predator – a sexual predator even – desensitised to his crimes by the brutality of life on the inside?

"And they call him 'Animal' because...?"

"Because he really likes animals," said Darren. "Obviously."

They turned off the main road and down a side street that Stephen immediately recognised as Darren's road.

"They had a little farm in the prison," said Darren. "A smallholding. Chickens. Rabbits. That kind of thing. Ed seemed to find his calling. His uncle's shop – which is now Ed's shop – sells mostly pet supplies these days."

"Ah, so he's on the straight and narrow now."

Darren thought about this for a short distance. "No, I wouldn't say that."

"And have you found your calling in life?" said Stephen, which he realised was a ham-fisted way of asking 'do you have a job, or do you still sponge off your mum?'

"You know," said Darren, "I've never really needed to find one. I help out at the church a lot. I help run the local cub pack with Mr Michaels, run it singlehandedly since he got arrested in Switzerland on terrorism charges."

"The cub leader is a terrorist?"

"Awaiting trial. There's probably a perfectly innocent reason why he was inside the Large Hadron Collider."

"Is that the St Michael's cub scouts we used to go to ourselves?"

"That's the one?"

Stephen's brow creased at the memories. "Wasn't that the one Nigel Herring got kicked out of for doing something unspeakable to a hamster."

"Might be."

"What did he do, exactly?"

"I can't tell you. It's unspeakable." Darren sniffed. "Anyway, I hear he developed a phobia of hamsters after that."

"What? He thought they were going to come after him for revenge?"

Darren shrugged.

Darren's house – technically his mum's – was a small semi-detached with a narrow garage to one side. The only light came from the upstairs landing window.

Darren went up to the garage door and took out a bunch of keys. It was a sturdy-looking lock.

"Anyway, I am, to my surprise," he said, "what they call independently wealthy. So, I don't need a paying job."

"You won the lottery?" said Stephen.

Darren pulled open the garage doors and turned on the light. The garage was lined with filing cabinets.

"You own the world's most expensive filing cabinets?" suggested Stephen.

"Not quite," said Darren. He squeezed between the cabinets. Stephen saw a pile of board games and roleplaying supplements. *Palladium*, *Runequest*, *Talisman*. One small box contained the throwaway party game *Truths and Dares*.

"Ha! I remember this," said Stephen, opening the snug lid. There was a thick wodge of white *truth* cards and an equal wodge of black *dare* cards. "We dared Lennox to ask a random girl out. Didn't they end up going out for four years."

"Something like that," said Darren. "Here."

"Is this the secret of your wealth?"

He pulled open a drawer, flicked through a hanging file and pulled out a plastic wallet, subdivided into nine protective sleeves. Each held an individually-sealed card. Stephen immediately recognised the border design on the cards.

"*Mana Clash*?"

"The *Potent Lotus* card," said Darren. "In the game, it taps into any kind of mana source you want. Sold one over the internet last month for four hundred pounds."

Stephen nearly coughed in surprise. "Four hundred pounds? For a trading card?"

Darren put the wallet back in the cabinet and, closing it, shuffled further in. He came up against a bicycle stored between the aisles and had to squeeze past. Stephen looked at the faded red bike with the wide basket on the front.

"You've still got that thing?"

Darren gave a shrug. "It was my dad's post bike. I've not ridden it for years."

"It's as old as we are."

Darren opened a new drawer and finger-walked through rows of wallets until he found the one he wanted.

"This," he said, "is a foil special from the *Dimensions* expansion set. Only ever released in Japan. This card, *Fortunes of War*, guess how much?"

"I don't know. Six hundred pounds."

"Two and a half thousand."

"You are kidding me!"

"I am not kidding you."

Stephen came closer, squinting at the playing card as though somehow scrutinising it might make its true value shine forth. But it was just a playing card with a glittery border and some nerdy rules gubbins beneath standard, fantasy artwork.

"Two and a half thousand," he whispered. "And to think we used to laugh at you buying all those cards off Ed."

"What's galling is that Ed told me he had found a supplier of *Dimension* packs, back in our late teens. Claimed he could get some for me. Never happened. I'd be a millionaire if that had happened."

"Life is full of what-ifs, I guess," said Stephen.

He looked at his old friend, squashed between a pink bike (it was pink, no matter what anyone said) and a filing cabinet, surrounded by thousands upon thousands of pounds' worth of geek gaming tat and wearing what was undeniably the most hideous jumper Stephen had ever seen. And he considered himself, grubby and penniless in a monk's habit, here only because he was on a mission from Hell itself.

"Nothing ever turns out like we think it will, does it?" he said.

"Too true," said Darren. "Now, let's find you a spare bed for the night."

Darren extricated himself from the confines of the garage, locked up and led Stephen inside. Apparently, Darren's mum had already gone to bed, so the two grown men literally tiptoed up the stairs and, in whispered conversation, discussed sleeping arrangements. Darren found Stephen a box room at the back of the house and together they unfolded a spring-loaded camp bed into the only available floor space.

"Sorry, it's not much of a room. I can get mum to tidy it in the morning," whispered Darren.

"It's great," Stephen replied honestly. It was, if anything, marginally more luxurious than the dormitory back at St Cadfan's.

Darren dug out a musty-smelling orange sleeping bag from a storage box and a cushion that would serve as a pillow and backed out, leaving Stephen to settle in.

Stephen tiredly slung his rucksack onto the bed and pulled out his clothes.

"Ew."

Something had happened to the shirts, trousers and socks within. They were full of holes and many of the holes were ringed by dirty crusty stains. It was like a band of grungy moths had worked their way through it all. A black hard lozenge fell out the bottom of the rucksack. Stephen picked it up and wondered why he had packed a liquorice stick before realising it was a dried-up slug. He dropped it in disgust.

"Well, I hope you had a lovely final meal," he said and put his ruined clothes to one side.

There was a tapping sound. He looked to the ajar door but there was no one there. The tapping sound came again.

There was a squirrel on the window sill outside. It had a roll of banknotes in its claw. Stephen stared at it until the squirrel gave him a blankly impatient look. He reached for the latch and pushed the window open. The squirrel immediately held the roll of money out to him.

Stephen took it. There were tiny flecks of red paint on the squirrel's claws.

"Where did you find this?" he said and immediately feeling stupid, followed up with the no less stupid. "Thank you very much."

The squirrel tutted as though to tell Stephen to not do it again and leapt away into the darkness.

Tuesday

Stephen woke, still tired and a little dazed.

He had not slept well. The room had been too quiet. All night, his sleeping subconscious mind had stumbled about like a man in the fog, wondering where the rest of the world had gone. In short, Stephen slept poorly because the snores, farts, sighs and nocturnal mutterings of the other monks in the dormitory were absent and, in a way that was both sweet and disturbing (mostly disturbing), he realised he missed them. It would have been better if his restlessness had been down to worry for Rutspud – a far finer and nobler explanation. Deciding that, yes, that would be the lie he would tell himself, Stephen threw on his habit and went downstairs towards the sound of conversation and the smell of bacon.

In the small kitchen diner at the end of a hallway lined with shelves of kitschy crystal animals, Darren was tucked into the corner table and tucking into a plate of bacon, eggs, sausage and beans.

"He is up," greeted Darren, spitting a fleck of bean onto the table. "I thought I was going to have to rouse you myself. Mum's just doing yours now."

At the gas hob, Darren's mum paused in the act of prodding a pan of pork products to fried perfection. She looked just as he remembered her and simultaneously utterly different. Had she always been so small and so very... mumsy? Certainly, she had always looked tired, but now she had the wrinkles to prove it.

"Morning, Mrs P."

"Good morning, Stephen," she said and wiped her hands on her apron as she appraised him. "Well, just look at you."

"All grown up, yeah," he said.

"I meant the..." She wafted her hand at his habit. "A man of the cloth in my house. I thought it was just a phase you were going through."

"That's what I said," said Darren.

"That is what he said," said Stephen.

"I've done you the full works," she said, and Stephen realised that the five sausages and four rashers of bacon in the pan were all for him. "You need feeding up. I suppose it's all gruel and cabbage water at the abbey."

Stephen didn't bother to explain that Brother Manfred was a culinary explorer, and that breakfasts at St Cadfan's had been known to include bacon muffins, egg and grape tacos, and the memorable and never repeated (yet eternally repeating) kippers in jelly.

"That looks lovely," he said.

"Cup of tea?" said Darren.

"Yes, please."

"He'll have a cup of tea too, mum," said Darren.

"No, I can get it," said Stephen. "You don't have to bother yourself."

"No, you asked. You'll get. Already doing it," said Mrs Pottersmore. "You sit down, out of the way."

Stephen knew there was no point arguing and put himself next to Darren at the dinner table.

"That's, um, another smashing jumper," he said.

Darren considered his garish knitwear. It was a representation of the story of Noah, with dozens of carefully-embroidered animals emerging from the ark.

"I like the rainbow," said Darren. "It's very striking."

"Mmm. Isn't it?" agreed Stephen, rubbing the after-images from his eyes. "And the animals. Are those dinosaurs in the background?"

"Maybe," said Darren.

"A theologically-challenging jumper as well," said Stephen.

Darren waved an eggy fork at him. "You required to wear the habit all the time?"

Stephen pulled a face. "My old clothes got damaged in storage. I'm a little sartorially embarrassed at the moment."

"We'll find some of Darren's old things for you," said Mrs Pottersmore.

"No, err, you don't have to," said Stephen, thinking there might be a problem finding anything that would fit and wouldn't cause permanent sight loss.

"I'll have a rummage through the clean linen," she said and put a heaped plate in front of Stephen. The layer of grease shone like a tropical sea.

"This looks lovely, Mrs P. You're very kind."

"Oh, I like to feed growing boys."

Yes, thought Stephen. And the more you feed them the more they grow. It was probably a good thing Darren had never given her any grandchildren. Social services would have had her in court for calorie-based child abuse.

Stephen cut up his bacon as Mrs Pottersmore went off to find him some alternative clothing.

"The jumpers," he said. "I've got to ask..."

"My mum likes knitting. I like to make her happy. And, you know what? I think they make the world a brighter place. Why do people seem to have a problem with that?"

"Actually, I was going to point out that they're very religious."

"They are."

"You've got into Jesus in a big way."

Darren nodded emphatically. "He's great, isn't it?"

"Jesus? Oh, yes. He's one of my favourite people. Top five easily. Even top three."

"Number one, surely," said Darren, alarmed.

"Quite probably. But you...?"

"Yes?"

"You were all into that occult stuff and I don't mean just dreamcatchers and joss sticks. You were a full-blown, Anton LaVey 'all hail the mighty Baphomet' what-have-you Satanist."

Darren's emphatic nod had become slow, shameful. "I was."

"And...?"

It was a difficult expression on Darren's face. Complex thought had never come easy to him. Stephen recalled that, in school lessons, algebra had given Darren cold sweats and,

65

depending on whether one believed the rumours or not, he'd once fainted in an exam trying to prove Pythagoras' theorem.

"I underwent a conversion," said Darren.

"A conversion."

"One of them road to Tabasco things."

"Damascus."

"Damascus? You sure?"

"Tabasco... I think it's in Mexico. Paul was a well-travelled guy but..."

"Right," said Darren. "Road to Damascus. That one."

"So, you saw the light," said Stephen. "People turn to God for different reasons..."

The difficult expression on Darren's face hadn't got any easier.

"Can I tell you something?" he said.

"Of course, you can."

Darren looked past Stephen to make sure his mum was out of earshot.

He's killed someone, thought Stephen instantly. He's killed someone and this whole Christian thing is a guilt trip. Stephen gave himself a mental shake. Why had he immediately assumed Darren's secret was a murderous one? It was preposterous. Or maybe, Stephen thought, it was just so transparent that a middle-aged bachelor living in his mum's attic would turn out to be a murderer. 'He was always so quiet, kept to himself,' the neighbours would say.

"You promise you'll hear me out?" said Darren. "You won't laugh?"

Laugh? Murder wasn't a laughing matter, so Darren clearly was not a killer – unless he was a *psychotic* killer who thought murder was hilarious and kept body parts in the freezer and wore women's heads as hats. Stephen looked at his sausages and put his knife and fork down.

"I won't laugh," he said. "But just so you know, I'm not a priest. I don't take confession, in case you were thinking of confessing to something..."

"I met the devil," said Darren.

Stephen looked at him.

"Like in a metaphor?"

"No, in my bedroom."

"But the devil was a metaphor. Like for drink or drugs. Or Angry Birds."

"No, it –" He snorted unhappily. "You said you would hear me out, Stephen."

"Sorry. Yes." He zipped his mouth and made a silent 'go on' gesture.

"I met the devil," said Darren. "He looked like a man, just like a man. He came to my door, a few years ago now, and he wanted to talk to me about a Satanic ritual."

Stephen so very much wanted to ask Darren why Satan would want to talk about a Satanic ritual. Did the devil think he was doing it wrong and had just come over to give him some pointers? Stephen held his silence and made a thoughtfully-interested expression.

"He was very rude," said Darren. "Vulgar. He mocked my beliefs, my rituals. He didn't recognise me as a true follower. He didn't even know that I had devoted my life to worshipping him. And then he showed himself to me."

"Showed himself?" said Stephen, hoping he wasn't going to need an anatomically-correct dolly for Darren to indicate which bits of himself the devil had shown.

"He showed me his true nature. His vile wickedness."

"I see."

"And then he opened a portal to the afterlife and jumped through. And like that – puff! – he was gone."

Stephen nodded, mulling things over. He was in a deeply tricky situation. Throughout much of the church's history, those who claimed to communicate with the infernal had been subjected to exorcisms, tortures and even death when, in reality, what they probably needed was someone to talk to, a bit of a lie-down and maybe some really powerful anti-psychotic drugs. The modern church still believed in demons, but it believed in mental illness and psychiatric medicine a heck of a lot more.

Stephen knew that if he was approached by one of the faithful with fanciful stories of spiritual encounters then his role should be a pastoral one, a counselling one, and a signposting service to the appropriate NHS department. And yet Stephen had a great deal of

67

personal experience with demons. He'd met them, he'd sat down and had a drink with them, he'd shared a bag of jelly babies and moonlit bicycle rides with them. To dismiss or diminish Darren's experience when he himself had left the monastery to search for his demon buddy, Rutspud, would be hypocritical in the extreme.

"I was so horrified by it all, I flipped," said Darren.

"You went mad?" said Stephen.

"No, I flipped. I switched teams: one day a Satanist, the next a Christian – a really *enthusiastic* Christian. I was never a Satanist. Not really. It was just my way of rejecting the values I'd been brought up with. A way of showing I didn't care what people said. 'Oh, there's fatty Darren Pottersmore, lives with his mum. Stupid Darren Pottersmore, whose dad ran off with some strumpet in Kingstanding...' Satanism was my armour against other people's cruelty. I didn't believe in Satan. I just didn't want to believe in anything anyone else believed in."

"You were a nihilist."

"Was I? Why, what do they believe in?"

"Nothing."

"Oh, that'll be it then. Huh. I heard that someone had set up a nihilist collective coffee shop or something in Boldmere."

"What's a nihilist collective coffee shop?"

"No idea but I thought it sounded dead clever."

Darren stopped and appeared to think long and hard. "Anyway, that's how I became a Christian. And Jesus, he's my armour now. He's got my back."

"Good for you."

"Do you believe me?"

"I do," said Stephen. "You sound like a fervent believer."

"I meant about the devil."

"I believe you believe," he said diplomatically.

"So, you don't believe me," said Darren.

"I didn't say that. I believe in the devil. I believe in demons. How each person perceives them is as unique as each individual." He made a show of looking over his shoulder to be sure Mrs Pottersmore hadn't returned. "Can I tell you something?"

Darren noisily utched his chair closer. "What?"

"You know I said I've come back here on a mission?"

"Your quest. Yes."

"Well, this quest, it's not entirely un-demon-related."

"Isn't it?"

"No. I've come back to Sutton to find out who has been carrying out demon summoning rituals."

"Summoning rituals? Plural?"

"At least one," said Stephen, honestly. "And it occurs to me that, with your insider knowledge, you might be able to help me locate them."

"Cor," said Darren, eyes unfocussed in wonderment. "I'd be like your sidekick, helping you out."

"Exactly."

"Watson to your Sherlock."

"That's it."

"Ron Weasley to your Harry Potter."

"If you like."

"Donkey to your Shrek."

"Perhaps."

"Samwise Gamgee to your Frodo."

"Yes."

"Spock to your Kirk."

"Uh-huh."

"Chewbacca to your Han Solo."

"Hmmm."

"Scarecrow to your Dorothy."

"Really?"

"Buzz to your Woody."

"Do you have many more of these?"

"Maybe," said Darren in a quiet voice.

Stephen speared a piece of sausage with his fork.

"Go on then. Get them out of your system."

Darren took a deep breath.

With an *urk*, a crunch and a stream of curses, Rutspud pulled himself back up into the three-dimensional world.

It had taken all night to work it out. He had thrashed and pushed and railed against his 2-D slice of reality, but thrashing and pushing and railing in two dimensions was of no use if you were trying to get into the third. It had required a rethink of all Rutspud's preconceptions. It was like... learning to ride a bicycle (now *that* was an interesting night on the grassy slopes of Bardsey Island with Brother Stephen). Natural instinct said to stay upright when cornering, but that way lay disaster. To cycle, one had to lean into the turn, push in a direction that seemed far from logical. So, it had been in Rutspud's pizza-flat prison. He just needed to reach out in a counterintuitive direction, flex back and up.

"*Urk!*" said Rutspud. "Satan's great dangling cods! Those demon-fiddling arse sores!"

"Yous should have listened to poor old Shafttoe," said the demon in the darkness across the way.

Rutspud tried to stand, forgot his limbs worked up-down, left-right *and* backward-forward ... and fell down again.

"A little light?" he wheezed.

Shafttoe clicked on his lamp. He sat with a *Take A Break* magazine in his lap and a biro clutched thoughtfully between his tombstone teeth.

"'Eighteen across: ant and blank, popular TV presenter, three letters,'" he read. "Ant and blank... Ant and blank... Ant and Bee? Bee would fit. Fly? You know any famous TV presenters, my friend?"

"What?"

"Can't see many insects doing TV, can you?"

Rutspud didn't hurry to stand again. He concentrated on counting his limbs and remembering what directions they moved in. He blinked a lot and stared at Shafttoe. The other demon had a pallor Rutspud didn't recall from the day before, a faded colourlessness – like a liver squeezed of all its juices.

"You all right there?" said Rutspud. "Looking a little peaky."

"I'm not a morning person, squire," said Shafttoe. "Also, wish-granting don't half take it out of you."

"Does it? I mean don't it?"

Shafttoe interlaced his fingers, cracked his knuckles with noisy machismo and then winced in pain. He gave Rutspud a filthy look as though he was somehow responsible.

"You try it sometime, you smug git! Having the powers of Hell running through you ain't no fun."

Rutspud frowned. "I thought you said this was a holiday."

"Swings and roundabouts, innit? To get what you want, you've gotta give a little."

That wasn't how things worked in Rutspud's experience and he had never heard such words from a fellow demon. There was no give-and-take in Hell. To get what you wanted, you had to steal it. In Hell, the path to the top led straight across the backs of your enemies and ambitious climbers wore spikes.

"This operation," said Shafttoe, flicking an inclusive finger between the two of them. "This is about teamwork. And there ain't no 'I' in fucking team."

"Between the 'k' and the 'n'?" suggested Rutspud.

Shafttoe was unimpressed.

"You think being squished into two dimensions is the worst Merilyn can do to you? Pah! You'll end up like Lackring if you don't start pulling your weight."

"Lackring?"

Shafttoe pointed at the box in the corner covered by the large, stained sheet.

"Here," said Shafttoe and, with arthritic awkwardness, stood up on his chair and used a rolled-up magazine to bat at the cross beams above his head. "Coming your way."

Someone had stored bamboo sticks and other long-handled implements by laying them across the wooden beams and the electrical wiring that ran along the ceiling. As Shafttoe slapped at the items, several slid forward precariously and then gravity found one of them and it spilled forward towards Rutspud. He clumsily caught it with a hand that still wasn't thoroughly reacquainted with X, Y and Z co-ordination.

Rutspud saw it was a fishing rod. In the sixth circle, they used them to feed oil executives to Yan Ryuleh Sloggoth and the other denizens of the Bottomless Pool of Demonic Horrors.

Shafttoe jerked his head towards the box in the corner.

"Come on then," he said. "Meet the neighbours?"

Rutspud reached out the fishing rod and poked at the covers. He snagged the tip in a tear in the fabric and pulled. As it shifted, he saw that, in the shadows, it was weighed down by something.

"Easy now," said Shafttoe.

"I am being easy," said Rutspud and tugged at the cloth until it fell to the floor in a sudden clatter of mechanical odds and ends.

It was cage, though not a particularly sturdy one. It didn't even have a bottom. It sat atop a magic circle, smaller than either Rutspud's or Shafttoe's, and at the centre of the circle hunched a demon covered in rolls of sagging skin, like someone had sucked half the meat out of a sausage and given it arms and legs as compensation. It looked like a waxwork model of a child had magically come to life and unwisely decided to sit next to a three-bar fire to warm up for a bit.

"Lackring?" said Rutspud.

The demon shushed him loudly. "Can't you see I'm on hold?"

Lackring waved something at Rutspud before putting it back against his ear. He rocked on his heels and skinny buttocks and crooned along with whatever he was listening to.

"*Too-doo doo-ah, too-doo doo-ah, pa rumpa-rumpa doo-ah...*"

"I'm new here," said Rutspud. "Shafttoe wanted to introduce me to –"

"Shush!" the demon squeaked, its pink eyes widening for a second. "I'm next in line! *To do-doo, to do-doo, to do-doo...*"

"Has he got a phone?" asked Rutspud.

"If you look more closely, you'll see our friend is making a telephone call with a dead rat," said Shafttoe.

Rutspud looked. His caged neighbour was rocking to hold music supposedly coming from the mummified remains of a small rodent.

"What happened to him?" said Rutspud. "Merilyn obviously, but what?"

Shafttoe stretched and resettled comfortably in his chair. "Our friend was not willing to play the game. He thought he was above such things."

"He refused to grant their wishes."

"Indeedy-do. We may be guests at this holiday retreat, but there must be some form of re-cip-ro-ca-tion. Our Lackring don't understand that, weren't willing to bend. Were you? Eh? Eh!" he called loudly.

Lackring didn't respond. Shafttoe shook his head in disgust.

"You think being squashed into two dimensions is bad, my friend? Hold out much longer and she'll break out the Enya."

Lackring gave a high-pitched wail and rocked faster. "*To do-doo! To do-doo! To do-doo!*"

Rutspud shuddered.

"Oh, you know the Enya, do ya?" said Shafttoe.

Rutspud nodded. "Lord Peter uses it to motivate demons who are stressed and depressed."

"Ah, well, us grafters in the third circle wouldn't know what Lord Peter gets up to in his high and mighty tower. But I suppose you lot airy-fairying around in Infernal Innovations get to mix with management."

Rutspud had been cunning enough to avoid many of the support mechanisms handed out to overworked demons by the current lord of Hell. A former-saint possessed of a human sadism no demon could hope to compete with, Lord Peter understood that the most terrible punishment can be made worse by dressing it up as a reward. In that spirit, he'd sent Rutspud for a course of 'kitten therapy' at Hell's Relaxation Centre. Rutspud had suffered a severe bout of the Enya while distracting his fluffy tormentors with Brother Stephen's laser pointer. The Enya was worse than kittens. It was the sound of deep-sea creatures exchanging schmaltzy greeting cards. It was the mating song of treacle and moonbeams. It was, to a demon's ears, utterly horrific.

"Hey, mate," Rutspud said to the gibbering demon, reaching out a hand that refused to stretch beyond the limits of his own magic circle. "There's no one here to harm you now."

"Don't play the game," said Shafttoe, "and there's worse they can do. It might start with the holy water and a little light violence. They might move onto the feather duster and a spot of the old Enya."

Lackring gave another wail at the very mention and whined to himself. "I'm next in the queue, *next in the queue!*"

"And when one of us gets a dose of the Enya then we all do. Everyone suffers for one individual's selfishness. It's not like they give him headphones, is it? And is that fair?" said Shafttoe. "I ask you, is it fair? No, it flamin' well ain't."

Lackring kept his back turned but Rutspud could read demons, even mad melty-looking demons with their backs turned, and Lackring was only pretending to not hear.

"All right, point made," said Rutspud.

"And don't think it stops with the Enya," continued Shafttoe bitterly.

"I said, all right!"

Shafttoe snapped open an entertainment magazine and pretended to read. Rutspud squatted at the limit of his summoning circle.

"Lackring," he whispered in his gentlest voice. "Hi, I'm Rutspud."

"Press one if you do not know the extension number of the person you are trying to contact," said the demon and pressed a trembling digit into the dead thing's belly.

"How long have you been here, mate?" whispered Rutspud.

Lackring didn't reply.

"Longer 'an me," said Shafttoe.

"And how long's that?" said Rutspud.

"When I arrived, it was him and Shotbolt here. I don't know how long they'd been here. We is immortal so..."

Immortal, not indestructible, thought Rutspud. Lackring was mad, as broken as a smashed clock, but Hell knew how to deal with insane demons: break them down for parts or give them a promotion. Demons only died when the powers that be were finished with them.

"Shotbolt?" said Lackring.

"Do you remember Shotbolt?" said Rutspud.

Lackring spun round on his bum to face Rutspud. His eyes were so crazed with pink weariness it looked like he was wearing candyfloss contact lenses.

"Would you look at this?" said Shafttoe, extravagantly ruffling his magazine. "Unexpected romance blooms in the *Celebrity Big Brother* house."

Lackring's eyes flicked to Shafttoe's.

"Thingy off of *Loose Women* is apparently enjoying a tender moment with disgraced cricketer Ben whatsisname," said Shafttoe – a sentence that made no definite statement but dripped with subtextual menace.

Lackring's eyes flicked back to Rutspud. His mouth cracked into a child-like smile.

"Yes!"

"Yes?" said Rutspud.

"I *would* like to answer a customer satisfaction survey after my call," he said and spun round to face the wall again.

Rutspud sighed and threw himself back into the centre of his circle.

"Now, what you have before you," said Shafttoe, still pretending to read his magazine, "are two salutary lessons."

"Do I?" said Rutspud, disinterested.

"That you do, my friend. It's like two magic mirrors, glimpses into your possible futures. You can be an ungracious guest," he said, gesturing over at Lackring, "or you can take full advantage of the opportunities before you." He gave a jaunty bow of his head, indicating himself.

"Those are the options, are they?"

"Those they are. Our masters don't have endless patience. They'll want you to start delivering the goods soon. In fact, I'd be recommending you volunteer next time they come down."

Rutspud gave him a shrewd look. "That's all very well, but I don't know anything about granting diabolical wishes. I have no powers."

Shafttoe gave a cough of laughter which turned into a full-blown coughing fit. He reached for his cigarettes, scratted around one of the last remaining ones and then remembered that occultist Mo had taken the matches away. He coughed, spat noisily into his open hand, paused to recall what he had been doing and gave a little concluding chuckle for Rutspud's benefit.

"Powers?" he said. "Course you don't have no powers. You are what is known as a conduit. It's like... it's like my eyes."

"Is it?"

Shafttoe flicked a page in his magazine. "'Nine months pregnant Megan is hoping for a boy. To show off her baby bump for what could be the last time, she poses in matching white underwear for a selfie in the mirror,'" he read. "I read it with my eyes and the words come out my mouth, yeah?"

"Yeah."

"I din't create this Megan, cos if I did I reckon I'd create her with a few more clothes on. I'm just a..."

"Conduit," said Rutspud.

"Precisely. That bit don't take no effort at all. What you will want help with is the razzamatazz."

Rutspud rolled his eyes. "The razzamatazz."

"It's the shine on the –"

"Apple, yes."

"It's the icing on the cake. Your basic occultist don't come to us for results. I mean, the results is important and that, but what they come to us for is an *experience*."

"Uh-huh."

"Now, you let Shafttoe teach you how to sprinkle your performance with a bit of the old razzamatazz and we'll have you living in the lap of luxury an' all." Shafttoe seemed to recall the wad of phlegm he'd coughed up into his hand. He inspected it for a moment and then wiped it on the arm of the chair. "Do we have a deal?"

Rutspud didn't trust Shafttoe. But, then, the number of individuals he trusted in the entirety of creation could be counted on one claw.

"Sure," he said. "Why not?"

Stephen scuttled to keep up with Darren as he turned the corner into Bush Road.

Mrs Pottersmore's search through Darren's cast-offs for clothes that would fit Stephen had resulted in a pair of oversized trousers, a *Lost Prophets* T-shirt and a jumper representation of the ascension of Christ that make it look like the Son of God was rising to Heaven on a robeful of silver-threaded fart power. Stephen declined and stuck with his monk's habit. He had long ago gotten used to wearing clothes that drew looks of derision, but he was only prepared to go so far.

"I appreciate the enthusiasm," said Stephen, "but can you at least tell me why we're going to a shop."

"A Satanist," explained Darren, "and I mean a good Satanist, is only as good as his or her tools."

"Tools?"

"Absolutely. You think you can just google for black candles and pentagrams?"

"Yes," said Stephen.

"True. But not the good ones. Satanists need suppliers and if someone's summoning demons then they'd need the equipment."

"And so, we're going to a supplier. Gotcha."

"Used to be my supplier. My dealer, you would say."

Stephen abruptly realised where they were going. That shop they were heading towards had gone through many makeovers. Stephen had known it variously as *Caldicutt's Ironmongery*, *The Sutton Angler*, *Ray's Video Emporium*, *The Hobby Store incorporating Ray's Videos* and *Boldmere Aquatics (and videos)*. The sign above the window now read, *Ed's Pet Supplies*.

"Wait," said Stephen. "Did I not say? Me and Ed, we've not been on great terms for a while."

"People lose touch. That just makes reunions all the nicer."

"No, but the thing is –"

77

But the thing would have to wait, because Darren opened the door and it announced his entrance with an electronic *meep-moop*. Feeling that absolutely no good could come of it, Stephen went in after him.

What struck Stephen first was the smell, a vivid aroma of mysterious origins. There was the rich fustiness of sawdust, the oaty fug of dog biscuit crumbs, a certain damp tang of aquatic creatures and an undercurrent of small-animal poop. It was a blast of aromatic nostalgia that evoked childhood's wonder and tragedy in equal measure: the delight of getting your first hamster (or goldfish or whatever) and the brutal reality of a shoebox coffin (or quick flush-and-a-prayer or whatever).

The shop wasn't as large as Stephen remembered it – time had shrunk it, as it did so many things – but Ed clearly hadn't let size hinder his business ambitions. The shelves on the walls and in the centre of the shop stretched floor to ceiling and were crammed with boxes and cages, aquariums and blue-lit habitats, pressed together with a wilful eclecticism, each living space marked with a dayglow label and exhortation to buy. Budgies (*£7 – going cheep!*) sat beside rats (*£3 – guaranteed plague free*) sat beside a tank of oysters (*£2 each – pet or starter*). Stephen stared down into the tank and his stomach grumbled.

Darren dinged the bell on the counter.

"Listen, maybe I didn't explain," Stephen began, but then there was a rustle at the bead curtain behind the counter and, like a little boy, he ducked behind a glass vivarium. It made a poor hiding place, as he was quite a bit larger than the bearded dragon inside.

"Good morning, sirrah," said the shopkeeper. "Long has it been since you've graced my humble establishment."

"Morning, Ed," said Darren. "It's been a while."

Stephen peered cautiously over the head of the bearded dragon. It had been a couple of decades since he'd spoken to Ed, at least ten since he'd seen a picture of him. He'd barely changed in that time. While Darren had ballooned in size and Stephen himself had filled out a bit, Ed was still a thin streak of not much at all. As befitted his ever-shifty nature, Ed looked like he could disappear by turning sideways. He was looking a little worn around the edges today.

"I don't think I've seen you in here since you came to sell off all your old demon-bothering kit," said Ed.

"That's a while ago now."

"Sold most of it to Asmondius."

"The level thirty demon?"

"The Satanist. Sold him a lovely pair of jinn bottles the other week. He runs *Hallowed Grounds*, that Satanic coffee shop on the Boldmere high street."

"I thought it was a nihilist coffee shop."

"Yeah," said Ed. "And it's a Satanic coffee shop too."

"But nihilists don't believe in anything," said Darren in the tones of one who had learned a fact and was keen to share it. "So, they believe in Satan *and* they believe in nothing?"

"I don't make the rules," said Ed. "And I don't go judging people neither." Ed pointed at Darren's Noah's Ark jumper. "Still into the old Jesus thing, I see."

"Very much so."

Ed's face twitched as though 'the old Jesus thing' was intrinsically less interesting than the 'demon-bothering'. "And what's the angle there?"

"What do you mean?" said Darren.

"What you get from it. I'm guessing the groupies aren't..." He twitched again.

"Everlasting life in Heaven with Jesus," said Darren.

"Ah. Okay. I suppose that's something." Ed cast about awkwardly, needlessly moved a display item from one side of his counter to the other, blew dust off his till and smiled. "So, what can I do you for? I've got the perfect pet for the religious man of today."

"Well, actually," said Darren but Ed had nipped back through the curtain.

Stephen put his head round the vivarium. "Psst!"

"What are you doing back there?" said Darren.

"I really don't think Ed wants to see me."

"Course he does."

"We parted on bad terms. You see, you know the thing with the policeman."

"The fight he got into?"

"Yes. I was there."

"You weren't," said Darren. "He never said."

"I wasn't there for long. I ran away before..."

The bead curtain rustled. Stephen hid. Ed placed a glass case on the counter. Darren looked at it.

"It's a frog," he said after some considerable thought.

"You have a keen eye and a keen mind. A veritable Richard Attenborough you are."

"I'm going to open a theme park off the coast of Costa Rica and use frog DNA to bring dinosaurs back from extinction?"

"What? No. I'm saying you have the intellect of a great naturalist, Darren."

"Ah. You mean David."

"I'm fairly certain you're name's Darren."

Darren shook his head. "How exactly would this be the perfect pet for a religious man?"

Ed threw his hands wide. "Think about it!"

"I am."

Ed whipped off the lid and scooped up the little brown amphibian.

"Frogs!" said Ed. "Ten plagues of Egypt. You could build up a collection. Very thematic. And every man needs a hobby. You got your frogs, your locusts, your...?"

"Ten geese a-laying? swans a-swimming?"

"Exactly. What d'you say?"

"Um, no," said Darren. "Thing is, I came in here for a reason."

"Of course, you did," said Ed. "Do tell."

Darren glanced back at the display case behind which Stephen was hiding. Stephen did his best to merge with the bearded dragon.

"I'm trying to find, well, *we're* trying to find some demon-worshippers in the local area," said Darren.

Ed frowned. "We?"

It was unavoidable. Stephen couldn't spend the rest of his life crouching behind reptiles. He stood up.

For one wonderful moment, Ed didn't recognise him. His eyebrows lifted in polite but formal welcome... and then memory came blundering in, trampling across Ed's genial expression in heavy boots.

"Stephen?"

"Hi, Ed."

"You!"

"Yes. Er, it's me."

Ed's lips pursed in a scowl and he automatically drew back his arm to fling something at Stephen. The thing in question however was an innocent frog and Ed remembered himself in time and gently returned it to its case.

"Look," said Stephen, "I wouldn't come bothering you if I didn't have to and –"

"Bother me?" said Ed angrily. "Bother me? I'm glad you wouldn't want to bother me! Do you know what he did?" he asked Darren as he came round the counter. "Do you?"

"I'm sure it's a long time ago now," said Darren reasonably.

"Let me tell you what a long time is!" said Ed. "Six months in prison! Six months!"

"And if I could go back and change things..." said Stephen but got no further because Ed had finally found something to throw at him. The hamster ball bounced heavily off Stephen's forehead. "Ow!"

"Let's not fight," pleaded Darren, stepping between them.

Ed tried to shove Darren aside, realised he was up against someone of significantly greater mass and inertia and, instead, squeezed past him. Stephen held up his hands in both apology and self-defence. Ed responded by whacking him on the bonce with a bag of bird feeder nuts which split open, throwing peanuts and sunflower seeds everywhere.

"Please," said Darren. "I'm sure you can put this all behind you."

Bad choice of words, thought Stephen as Ed whipped him with a heavy plastic tube that featured a smiling guinea pig.

"Oh, it's all behind Stephen," said Ed. "Couldn't see him for dust, could I? Deserted me to get beaten up, robbed."

"I did it for you!" said Stephen.

"What? Ran like a fucking coward?"

"I took the suitcase! Not Nigel. I did! The police were coming!"

"Balls, you did!" yelled Ed.

81

Birds and mammals of all persuasions and a few surprisingly vocal reptiles screeched and cried out at the noise and violence. Stephen ducked a cascade of dried pigs' ear chews and ran for the door.

"You ruined my life!" Ed screamed after him.

Without enough breath for a final apology, Stephen dashed out the exit and didn't stop until he was at the corner of Bush Road. When Darren found him, five minutes later, Stephen was still pulling peanuts out of his hair and hood.

"That didn't go very well," said Darren.

Stephen threw the nuts on the ground and gave him a look. "You think?"

They walked to the Boldmere high street, Stephen still pulling the occasional seed from his hair.

"So, what's this *Hallowed Grounds* place then?" he said.

"It's that coffee shop," said Darren. "The one I mentioned. If that's where all the local Satanists hang out these days..."

"I can't believe that 'all the local Satanists' is even a meaningful phrase."

"The world moves on," said Darren. "Things change. Anyway, maybe we can ask around. You know, like private detectives. We go in like a pair of regular joes, ask the bartender some questions..."

"Bartender?"

"Sorry. Getting into character. Although I do recall they sell a range of craft beers."

"What the hell is craft beer?"

"That one pass you by, huh? I believe it's kind of like real ale but with fancy labels on it. Hipsters drink it."

"Yeah, I'm not overly clear on what hipsters are either."

"That's okay," said Darren, as they turned into the Boldmere high street and the long parade of shops. "No one is."

"Fashions change so fast," said Stephen. "God, I sound like an old man. Hey, what happened to Blockbuster?"

"What?"

Stephen pointed along the high street.

"There used to be a Blockbuster Video there, between the shoe shop and the bakery."

"It closed down," said Darren.

"They moved it?"

Darren put a comforting hand on Stephen's habit sleeve. "They closed."

"What, all of them?"

"All of them."

"Why?"

"People don't really watch DVDs anymore. They certainly don't rent them."

"I know," said Stephen, but still... And that's where Woolies used to be."

"That's been gone a while now."

"And there used to be – what was that phone shop called?"

"Phones 4 U?"

"Right." Stephen stared at the high street. "You turn your back for one minute..."

"One minute?"

"All right, five years, and everything changes. And now it's all charity shops and cafes and –" He laughed. "And yet that crappy second hand bookshop is still there."

Darren looked across the road at *Books 'n' Bobs.* "I know the guy who runs it. We used to go to the same wargaming club. I've sold him some of my old books over the years but most of that stuff in there is tat. Here it is."

Stephen was still looking across the road. A small team of squirrels were mending a pothole. Two were manhandling – squirrelclawing – a pot of bubbling tar into position, directed by a foresquirrel wearing a helmet fashioned from a bottle top. The others stood around watching, tools in hand. The squirrels were going about this repair work entirely unnoticed by humans.

"You see that?" he said to Darren.

"What?"

Stephen looked back. The squirrels had gone.

"Nothing," he said.

"Good." Darren stood at the door to the coffee shop. He shook himself down like an am-dram actor doing warm-up exercises. "How do you want to play this?"

Stephen suppressed a smile. "Play this? We're just going in for a drink, Darren." *Hallowed Grounds* had a narrow shop front, barely wide enough for a door and a slim window. "If we happen to meet this Asmondius and he can point us in the right direction then that's great. But, as far as anyone's concerned, we just regular customers, like everyone else."

Stephen stepped into the coffee shop. A dozen heads swivelled to look at him.

"Or not like everyone else," he murmured to himself.

It was like the world's hardest game of *Guess Who?*

Does he have a beard? Yes.

Is it the long and well-groomed beard of a fashion-conscious lumberjack? Yes.

Does he have tattoos? Yes.

Are the tattoos of foreign and idiosyncratic ideograms? Yes.

The sort that might be secret and ancient wisdom and might be a list of menu starters? Yes.

Does he have piercings? Yes.

Does he have sufficient piercings that you have to assume he has others of a more intimate nature? Yes.

Is his dark and brooding look carefully and expensively constructed to look like he has a total indifference to material goods? Yes.

Is he staring at me? Yes.

Stephen gave the room a cheery smile and a "good morning" that caught in his throat and turned into a cough. He put his head down and headed to the counter with Darren in tow and all eyes following them. Stephen made a show of looking at the various muffins and granola bars in the display case.

The barista – Beard, check. Tattoos, check. Piercings, check. – gave him a courteous nod.

"How are we today, sir?" he asked.

"Yes, very well, thank you," said Stephen. "You?"

"Oh, life is but a brief guttering candle between two infinite darks, sir. You know how it is."

"Um, yes?"

"And what can I get you today?"

84

Stephen looked at the coffee price list. The drinks had names like *Espresso Elevator to Hell*, *Morning Ritual* and *Bean-elzebub*.

"Anything you'd recommend?" he said.

"The *Prince of Dark Roast* filter coffee is very nice. It's a simple blend of foraged organic beans from Zimbabwe, roasted to an authentic Chokwe recipe and brewed with locally-sourced, raw water."

"Raw water?"

"Unfiltered and untreated."

"Oh."

"We get it from the canal."

"And does that make it taste better?" asked Stephen.

"All experiences are equally meaningless in a cold and godless universe, sir." There was a glint of madness in the barista's eye, albeit a madness that was very polite and customer-focused.

"Oh, well, that sounds delicious then," said Stephen. "One of those."

"And sir?" said the barista, looking past him at Darren.

"Just a tea for me," said Darren.

The barista's gaze hardened a fraction. "Does sir see tea on the menu?"

Darren studied the menu board. "A *Devil's Brew*?"

"And one *Devil's Brew*. Coming right up."

The barista turned to the vast chrome machinery behind him and began the lengthy process that apparently went into making a simple coffee. Stephen unrolled a note from the money Brother Manfred had given him.

"Has Asmondius been in recently?" asked Darren in the least nonchalant nonchalant tone ever produced by man.

"Asmondius?" said the barista innocently. "I couldn't say."

Stephen felt the presence of at least two people behind him. I bet they could say, he thought. In his mind's eye, he pictured two hulking body builders, the nihilist-Satanist equivalent of hired thugs. Stephen automatically huddled. Maybe, he could pretend he wasn't with Darren, that he was just a passing monk popped in for a perfectly ordinary half soy decaf gingerbread Frappuccino...

"Who wants to know about Asmondius?" said one of the hulking presences.

Stephen sighed. "We do," he said and turned.

The two men weren't half as tall or musclebound as Stephen had imagined, but they were certainly younger and more athletic than him. They were standing uncomfortably close, deliberately so, and there were little details that added an extra level of menace. The one on the right was missing two of his top teeth which, whilst acknowledging that he himself might be prejudiced against those with dental health issues, Stephen saw as a clear sign of someone to steer clear of. The one on the left, though still dentally complete, had upped his danger quotient with some prominent and vicious-looking piercings.

"You've got a piercing in your eyelid," said Darren, impressed.

"S'right, bruv," the man replied.

"Doesn't it rub against your eyeball?"

"Constantly," he said. "Most painful piercing there is."

Toothless looked at him. "Like balls it is, Cain. My mate got his uvula pierced."

"Did she?" said Darren.

"He."

"Oh," said Darren, confused. "I didn't think men had..."

Cain made a dismissive noise. "Uvula's nothing, Baal. I'm thinking of getting my liver done."

"Liver?"

"S'right. Internal piercing. They have to open you up, do it and stitch up again."

Stephen held back on the obvious 'why?' and saw Darren's lips creased to form the same question.

"You guys know Asmondius?" Stephen leapt in.

"Who's asking?" said Toothless Baal.

"My name's Stephen. I'm a monk." He gestured at his habit as his credentials. "And I'm hoping that Asmondius can help us with a little problem."

This caused the pair of them great mirth.

"You don't know Asmondius, do you?" chortled Baal.

"No?" said Stephen.

Cain with the eyelid piercing grabbed Stephen roughly and steered him towards a door at the back of the shop. "Let's go see him, yeah?"

"You too, lard bucket," said Baal, prodding Darren.

"No need to be offensive," said Darren. "It's wrong to mock people for things out of their control. I'll have you know that I'm overweight because my calorific intake vastly exceeds any energy I expend."

"Your drinks," said the barista, hurriedly offering two cups before his customers could be whisked away.

Stephen took his coffee and gazed into its decidedly dark depths.

"Any milk?"

"Soy, oat, almond or coconut, sir?"

"Cow?" suggested Stephen.

"Sir is a monster," said the barista and Stephen was propelled through the door, his coffee unmilked.

When the occultists came, Rutspud was prepared. Prepared in this instance meant prepared to act like a capering buffoon under Shafttoe's instructions. As the occultists descended the steps, he adopted what Shafttoe had called 'Mephistophelean Pose #4' but Rutspud thought of as 'blimey, this suit is too tight'. To his side, the covers had been thrown back over Lackring's cage and the electrical odds and ends that had fallen down with it pushed into the shadows. Across from Rutspud, Shafttoe stood in his own circle giving what Rutspud assumed to be stage directions in an incomprehensible language of grimaces and facial tics of his own devising.

Mo slowly closed the ceremonial book. Winnie gave a final liturgical 'mmmbop'. Merilyn's sunken but gimlet-sharp eyes, looked from one demon to the other.

"How's your back passage, Winnie?" she said.

"What?" said the dumpy occultist, momentarily alarmed. "Oh, yes. The squirrels have done a bang-up job. And I was on the high street just now and saw some of them clearing away some bird feed."

"Bird feed?" said Mo.

"Yes. Nuts and seeds. I think someone had spilt a bag. But, yes, much tidier now, thank you. I mean, thank *you*, Prince Shafttoe."

Shafttoe, locked in his pantomime demon crouch, gave a stiff bow. He looked like he was trying to push out an agoraphobic turd.

"Don't thank him," said Merilyn sharply. "He was doing his job. There's too much thanks about these days."

"Oh, I like to see good manners," said Mo.

"A bit of Ps and Qs never go amiss," said Winnie.

"We *all* like to see good manners," said Merilyn, swiftly asserting her eminence in the field of good manners, "but thanks has to be deserved. I've seen you waving thank you to cars that stop at the zebra crossing."

"I always wave," said Winnie.

"It's the law. They have to stop. You thank someone for something and they think they had a choice."

"But some of them don't stop, do they?" said Mo, aiming for a middle position.

"And they are lawbreakers," said Merilyn. "But thank those who obey the law and they'll start thinking they don't have to."

"So, you don't wave to cars at crossings?"

Merilyn turned on her fellow occultist. "For what? 'Thank you for not illegally mowing me down'? Do I see car drivers thanking me for not leaping without warning into moving traffic? I do not. I respect their right of way. They respect mine. Thanks does not come into it."

"But you leap into traffic and you're going to come off worse than the car," said Mo.

"Much worse," said Winnie.

Merilyn smiled one of her cold smiles.

"So, we thank the car driver because they have the power to hurt but they do not thank us because we're nothing but a potential dent in their bonnets? Might makes right?"

"Um," said Winnie.

88

Merilyn stepped into the centre of the room, black robes swirling dramatically behind her.

"Courtesy and respect should flow up the social hierarchy. Children should respect their elders. Tradesmen should know to come to the back door of the house. Cars should stop for decent folk and not expect thanks. Servants should cower and grovel." She turned smartly to Rutspud. There might even have been an aristocratic heel click. "Rutspud," she said.

Shafttoe gave Rutspud some silent eyebrow waggles of encouragement.

Rutspud, as rehearsed, hunched up like a bodybuilder who'd overdone the steroids and put on a deep and gravelly voice which he'd argued made him sound like he had bronchitis but Shafttoe assured him sounded dramatic and foreboding. Neither of them was sure what a foreboding voice actually foreboded but they ran with it anyway.

"In my demonic kingdom, none dare command me. I reign supreme," he intoned, trying not to look like the idiot he felt. "When I was summoned by your august majesties, I did not know you were puissant individuals. Lord Rutspud offers his sincerest apologies."

Merilyn looked down at him. Well, he thought, at least that's given her pause for thought.

"Lord Rutspud," she said. "You've been promoted since we last spoke."

"I am lord of the sixth circle of Hell, ruler of the city of, um, P'tang."

"Didn't we have the lord of the sixth circle in here before?" said Merilyn, in a tone that was perhaps meant to come across as lightly amused and missed it by miles.

"I am now your servant," said Rutspud. "Command and I shall do your bidding."

"Yes. Yes, you shall." She held his gaze.

Rutspud did his best to appear dreadfully powerful yet compliant, which wasn't easy given that he was also fighting down the desire to jump up and slap this git good and hard.

"It's a sorry world when the foulest demons of Hell show better manners and civility than the youth of today," said Merilyn.

"My boy is a polite little boy," said Mo.

"Your boy is many, many things," said Merilyn. "But this world is going to Hell in a handcart and it all started when people stopped showing respect to one another. Thinking obeying zebra crossings is optional..."

"Throwing bird feed all over the pavement," put in Winnie.

"The other day, the lad in the supermarket called me 'mate'," said Mo.

"Really?"

"Not 'madam'. Not even 'missus'. Mate! I was horrified. And then when I told him I didn't need all the plastic packaging around my bananas and wanted him to take it off, he looked at me like I was mad!"

"Well, really," said Winnie.

"It's not as though bananas don't already come in their own protective wrapping, is it?"

"No respect for others," said Merilyn.

"For themselves," said Winnie.

"For the planet," said Mo.

"It's the disposable culture we live in."

"*I* recycle *my* tea bags," said Merilyn.

"They use something once and throw it away," said Mo.

"Put it in the little green recycling caddy I do and put it out for the dustman."

"Huh! Most of them don't seem able to put their own litter in the bin."

"They think it's someone else's job."

"It shouldn't be up to the squirrels to tidy up their mess."

"Otherwise, how will they learn?"

"Nuts and seeds. Nuts and seeds all over the pavement!"

"How would they like it if someone collected all the rubbish they'd dumped and left it on their doorstep?"

"I wish someone would." Merilyn caught herself at the end of that sentence. "Yes, I wish someone would."

She looked down at Rutspud.

"Your command?" he asked.

Merilyn's puckered sphincter of a mouth wrapped itself around each carefully-chosen word.

"We command that every piece of improperly-discarded waste crawl back to the person who threw it away. Every dogend, every crisp packet, every mattress dumped in a hedgerow –"

"Ooh, that does get my goat," said Winnie quietly.

"– every single piece should make its way back to the offender for correct and proper disposal."

"Righty-ho," said Rutspud. "Let's do this."

Merilyn raised her arms and began to chant. Rutspud had heard it before, although he had been two-dimensional at the time and in no fit state to enjoy it. Mo and Winnie flanked Merilyn and joined in with the gibberish incantation. Rutspud felt he ought to be playing some role but was unsure what was expected of him. He adopted a receptive pose and tried to give off some generally positive body language.

"Okay, and what do I do now-*waaaah....*"

The feeling began in his feet and travelled rapidly up his legs, a numbness, as though he was being vibrated at high speed except there was no movement. There was a sucking sensation but not applied to his whole body, as though fifty percent of his molecules had decided to migrate south for the winter. It was indescribable, although Rutspud would have been quick to describe it as 'definitely unpleasant'. And that was only the beginning.

There was a searing blue flash and then the power – the *wish* – passed through him. Shafttoe hadn't lied, not really. The wish-granting business simply meant being used as a conduit for the powers of Hell, just as the human digestive system could be used as a conduit for water under pressure. But this... This was an acid enema.

The light and the power vanished, but the pain – Balls, the *pain!* – continued. Rutspud collapsed, sapped of all energy and drained of something that he suspected was more intrinsic and vital. His breath came out as a rasping moan.

"Very good," said Merilyn.

Rutspud couldn't lift his head to look at her.

"Have you killed him?" said Winnie.

"I think this one is made of steelier stuff than the pathetic specimens we've had before. What do you think, Shafttoe?"

"As you say, mighty one," said Shafttoe servilely. "As you say."

91

Footsteps sounded on the wooden steps as the occultists departed.

"There you go," said Shafttoe. "Passed the initiation. Paid your dues. Part of the club now, yeah?" There was an unmistakable note of pleasure in his voice.

Rutspud tried to respond but could only manage an embarrassing mess of vowels and gave up.

"What don't destroy us makes us stronger," said Shafttoe. "That's what Nietzsche said, wasn'it? Although... having met the man since his death, I don't reckon he believes that no more."

Cain led the way up a steep flight of stairs. Stephen and Darren had little choice but to follow.

"Anyway," said Baal at the back of the line, "my mate, Obsidian, he got his ball pierced."

"His sack?" said Cain. "Nothing. I've got that."

"Not just his scrotum. His testicle. A bar right through it. Says it's bloody agony. That's a proper piercing."

"Tell you something that's better," said Cain as he reached the top of the stairs.

"Better than having a bollock pierced?" said Baal.

"Much better."

Against his better judgement and the fact that he had other things to worry about, Stephen was curious what could possibly be 'better' than a piece of metal inserted in a testicle.

"You know you can get your eyeball tattooed?" said Cain.

"Course," said Baal.

"They inject the ink right in there."

"I know. I know."

"My bruv, Raven, he had them inject his balls with permanent ink. Both of them."

"What?"

"It's true, mate. And now he spunks black."

"Black jizz?"

"Black jizz. He showed me."

"Cool."

Stephen considered there were any number of words he could have responded to that information with. 'Cool' was not one of them. But he was a big believer in not passing judgement on others, even idiots, and kept his thoughts to himself.

Cain stepped through a door. There was brief, muttered conversation and he beckoned them in.

Stephen didn't know what to expect from the private chambers of a Satanic group leader. His mind immediately leapt to the clichés: black drapes, silver pentagrams, greasy black candles and greased-up virgins. Stephen suspected that he had watched too many Hammer horror movies in his youth.

The room was, in reality, very much more the office of a coffee shop manager who also happened to be a nihilist Satanist. Boxes of vacuum-packed coffee beans and other supplies were stacked at the back by the fire door. A noticeboard behind the main desk held a large and complex staff rota, a couple of greetings cards wishing the recipient a happy Walpurgisnacht and a poster cheerily reminding one and all that 'No one gets out of here alive'. Above the noticeboard, someone had mounted a pair of crossed samurai swords – a décor choice favoured by samurai and sad loners everywhere. The desk held a set of in-trays, a computer tablet, a pair of ornate glass bottles and what Stephen reckoned was a genuine human skull. It was brown, cracked and, like Baal, missing numerous teeth. The fingers that currently drummed on the skull were covered in heavy silver rings.

The owner of the fingers, the rings and, Stephen assumed, the office, the desk and the skull (though not its original owner, obviously) definitely had the appearance of a Satanist, by which Stephen meant he had the bald head, neat beard and sharp cheekbones of an evil stage hypnotist. He wore a black tie over a black shirt, a look that could so easily come across as 'Italian waiter' and was quite tricky to master.

"An actual monk?" he said, around the wad of gum he was chewing. "Thank you, Cain."

"Mr Asmondius, thank you for taking the time to see us," said Stephen, nervously.

"I had expected you sooner. Still, 'none shall know the day or the hour', eh?"

Asmondius had a languorous and nasal voice, cultured in tone (and all the more irritating for it).

"Sooner?" said Stephen.

Asmondius waved a beringed hand at Darren. "And who's your colleague in the hideous knitwear?"

"Darren's helping me with a personal matter."

"I bet he is."

"I'm trying to find someone who might have carried out the Rite of Ukahdo. It's a summoning ritual used –"

"I know what it is!" snapped Asmondius and then, "Wait. You haven't come to threaten me?"

"Threaten you?"

"Or plead with me? Or bargain?"

"I'm sorry. I don't fully understand..."

Asmondius sat forward, his fingers steepled together. "I have spent the last month performing the rituals of the Abugor Vipos, a direct attack on the spiritual body of the Christian church. You – you! – have come here in response to that attack."

Stephen pulled a face. "Ooh. I am sorry. No, I don't really have that kind of authority."

"One month!"

"Yes. You've put in a lot of hard work, I'm sure."

"Nights I have devoted to becoming a magical canker at the heart of the church."

"I understand. I'm sure the church will..." Words bubbled up inside Stephen and every rational and fearful thought within him told him not to say them, but they were irresistible. "Are you sure the church knows?"

"What?"

"About your, um, attack? Have you notified them?"

Asmondius picked up the skull and slammed it down like an inefficient gavel.

"I have drawn the sigils and invoked the spirits!" Asmondius picked up one of the bottles on his desk. It was large, bulbous, thin-necked and covered with a swirling network of engraved symbols. It might have been an antique, it might have been mass-produced in a Chinese glassworks and sold for a tenner at a New Age craft fair – it was so hard to tell these days. "I will bind jinns of Hell in these bottles and unleash them on unsuspecting clergy! I have been the worm in the very gut of their being! Priests and nuns have wept in their sleep as my shadow passed over them! I am the weight on the pendulum, sending the whole sick edifice of Christianity to swing out of true!"

He stopped at a slurping sound. Stephen looked at Darren, who was sipping noisily at his tea. Darren glanced from Stephen to Asmondius mid-sip.

"Sorry. Didn't want it to get cold," he whispered. "It's very nice by the way. Mr Asmondius, is it true that you're both a nihilist and a Satanist?"

"What?"

"I was just wondering how that works. Do you believe in Satan? Or do you believe in nothing?"

"Nothing! Nothing has any meaning. Life is a scream in the void. There are no truths! There is no purpose! Those priests and popes who claim to know truth are liars and charlatans and I stand beside all forces that oppose them!"

"Sure, but if you do believe in nothing then being a Satanist is kind of pointless and I –"

"What are they doing here?" Asmondius demanded, now of Cain and Baal.

"The Rite of Ukahdo," said Stephen. "I'm trying to find someone who has used it."

Asmondius snorted. "They'd need the text of the Krakovian *Livre des Esperitz* to start with. That's a rare book. I've never seen a copy. Why do you care?"

"As I mentioned, it's a personal matter." Something crunched under Stephen's foot. He shifted his sandals. Peanut crumbs. Damn, he was still shedding them! Stuck in the lining of his robes somewhere? A second, uncrushed peanut rocked on the floor , as though it had just been dropped. "Um, I'm helping a friend," said Stephen.

Asmondius sneered. "Help? A member of the church, help? I know you lot well enough. The only ones you help are yourselves. *I've* suffered abuse at the hands of the church. I know exactly what you priests are like. Greedy. Gluttonous. Proud. Avaricious. Lustful!"

He spat his gum out onto the floor.

"Unhygienic," said Darren.

"How can you live with yourself?" said Asmondius.

Stephen didn't answer. One, because he assumed it was a rhetorical question and, two, because he knew there were people who had been mistreated by the church and suffered terrible abuse. Only a fool would deny that such things had happened, and only greater fools would try to cover it up. And they had tried. And they were fools and worse than that for doing so. Stephen didn't answer because this man might be entitled to his rage. His own faith wasn't so fragile that he needed to argue with a man in pain.

"You are a tool of evil and corruption," said Asmondius. "You are a pervert and an abuser. You are a moron for worshipping a God that science has disproved at every turn, whose will is unknown and whose actions are fucking abhorrent."

There was a tug on Stephen's sleeve. Darren gave him an imploring look.

"What?" Stephen whispered.

"Aren't you going to say something?" Darren whispered back.

"God does not need me to defend him," said Stephen quietly.

"God is beyond defending! His religion has fucked over the people of the world at every opportunity! The Crusades! The AIDS epidemic in Africa! The subjugation of women!"

"That thing what Reverend Chiverton did to you, sir," offered Baal helpfully.

"Yes! And that!"

Reverend Chiverton. The name rang a bell, but Stephen couldn't quite place it and let it go.

"Your damned God demands worship and he doesn't deserve it!" said Asmondius. "Renounce him now. Do the right thing."

"I can't renounce him," said Stephen.

"Why ever not?"

Stephen met Asmondius's gaze. "Because I love him."

Asmondius was taken aback. "You love him? Love God?"

Stephen nodded humbly. "Absolutely."

"After all he's done? After all the fucking evil things God has done?"

Stephen paused, held his tongue a second and sought out that still centre in himself. He adopted a forthright stance and, in doing so, crushed another peanut. There were several on the floor near his feet now. Where were they coming from? He cleared his throat.

"I love God. I also love beer."

"What?" said Asmondius.

"Obviously not in the same way but I love beer. And God is a bit like beer."

"Is he?" said Asmondius.

"Is he?" said Darren.

"You can find beer in any number of places. You can make it yourself. Anyone can make beer. But you can also buy it from a brewer. A big, organised brewery. Some people think buying beer from a big brewery is somehow wrong but, you know what, they've got history and experience and expertise on their side."

"Oh, I get it," whispered Cain. "It's like the church, innit." Baal shushed him into silence.

"And like beer, God can fuck you up," smiled Asmondius.

"You can over-indulge," agreed Stephen, "and things can go wrong. People overdo it, and this makes them confrontational and violent. And then they blame the beer. It's not the beer. It's the person. If you're fighting on the pavement outside a nightclub at three in the morning, that's not the beer's fault, that's your fault."

"But we don't need beer in our lives," said Asmondius.

"Nope," agreed Stephen merrily, warming to his theme. "And some people live very happily without beer. Good for them. But I like beer. I love beer. It makes my life better."

"Ha! You're an addict. An alcoholic."

"Not really. I like beer for what it is. I like the fact that it brings people together. I like the fact that if two people who've had an argument sit down with a beer and talk things through, they will see they have more in common than they thought. You see, that's the thing."

Asmondius raised an eyebrow.

"Beer doesn't demand praise," said Stephen. "It doesn't demand worship. Why would it? It's beer. But sometimes beer is so amazing, so wonderfully good, that you can't help but praise it."

"Yeah, but beer doesn't claim to be an all-powerful and mystical creator."

"Oh, I don't pretend to understand either God or beer. They're both ineffably mysterious."

"Beer is just beer!"

"Sure," agreed Stephen. "I enjoy beer. I can make beer. But there's still a mystery that defies explanation. And there are some people who will tell you that how *you* like your beer is wrong, that what you've put in it is somehow impure. 'You can't drink that. It's all artificial' or 'It's not as authentic as *this* beer.' Those people only like one beer or one way of making beer. You know what? That's fine. You enjoy beer your way and I'll enjoy it mine."

"The number of wars caused by petty differences!" said Asmondius.

"Wars caused by beer?" whispered Cain.

"He means religion," whispered Baal. "He's being all figurative."

"Some people try to force you to accept their way of enjoying beer," said Stephen. "The details become more important than the beer."

"Real ale wankers," nodded Baal.

"It's not the beer's fault if people get all uppity about it," said Stephen.

"Are you saying that ISIS are like real ale wankers?" said Darren.

"Well, they don't drink alcohol, do they?" said Cain. "They're like... like..."

Stephen looked at the half soy decaf gingerbread Frappuccino in his hand.

"Coffee wankers?" he suggested.

"You think I give a shit about the excuses you make on your God's behalf?" said Asmondius. There was something vaguely familiar about the Satanist's nasal whine, an evocation of an old, old memory. Asmondius pulled out a pack of chewing gum and popped a tab into his mouth. "Now, you made two mistakes coming in here with your moron of a friend."

"Hey," said Darren softly.

"First, you were stupid enough to think that we who have devoted our lives to opposing God would help you with your trivial request. Second, coming in here dressed like that."

"My other clothes were ruined by slugs," said Stephen. "Or possibly very messy moths."

"The boys know how much I hate the church. The mere sight of robes of office –"

"After what old Reverend Chiverton did to you," said Baal.

Old Reverend Chiverton. Old Chivers, thought Stephen. The St Michael's scout leader when they'd been kids?

"Church robes. It's like a red rag to a bull to me. And as for that retarded jumper."

Darren put his hands defensively to his knitted Noah's Ark top.

"It's unscientific," said Asmondius, chewing noisily. "It's unhistorical. Are those fucking dinosaurs in the background? It's visual proof of how stupid your whole religion is."

"I'm not saying it actually happened like that," said Darren. "All my mum's knitting has an allegorical aspect to it."

"Shut it, tubs! Now, Cain and Baal here are going to take you outside."

"Well, thank you for your time," said Stephen.

"No, they're not going to let you go. Not looking like that."

"Not looking like...?"

A sharp tapping at the fire exit door momentarily drew Stephen's attention. It wasn't very loud, probably no more than a windblown branch. He would have ignored it, particularly given the apparently imminent prospect of actual violence, but it was followed by more taps in quick succession, a tattoo of rat-a-tat-tats.

"What the...?" said Asmondius.

Baal pushed open the door. A small but significant mound of nuts and seeds fell in through the gap and rolled lazily across the floor towards Stephen.

"What the...?" he said. He looked down. A dozen or so nuts were nuzzling up to the soles of his sandals, like lambs pressing against their mother for warmth. "Are they following me?"

"What is this nonsense?" said Asmondius, coming round his desk. He stopped as he put his shiny black shoe in the gum he had previously spat. "Aw, shit," he said, peeling it off and stickily throwing it away into a corner. "See what you fuckers did?"

"We?" said Darren.

Peanuts rattled up the metal fire escape and rolled across the floor toward Stephen, followed by a squirrel that was fighting to hold a bunch of nuts in its claws while others kept rolling out of its reach.

Asmondius gave a yelp and, with almost feline reflexes, leapt onto his desk.

"It's a rat!"

"I think it's a squirrel," said Baal, reasonably.

"You can see it too?" said Stephen. "I was starting to think I was imagining it."

"Get rid of it!" yelled Asmondius fearfully. "Look! Look at its teeth!"

"Nigel?" said Darren.

"That's who it is!" said Stephen, realising why Asmondius was so familiar. "It was driving me insane."

"The squirrel's called Nigel?" said Cain.

Stephen turned to him. "Asmondius. Nigel Herring. The year above us at school."

"That's not my name!" screamed Asmondius.

"Got kicked out of the scouts by old Chivers for doing something unspeakable to a hamster," said Darren.

"LIES! LIES!"

"I thought he excommunicated you for challenging the church's teachings?" said Cain.

"Nah, it was definitely for the hamster thing," said Darren. "One of his mates put a hamster in his gym kit for a laugh and the whole school heard the screaming when he found it."

"You weren't there! You don't know!" said Asmondius and then shrieked as the squirrel hopped closer, trying to collect nuts that were rolling towards Stephen's feet.

100

"I'm like some sort of nut magnet," said Stephen, mystified.

"You fucking let that rat in here!"

"We didn't. We really didn't," said Darren.

"Baal. Cain. Hold 'em..." Asmondius, still standing on his desk, tried to free a samurai sword from its mounting on the wall. The wire ties seemed to be hindering his shaking fingers.

"Let's not do anything hasty," said Stephen.

"Yeah, I'm not sure I signed up for this," said Baal.

"Nah, bruv," said Cain. "Can't be a devil worshipper without a bit of blood-letting."

"I dunno. I got into it because of the whole bleak-emptiness-at-the-heart-of-the-universe vibe," said Baal. "And for the chicks."

"And the chicks, obvs," agreed Cain.

"Hold them!"

Asmondius (the Satanist formerly known as Nigel Herring) had lost all of his Satanic-master-slash-evil-hypnotist cool and was now just a tattooed beardy in an Italian waiter suit trying to pull a sword off the wall.

The sword snapped with a ping and came free, leaving behind four inches of its tip still attached to the mounting. But it was still a fearsome weapon.

"Now," growled Asmondius, "I'm going to gut you like – Oh, sweet Jesus! What's that?" He pointed the sword at a furry, alien lollop rolling toward him out of the shadows and screamed. His scream of terror faded to a high-pitched squeak when he realized his attacker was a wad of fluff-encrusted chewing gum.

"What da fuck?" said Cain.

"Is this God's doing?" whispered Darren.

"Let's not hang around to find out," said Stephen, and shoved Darren towards the fire exit.

Asmondius tried to step on the sticky monster, but it scooted away like a terrified roach. He chased it, stomping and missing, until it disappeared into a shadow. Then he turned to take out his frustration on his prisoners and saw that they were gone.

Darren and Stephen were already outside on the fire escape when Asmondius started yelling. They rattled down the rusted stairs toward the alley, followed by a *tink-tink-tinking* cascade of animated peanuts.

"It's going to sound weird," Darren puffed as they ran down the alley, "but I expected Satanists to be a lot friendlier than that."

"Funny," huffed Stephen. "I know what you mean."

At the end of the alley, they turned right onto the Boldmere high street and slowed to a pace that aimed to be both inconspicuously casual and briskly efficient and thus failed to be either.

"Are you continually dropping bird food?" asked Darren.

Stephen looked back at the queue of seeds and nuts skittering along behind them like a line of polite dots. "I think they're following us," he said.

"You're nuts," said Darren.

"Well, they're technically Ed's... Do you think *Baal and Cain* are still following us?"

In reply, a voice shouted, "That way, bruv!"

"Don't think so," said Darren and, as one, they broke into a run.

Stephen and Darren were not seasoned runners. Darren had weight against him (not to mention circumference and volume) and Stephen, though comparatively svelte, had been living on an island where you couldn't build up a decent sprint without running into the sea. Within thirty seconds, they were both thoroughly out of breath though hardly any distance beyond the end of the high street.

An old lady with a tartan shopping trolley gave the two of them a curious and critical stare.

"Is this a fancy-dress thing?" she said.

"No, we're being chased by angry nihilists," said Darren.

"And what are they angry about, young man?"

"Nothing?" suggested Stephen.

"And what are these?" she said, gesturing at the long line of nuts that was definitely following Stephen.

"That might be God's doing," said Darren.

"Debatable," said Stephen. "Come on."

They slalomed through midweek shoppers, hoping to spot a police officer – even a traffic warden or PCSO – they could report their pursuers to, but Boldmere high street was either too sweet a slice of suburbia to need patrolling or not important enough to warrant protection. Stephen scanned ahead for hiding places but, unless they fancied trying to hide in dustbins or do a Scooby Doo and nip into a shop and pretend to be display mannequin, there were no options.

"Through there!" panted Darren.

"Where?" said Stephen.

Darren nudged him sideways, through a side street between two converging main roads. On the corner ahead, there was a pub.

"I know that place," said Stephen.

The Boldmere Oak was much as Stephen remembered it. The black paintwork and brass signage above the smeary leaded windows were the same, perhaps a lick of paint had been applied here and there. He thought he'd seen something in the news about this area being massively redeveloped for a new church, but clearly that hadn't happened at all and Stephen couldn't remember any details.

"Lennox used to sneak us cans from the bar," he said, overcome by a momentary wave of nostalgia. "And we used to sit among the empty beer barrels and drink Fanta and..."

Darren pushed at the door. It didn't open. He grabbed the handle and rattled it to no effect.

"He's not opened up yet!"

"Oi!" yelled Asmondius. "You're dead men!"

"Damn it all!" said Darren and propelled Stephen round the building.

There was a scrubby patch of land behind the pub that had always been known as the 'beer garden'. (This was a euphemism pushed to the breaking point.) Against the pub wall was a covered area that someone might daringly call a veranda (but they ought to be jolly ashamed of themselves if they did). Empty metal beer barrels had always been stored on the veranda, stacked three high with space enough behind them for four teenagers to sit quaffing pilfered Fanta and talking teenage nonsense. That space was still there and just large enough for two men on the run to squeeze into.

Darren forced himself into the larger space between four barrels. Stephen pressed in next to him, face squashed between barrel and brick wall. Bootsteps crunched on gravel nearby.

"Don't move," he whispered.

"I can't," Darren whispered back.

Stephen held himself still and tried to will himself invisible. An entirely inappropriate thrill of excitement ran through him, as though his body had confused this with a childhood game of hide and seek. He also needed a wee. Hiding always made him need a wee.

The bootsteps moved off.

"Have they gone?" said Darren.

Stephen shushed him.

"I don't know," said Baal, distantly. "They could have run off down the Chester Road."

"They weren't that far ahead of us," said Asmondius.

"Peanut!" said Cain.

"What?"

"Look," said Cain.

The voices stopped. Stephen closed his eyes as he had years before, in the magical hope that darkness would make him harder to spot. Silence reigned.

"I do think they've gone," whispered Darren.

Without warning, the barrel in front of Stephen smacked into his face and bounced his head off the wall. The other barrels came down quickly, pulled away by strong and vindictive hands. Stephen's skull buzzed with a noise that promised pain in the very near future. He put his hand to his forehead to feel for blood and missed – which was a worrying sign.

Asmondius held his samurai sword. Cain was armed with a length of copper piping he'd picked up along the way. Baal, who was perhaps the least keen to deal out grievous violence in public, was unarmed.

"You are dead men!" spat Asmondius.

"Um," said Darren.

"All men are but walking shadows and all lives are without meaning," said Baal. "If that's any consolation."

Stephen was too concussed to respond, apart from a vague. "My head... oh, the nuts..."

He bent. He wasn't sure if he was reaching down for the bird food rolling towards him or just beginning a slow slide into unconsciousness. His body was keeping his brain on a need-to-know basis and apparently this was one of the many things his brain didn't need to know.

"I don't know what holy juju you've been casting," said Asmondius, "but it fucking stops now."

"You don't need to hurt us," said Darren and raised his hands in surrender as Asmondius raised his sword.

"No, they really don't," said a new voice.

Baal turned. A large hand grabbed the other end of his length of pipe and twisted so that Baal was suddenly on his knees with his hand still holding the pipe and his arm bent up behind his back. The pipe was yanked free.

Asmondius swung round with his sword but the pipe came up and smacked him viciously on the underside of his wrist. The sword flew from his grip and their angel of mercy snatched it from the air – an action that should have ended in a loss of digits but actually resulted in the man holding two weapons while his opponents had only a twisted shoulder and a possibly fractured wrist.

"And you?" he said to Baal.

"Man," said the Satanist, backing away, "I am not even here." He pulled at Asmondius's shirt and helped Cain to his feet. "We're leaving," he said emphatically.

"We are not –" began Asmondius, but Baal shook him to bring him to his senses.

"We're leaving, sir, and going to have a quiet sit-down somewhere."

They fled.

Stephen watched them run off with blurring vision. Part of him wanted to crash to the floor and sleep. Another part of him wanted to vomit and not stop vomiting until the pain in his head went away.

"And you two?" said their rescuer. "Why are you hiding round the back of my pub?"

He was tall, broad-shouldered and carried himself with a confidence Stephen immediately envied. But then, he'd always been taller, bigger and more confident than the rest of them.

"Nox the Destroyer," mumbled Stephen and fainted.

Something slapped against Rutspud's cheek. It was hard, and it hurt.

"Call for Mr Rutspud," said Lackring.

"Nrgle."

There was a tug. The hard thing fell off and scraped away across the floor. A second later, it landed on his face again. It was still hard, and it still hurt.

"Ow. Fggoff!"

"Call for Mr Rutspud."

Rutspud sat up and instantly regretted it. Everything solid inside him creaked, and the rest seemed ready to leak out and abandon his ailing body.

The hard thing that had hit him was the shell of an old telephone handset. Rutspud picked it up automatically. A fabric-covered telephone wire stretched from the handset to Lackring's circle.

Lackring sat in his uncovered cage and watched Rutspud. There wasn't a smile on the demon's face, not quite, but he looked like he was prepared to smile if the situation called for it. Rutspud saw that the other end of the telephone wire was tied to the tail of the very dead thing in Lackring's hand.

"Why have you tied your rat to... to this?" Rutspud asked.

"Call for Mr Rutspud," said Lackring, the threatened smile broke the surface for an instant, but only an instant.

"Yeah, I get it but..." Rutspud sighed and put the dead telephone handset to his mouth. "Why are you doing this?"

"I thought we should talk," said Lackring into his ratphone. "This is a secure line. No one's listening in."

"Riiight."

Rutspud looked over to Shafttoe. The recliner chair was tilted full back. Shafttoe was laid out with a copy of *Hello!* magazine draped over his face. Demons didn't sleep, but they could create a good facsimile with enough practice. Shafttoe was even snoring.

"Can you hear me clearly?" asked Lackring. "I think this might be a bad line."

"You are aware that this is just a piece of dead wire with half a telephone on one end and a crazy guy on the other?" said Rutspud.

Lackring tittered. "It's okay. I'm only pretending to be mad. I find they leave me alone that way."

"Oh," said Rutspud and then, "Oh."

"Of course, I wouldn't dare say that in public but unless they've got this line bugged they're not going to find out."

"Okay," said Rutspud. "Completely bonkers. Got it."

"I'm Lackring. Used to work in the Pit of Michelin-Starred Chefs Who Tell You That You're Eating Their Food Wrong."

"Ah. Know it well. How long have you been here?"

Lackring's saggy face screwed up in furious thought. "What century is it now?"

"Twenty-first, I think," said Rutspud. "Why? When did you arrive?"

"It was a Tuesday," said Lackring and when there was clearly nothing else forthcoming Rutspud threw the telephone at Lackring's head.

Lackring didn't even flinch. He picked up the telephone handset and tossed it back into Rutspud's circle.

"Call for Mr Rutspud."

"I'm not talking to an idiot. I can talk to myself if I want to do that."

"Call for Mr Rutspud."

Rutspud sucked his teeth and picked up the handset.

"I'm not sure I want to talk to you," he said.

"I could tell you about my escape plans."

"You have an escape plan?"

"Not just one. I have loads!"

"Okay," said Rutspud. "Let's not get over-excited. You're clearly a fruit loop and I've had enough disappointment for one day."

"No. They're brilliant," said Lackring.

"What? All of them?"

"Uh-huh."

"Okay. Hit me with the best of them."

Lackring did a little hand tapping drum roll on the wires of his cage. "Operation Succubus!"

"It's got a title. Good. Good. What's the actual plan?"

"You know succubuses?"

"Female demons? Yup. Met a few."

"Sent to the world of men to seduce, torment and destroy?"

"Yes, indeed."

"We use a succubus to seduce our captors and force them to let us go."

Rutspud considered the merits of this. "Um. And where do we get a succubus from?"

"Ah! That's the clever bit. I've seen the pictures in Shafttoe's magazines. All I need is a little black number – that's a dress apparently – and two half-coconuts."

"Well, dip me in a font and call me holy. That's definitely an interesting plan – apart from the lack of a dress, a coconut and any credibility on your part. I think I'm going to hang up now."

"Wait, wait, wait. I've got more," said Lackring.

"I don't know if I can take any more," said Rutspud. "I think I just need to lie down and wish I was dead for a while."

"You want an escape with a bit more precision, I can tell."

"And fewer coconuts."

"Then I have one which will have you out of your summoning circle in moments."

Rutspud reminded himself not to get his hopes up and said, "Do go on."

"First of all, describe your summoning circle to me, just so I can get a mental image."

"Mental image? You could just look and... Yes, yes, of course," he said wearily. "It's a big painted circle. Lots of symbols around the edges. Sigils of Mu. Pandemonium runes. Shafttoe says it's the Rite of Ukahdo."

"Oh, Shafttoe. I haven't seen him in ages! How is he?"

Right over there, you loon, thought Rutspud.

"The Rite of Ukahdo requires that you be summoned into a circle," Lackring continued.

"Yes."

"A circle. Not a square or an oblong or a squiggle."

"Got it."

"But a circle, an actual and perfect circle can only exist as a concept. All the circles we see in the world are just imperfect copies, shadows on the wall."

"Sure," said Rutspud. "It's impossible for anyone in this world to draw a perfect circle. I see that."

"Therefore, logically, you are not inside a circle at all."

"I'm not," said Rutspud cautiously.

"Which means you can walk right out of your summoning circle, well summoning-thing-that-looks-like-a-circle-but-really-isn't."

"I've tried."

"Ah, but you've not tried now that you know it's not really a circle."

"Fine. Let me give it a go."

Rutspud stood on aching legs and, trying to hold onto the notion that the circle he was inside was no such thing, walked out. His legs refused to carry him any further than the edge of the circle. He took a couple of steps back and did a little shuffling run-up to no effect. He leaned his upper body forward in an attempt to simply fall through the barrier. He slid down to the ground, every inch of him still inside the circle.

"Did it work?" said Lackring.

Lackring sat five feet away, watching him.

"You're an idiot," said Rutspud.

Lackring clutched the dead thing ever tighter to his ear. "Did it work? Rutspud! Are you there?"

Rutspud threw the telephone handset at Lackring again.

"I think we've been cut off. Are you there?" said Lackring.

Rutspud crawled back to the centre of his circle, curled up and wished he was dead for a while.

Stephen sat in a booth in the saloon of the Boldmere Oak with a bar towel full of ice pressed to his forehead. He winced every now and then and inspected the towel for blood, always disappointed that what he found didn't match the severity of his throbbing headache.

Lennox came over and placed two lemonades in front of Stephen and Darren.

"You're very kind," said Darren.

"That'll be two pound forty," said Lennox.

"Right," said Darren and dug in his pocket for spare change.

"So, you're the landlord here now," said Stephen.

"Landlord, owner, businessman and pillar of the community," nodded Lennox.

"You've come up in the world," said Stephen. "Bourgeois, one might say."

"Oh, you're a funny boy," said Lennox. "You want more ice in that towel?"

"Yes, please."

"Go screw yourself," Lennox grinned but went to get some anyway. "But, yes, I have done what we all said we would never do and I turned into my dad."

"Where are your folks these days?" said Darren.

"They retired and now divide their time between here and Trinidad, visiting my grandma."

"Your grandma?" said Stephen, recalling pictures of a wizened little thing in a floral dress on a sun-kissed front porch. "She must be..."

"Dead," said Lennox, passing him a fresh towel of ice.

"Oh. Oh, right. But your parents still visit."

Lennox shrugged coolly. "The cemetery is less than a mile from Maracas Beach and some fine creole restaurants."

"I'm sure that's very consoling in their time of grief," said Darren.

"And you? What have you been up to?"

Stephen tugged on his habit. "I'm a monk."

"I kind of figured that. Didn't think you'd lost a best or something." He pointed at Darren's vivid jumper. "I can see you lost a bet."

"No, I didn't."

"Your eyesight?" suggested Lennox.

"I'll have you know that this is one of my favourite jumpers," Darren sniffed.

"One?" said Lennox. "Wow. But what brings a monk to Boldmere?"

"He's on a mission," said Darren.

"From God?" said Lennox.

Quite the opposite, thought Stephen.

"I'm trying to find someone," he said.

"Some Satanists," said Darren.

Lennox jerked a head towards the rear of the pub. "Hence the run-in with the charming chaps out back?"

"Yes," said Stephen. "But I'm only looking for the Satanists or occultists or whatever because I'm trying to find a friend."

"What friend?"

He pulled a face. "It's complicated. Sort of a long story."

"You hear a lot of long stories in pubs," said Lennox. "Most of them are shit. But I'll take a punt on yours."

The saloon door opened and a trio of older men walked in – one with a little dog on a lead.

"Regulars," said Lennox. "Let me serve them and then it's story time."

As Lennox went off, Stephen put the ice down. He'd stopped bleeding and the ice was doing nothing for his headache apart from distracting him by making his hand cold. Something nudged against his foot. A thick line of nuts and seeds, much of it crumbs now, surrounded his sandals.

"Insane," he said, swept them up into his hand and then didn't know what to do with them.

111

"Hang on," said Darren. He went into his pocket and pulled out a doggy poop bag. Stephen emptied the rubbish in there and stuffed the bag in his pocket.

"You don't have a dog," said Stephen.

"But you never know when you might find some poop that needs scooping. I can't believe some people don't clean up after their dogs. Although the ones who just bag it and tie the bag to a tree are just as bad." He gave a meaningful nod to the dog owner at the bar.

Stephen realised he had met the dog before. The flat-nosed pug had been in the hands of a woman with a thin body like a dangling skeleton. "I think his wife told me to go to the homeless centre last night," said Stephen. "I don't think she wanted me to accidentally walk down her road and bring the house prices down."

"That's Alvin Rees," said Darren. "His wife's a friend of my mum's. Bags his dog's doings and chucks it in a hedge when he thinks no one's looking."

"Some people," said Stephen and picked up his lemonade.

"Some people," agreed Darren and chinked his glass against Stephen's.

A small but constant flow of customers kept Lennox busy for the next hour. Stephen was happy to sit and nurse a lemonade and contemplate his failure to find Rutspud. Lennox's daytime customers seemed to be primarily retired old boys, here out of habit or because they'd been kicked out for the day. Most of the rest looked like they were training up to be retired old boys, favouring a spot of midweek drinking over going to work. In many ways, Stephen realised, they were like the monks back on Bardsey Island. Give them pews instead of bar stools and swap out the pints for cups of Brother Manfred's herbal tea and they would look at home at St Cadfan's monastery.

Lennox made running a pub look easy. The only time he broke a sweat was when he kicked the Lambrini drinker out of the door.

"I used to be someone, you know," yelled the Lambrini guy from the pavement. "They used to worship me!"

"Yeah, yeah," said Lennox, dusting his hands for good riddance.

"There's a man you'd want at your back in a fight," said Darren. He looked suddenly at Stephen. "Sorry. I didn't mean to..."

"What?" said Stephen.

"The thing with you and Ed."

"Oh, right." He smiled but it wasn't a happy smile and it died almost instantly.

"I didn't know anything about what happened that night," said Darren. "I only heard from friends of friends that Ed had got arrested for breaking a policeman's nose and later sentenced to a stint in prison."

Stephen nodded grimly.

"You want the backstory? With wibbly-wobbly flashback effects and harp music?"

Darren gestured for him to proceed.

"Okay, so we were seventeen," said Stephen. "And we were drunk."

"Drinking underage," said Darren.

"Back then, you could just about get away with it in a pub, instead of having to drink in the park or sneak crème de menthe from your parents' drinks cabinet. You were always too goody-two-shoes to join us, and every publican knew Lennox was a landlord's son. So, it was just me and Ed. Anyway, Ed had met a bloke in the pub, some absolutely dodgy scruff-monkey called Nick."

"Dodgier than Ed?"

"*That* dodgy. And Nick was waiting for us at the pub. Ed gave him a thick wodge of notes, more money than I'd seen in my life by that point. And Nick gave Ed a cellophane-wrapped brick. Ed shoved it in this suitcase he had brought along which – him being Ed – I didn't want to know what was in there. Could have been drugs for all I knew."

"Don't think so," said Darren thoughtfully.

"Dodgy Nick left, and from that moment on Ed was just buzzing. It was like he'd made the deal of his life. We drank up our ciders and Ed said we should get a tray of chips to celebrate. His treat."

"And that's why you were both in Large Mike's."

113

"Right. Nigel and his drongo mates came in. We'd all grown up a bit by then... We usually ignored them and they usually ignored us. But, that night, Ed was high on his own criminal endeavours and we were both three-pints drunk. And there was fight."

"What about?" said Darren.

Stephen blinked, eyebrows raised. "You know, I've no idea. Someone looked at someone the wrong way? I think it started when someone said, 'are you looking at my chips?' Someone was busting for a fight and someone else wasn't going to back down. And it just happened."

"Showdown in Large Mike's."

Stephen grunted. "More like handbags at dawn. None of us – *none of us* – were actually any good at fighting. Nigel was no more of a hard man than Ed."

"He was swinging that sword around like –"

"Like a dweeb who thinks swords are cool. No, the fight in the chip shop was pathetic. A bit of shoving, a slap or two and then that stupid hugging thing people do. It could have been over in thirty seconds with nothing worse than a ripped collar or a ketchup stain, but the chip shop owner starts shouting and screaming and runs outside just as a police car comes along."

"Bad timing."

"That's all it was," said Stephen. He swirled his lemonade. The ice had long since melted. "And I made a snap decision. The police were going to come in. I could help Ed, try and pull Nigel and his mates off him. Or I could do the sensible thing and stay out of the way and explain Ed's side of the story when the police came in."

"But, Ed said..."

"Yeah. I ran. I grabbed the suitcase and I ran. Ed never saw me take it. He thought one of Nigel's mates had nicked it and run off, but it was me. I slipped out before the police were even out of their car. You understand why I did that?"

Darren nodded wisely and then shook his head.

"I thought everyone was going to get arrested," said Stephen. "Everyone *and everything* taken down to the station. Getting into a scuffle was one thing. Having a suitcase full of... *stolen* things was another. I ran out to save Ed getting into deeper trouble."

"Oh, that makes sense!" said Darren. "Oh, that's quite clever."

Stephen nodded and sipped tepid lemonade.

"Thing is..."

"Yes?" said Darren.

"That's the version of events I tell myself. That's the comforting lie."

"What do you mean?"

Stephen sighed. It should have felt better to finally admit this to someone, but it didn't.

"I did run out with the suitcase. That was the decision I made. But I didn't do it to protect Ed."

"Why did you do it then?"

Stephen made himself meet Darren's gaze. "Because I was a coward, Darren. Because I was frightened. Because I couldn't bear the thought of the look on my mum and dad's face if their son got arrested."

"But the case..."

He nodded. "The brain is an amazing thing and when the adrenaline's flowing it can leap to wonderful solutions. I ran because I wanted to escape – I did desert my friend when he needed me – and I took the suitcase to provide me with the self-justification for doing so. Aren't I fucking clever, eh?" he said bitterly.

Darren said nothing. That was probably the best thing he could have done. He didn't condemn Stephen; Stephen could do that himself. He didn't offer excuses or forgiveness; there was none to be given, not by Darren. He just sat there, a solid lump of friend wrapped in vomitously ugly knitwear.

"What happened to the suitcase?" asked Darren eventually.

"I ran down the road with it. I ran for a long time. I was on the bridge by the canal when another police car came by. I didn't know at the time that while the police were making arrests at the chip shop Ed had drawn his arm back to punch Nigel and accidentally broke a policeman's nose with his elbow. They'd called for backup. A car came along the road, all sirens and blue lights and, in a panic, I threw the suitcase into the canal."

Darren closed his eyes.

"How much did the suitcase weigh? The block within it?"

115

It was an odd question.

"Um, two or three pounds?" suggested Stephen.

Darren held out his hands and weighed an imaginary bundle thoughtfully.

"It's not one of the key elements in the story," Stephen pointed out.

Yeah, but..." Darren stuck out his bottom lip. "I think I know what was in that suitcase."

"What?"

"Mana Clash cards. The *Dimensions* expansion sets that you could only get in Japan."

Stephen's throbbing head whirled. "L-like that card you had worth two grand?"

Darren nodded and weighed his imaginary bundle again. "Probably a thousand cards. Maybe more."

Maybe more than a thousand cards worth maybe two thousand pounds each. The maths was vague but, whatever way he sliced it, the numbers were big.

"I threw it in the canal," said Stephen in hollow shock.

"Yes, you did," said Darren neutrally.

The two men drifted into silent thought on the significance of that and were only brought back by Lennox shouting at one of his patrons.

"Oi! Alvin! Tidy up after yourself!"

On the other side of the room, the man with the pug looked round. A neatly tied poop bag sat on the polished floorboards in the middle of the saloon.

"It's not mine," said Alvin.

Stephen peered. The contours of the bag spoke evocatively of lumpy squishiness inside.

"Does anyone else in here have a dog?" said Lennox. "No."

As Stephen watched, the bag flopped over by itself towards Alvin.

"You see that?" said Stephen.

"See what?" said Darren.

"That. The bag. It was like...." It was like a jellyfish throwing itself up a beach, trying to kickstart evolution.

"It's not mine and I'm not picking it up," said Alvin. "You can't make me. We don't live in Nazi Germany, you know."

"No, we live in a liberal western democracy, Alvin mate," said Lennox. "Which means you're free to take your business elsewhere if you don't pick it up."

"Well, really!" said the affronted dog owner. "Very well! But I'm only doing this because I'm public spirited."

He went to pick up the bag of poop. It seemed to almost leap into his hand. The pug yipped.

"Something strange going on," said Stephen.

"What?" said Darren, oblivious, swivelling round to catch sight of the strangeness. "Is it the End Times?"

"What?"

"Are you seeing signs of the End Times?" said Darren. "I always keep an eye out and report anything I see to Reverend Zac at church. He's always very interested – gets that faraway look in his eye when I tell him, like he can really picture it."

"No. I don't think it's the End Times," said Stephen. "But I wonder..."

"What?" said Darren.

There was a suspicion in Stephen's head, a suspicion that was more like a succession of questions. At the heart of it all was 'Where's Rutspud?' But surrounding that was 'Is he all right?' and 'What's going to happen to him?', 'What do the people who've summoned him want with him?' and 'To what use can you put a summoned demon?'

"I think I need to be honest with you," he found himself saying.

"About what?" said Darren.

"My friend. I told you I had come here on a mission, to find someone who was doing summoning rituals, to find a friend..."

"Yeah?"

"Well, my friend is... well, he's..."

A stool scraped, Lennox plonked himself down and clapped his hands on his knees in a way that meant 'and that's that'.

"Florence is come in to start her shift. I'm all yours for a bit."

"Florence, your niece?" said Stephen. "Little baby Florence? Tending bar?"

Lennox laughed. "Not so much a baby these days. And she used to be in the military, so she knows how to handle herself."

Stephen looked over to the bar but could see only flashes of hands pulling pints, a white smile chatting with the customers.

"I don't suppose I need to warn you away from my beautiful niece, do I?" joked Lennox, fingering the edge of Stephen's habit. "You've not been kicked out of the monastery, have you?"

"No," said Stephen. "No, I'm just here on a visit."

"Ah."

"He's on a quest," said Darren. "He's looking for a friend."

Lennox raised an eyebrow.

Stephen gripped the edge of the table. "I'm going to tell you both something."

"Okay," said Lennox.

"It's going to sound mad but I'm not making it up. And I'm not mad. I'm sane, boringly sane, you know I am. And I've not gone and switched to some crazy religious sect. What I'm about to tell you is true. Factually true. Not a metaphor. Not a wind-up. True."

"Got it," said Darren.

"Message received," said Lennox.

Stephen took a deep breath and said, "The friend I've come here to find is a demon."

Neither Darren nor Lennox laughed. Neither waved him away. Neither looked surprised or frightened. Stephen pressed on.

"His name is Rutspud. He works in the sixth circle of Hell. We became friends when he found a secret staircase leading from Hell to the cellars of St Cadfan's."

Stephen looked from one to the other. They were still listening.

"He was summoned by Satanists or diabolists or what have you a few days ago. I have reason to believe they are here in Sutton Coldfield or somewhere near here. I've been tasked by Belphegor – he's a duke of Hell, I think – to find Rutspud, free him and bring him home. But I don't worship the devil or anything. I'm still a, you know, one of the good guys. But Rutspud is my friend and that's why I'm here."

He stopped. Lennox was nodding, not agreeing, but thinking. Darren's face was a blank slate.

"Do you believe me?" said Stephen.

"Sure," said Darren.

"Totally with you," said Lennox.

Something imploded in Stephen's mind. He hoped it was just emotional shock and not an aneurism brought on by his head injury.

"B-but I just told you that my best friend is a demon."

"Bit hurt," said Darren. "I thought I was your best friend."

Stephen growled. "The demon bit! My friend is a demon. Don't you have a problem with... I mean, it's insane, right?"

Darren calmly drank the last inch of his lemonade. "I told you already. I believe in the devil. I've met him."

"Yes, but this is real! I... Lennox, come on. Demons, devils. You're okay with this?"

"I am," said the barman. "I've seen the devil."

"You too?"

"He comes in here sometimes."

"What?"

"This is his local."

"What?!"

"He was here this morning. Red skin, hoofs, the whole thing. I'm surprised you missed it."

The sensation of mind-blowing disbelief had spread from Stephen's head to his chest. He wondered if he was going to have a heart attack and then realised that he had forgotten to breathe.

Lennox put his hand on Stephen's, swallowing it in that huge, rock-steady grip.

"Stephen. Mate. We get it. We hear you. You are, unlikely though it may seem, bezzy mates with a demon from Hell. And you've come here to find him. And we're here to help."

"Absolutely," said Darren.

Lennox looked round. "And you've got all of the old gang here now to help you."

"Well, we haven't got Ed," said Darren.

"Saw him this morning," said Stephen. "It didn't go well."

"I mean, all the old gang are here *now*," said Lennox and tilted his head.

Stephen looked round. Ed stood in the doorway of the pub. He looked at Stephen with a tight, difficult expression on his face.

"Oh," said Stephen. He stood. "Ed, listen. All I can do is apologise and –"

"Is it true?" said Ed. "Did you really take the suitcase?"

"Er, yeah."

"To stop the police finding it and..."

Stephen looked back to Darren and swallowed hard. He nodded to Ed.

"Yeah. I thought you were going to be in even more trouble and..."

Ed laughed, suddenly and surprisingly. "And I thought you were just a bloody coward, mate."

"Well..." said Stephen. His cheeks suddenly felt hot with the shame.

"But you weren't," said Ed.

"Ah."

Ed stepped up and clapped Stephen on both shoulders.

"I should have thought better of you."

"Oh, you really shouldn't."

"You were being a mate. A good mate."

Stephen made inarticulate sounds.

"All these damned years..." Ed shook his head. "You heard what happened to me."

"Prison."

"Well, young offenders. Which is probably worse. I dunno. But I've turned things around."

Stephen put out his hand in an impressed gesture. "You, the respected businessman."

"Respected?" coughed Lennox.

"Fuck you, barman," grinned Ed. "I think this calls for drinks all round." A fifty pound note appeared in his hands. "Lager? Lager. Lager?"

"I'm just on the lemonade," Darren began.

"Lagers all round it is," said Ed cheerfully and went to the bar. "Oi. Florence. Looking gorgeous as ever, I see."

Stephen turned to Darren and looked for condemnation in his friend's face. There was none. Bloody Darren, as unjudgmental as Christ himself. Or just oblivious to what was going on around him. Either way, it wasn't what Stephen wanted.

"Glad to be back home in Sutton Coldfield then?" said Ed, wiping beer foam from his lips with the back of his hand.

"Um. It's unexpected," said Stephen, drained the last of his current pint and started on the one that had somehow appeared when he wasn't looking. "You know what they say. You can never truly go home."

Darren gripped the table and gave the room a suspicious and narrow-eyed scan. "You mean, this place isn't...?"

"I mean, places change, and nothing is like it once was. It's like.... it's like Wagon Wheels."

"Aw, I used to love Wagon Wheels," said Ed.

"My mum used to give me them in my pack-up," said Darren.

"Ooh, hark at the middle class boy who got Wagon Wheels in his packed lunch," sneered Ed.

"What did you get?" said Darren.

"Well, not chocolate," said Ed. "And if it was chocolate, it'd be a Blue Riband or a supermarket knock-off Penguin at best."

"I don't think Wagon Wheels are any more la-di-dah than Blue Riband or Penguins," said Darren defensively.

"I would have loved to have Wagon Wheels in my pack-up," said Stephen.

"What did you have then?"

Stephen thought about it. "Viscounts, I think."

"Viscounts?" said Ed.

"What? Mint Viscounts?" said Darren.

"In the foil wrappers?"

"Cor."

"They were definitely more middle-class than Wagon Wheels."

"They're not," said Stephen.

"They are too. That's 'would you like a Viscount with your cup of tea, vicar?' posh, that is," said Ed.

Lennox came over. He was shuttling between the table and the bar, assisting baby Florence as needed but keeping his friends company. He was the only one of them not drinking. There were seven empties and three part-drunk pints on the table.

"Are we on our third round already?" said Stephen.

"Some of us," said Ed. "Ere, Lennox. Settle an argument. Out of Wagon Wheels, Viscounts and Blue Ribands, which was the poshest biscuit?"

Lennox gave it serious thought, actual chin-stroking thought.

"Poshest, Viscount. But best, Wagon Wheel. Your Viscount is the Radio Four of biscuits. But your Wagon Wheel is like a fifty-inch plasma screen showing Sky Sports."

Ed nodded appreciatively. "Anyway, Steve-o, what about them?"

"About what?"

"Wagon Wheels. You said, 'It's like Wagon Wheels.'"

"They're smaller than they used to be," said Lennox.

Stephen pointed. "That. Everyone thinks they're smaller now than they used to be."

"They are!" said Ed.

"They are," said Darren.

"We had this very same debate at St Cadfan's. Two days we sat in heated argument."

"Not as long as your custard cream versus bourbon debate," said Darren.

"Not quite. And we ended up having a conference call with a production manager from the biscuit company who assured us there had been no change in size of the British Wagon Wheel since the war."

"Bollocks," said Ed. "They're tiny now compared to what they once were."

"Or our hands have just got bigger since we were kids," said Lennox.

"Apparently so," said Stephen. "And coming home's like that."

"Everything's smaller?" said Darren.

"Everything's different," said Stephen.

Ed had his phone out. "You're chatting shit, Steve-o. I'm looking this up. Same size, as if! This is some Matrix blue pill red pill crap."

"So, you're a monk," said Lennox.

"Eagle-eyed as ever," said Stephen, brushing his habit and finding a wet beer splodge. "I was a novice for a couple of years and am now a brother of St Cadfan's monastery."

"And this is on that Welsh island?"

"Bardsey. Island of twenty thousand saints, they say."

"Big place then?" said Darren.

"Let's just say that if Google ever decide to do Street View for Bardsey they'd better work out how to attach cameras to seagulls."

"Must be some attraction to coming back to civilisation then," suggested Lennox. "There must be stuff you miss."

Stephen gave it some thought. "Big town stuff, I guess, like the cinema."

"You don't watch movies?"

"Yeah, we can watch movies. We have the internet. But that's not the same. Remember when we used to go to the cinema when we were teenagers. *Ghostbusters. Indiana Jones.*"

"We all snuck in to see *Jaws 3* underage," said Lennox.

"Nah, that was *Jaws – The Revenge*," said Ed. "The awful one with Michael Caine."

"That's right," smiled Darren, remembering. "You almost wet yourself in fright."

"Did not!" said Ed. "Might have pissed myself in disgust at Michael Caine's acting."

"You refused to go swimming for months after," said Lennox.

"That's only because Duncan Henderson said he'd got the squits in the pool and they never cleaned it out."

"That," said Stephen. "I miss that."

"Duncan Henderson's squits?" said Ed.

Stephen slapped his shoulder. "The cinema. Mates. Good times."

"I'll drink to that," said Ed and raised his pint. Darren raised his. Stephen found his amongst the growing mass of empties.

"Good times."

Lennox stacked the empties.

"And takeaway," said Stephen.

"You don't get that on your little island?" said Darren.

"Nearest chip shop and pizza place is a thirty-minute boat ride, assuming the weather's on your side. Nearest kebab or Indian

123

or Chinese... another hour to the next town round from Aberdaron. I miss kebabs."

"Then that's what we're doing later," said Ed firmly.

"You're on," said Lennox and went back to the bar. "Oi! Alvin! What did I say?"

"What?" demanded the man with the pug dog.

Lennox tapped the floorboards next to not one but two dog poop bags that had found their way into the pub.

"They're not mine, I tell you!" said Alvin.

"I am five seconds from barring you and your dog, mate!"

"That's discrimination."

Lennox put the glasses down on the bar. It was a simple action but from the big guy it was as pointed and meaningful as if he'd slipped on a pair of boxing gloves.

"Alvin, under the Equality Act there are nine protected characteristics under which I – we – are forbidden to discriminate. I could not refuse to serve a person on the grounds that they are a woman. I could not refuse to serve a person on the grounds that they are gay or Muslim or French. A one-legged pregnant transgender Swede could come in here and I would be legally obliged to – and happy to – serve them the non-alcoholic drink of their choice and invite them to take the weight off their foot."

"Yes, but –"

"You, dear patron, are in danger of being barred, not because you're male, white, hetero or cisgender – all of which are also protected characteristics – but because you have an ugly little dog and there's little bags of dog crap on my pub floor."

"But they're not mine and –"

"If you want to take them away and do DNA tests, we'll get the pair of you on Jeremy Kyle and I can make a public apology," said Lennox. "Until then..." He pointed at the offending bags.

"Definitely strange," said Stephen as the man reluctantly picked up the bags.

"You're sure it's not the End Times?" said Darren.

"The Book of Revelation is distinctly lacking in references to dog poop. But there's those and the nuts that..." He hesitated. He didn't want to say that the discarded nuts had followed him here, but he was sure they had.

"You see?" said Ed, coming back to the table with three more pints. "You don't get that kind of entertainment on a tiny Welsh island."

Stephen did a double-take. "I didn't even see you get up! Is this your superpower, making beer magically appear?"

"See? I bet you miss this," said Ed.

"We have beer on Bardsey," said Stephen. "We buy some in. We brew our own. Seaweed beer is an acquired taste but, once you've acquired it..."

Ed shrugged and nearly dropped the beers.

"I just can't picture it. You, shutting yourself away from the world on a tiny island."

"I'm not shut away," said Stephen. "Where have you been today?"

"Me?" said Ed. "The shop. I've been working."

"And you live in the flat above. So, today, your world has been the distance from your shop to this place. That's not even a mile."

"Yeah, but I can go anywhere I want."

"Do you though?"

"The shop and... other business enterprises keep me busy. But I have all my animals and... that's something."

"Bardsey is home to the Yellow-Crested Merlin Stilt, one of the rarest seabirds in the world."

"Really?"

"Mostly on account of it being the world's worst parent. We have to spend considerable time stopping them accidentally murdering their own chicks. We've also got a number of peacocks on the island, much favoured by the former abbot, although their numbers are dwindling."

"Oh, why's that?"

"A distinct shortage of peahens," said Stephen.

"What's a peahen?" said Darren.

Stephen looked at him. "A lady peacock, Darren. Pea-hens and pea-cocks."

"No," said Darren doubtfully. "I'm sure that's not right. Peacocks are the birds."

"And they're the boys," said Stephen. "Cocks and hens. Male and female."

"It's like chickens," said Ed. "Chick-hens. And cocks. Oh, I tell you what, if you ever want to see the biggest black cock..."

"Woah! Stop!" said Stephen. "Where did...? What...? Why would you think...?"

"I'm just saying," said Ed. "Big black cock which must be..." He put his hands out.

"I don't want to know."

"But let me tell you this big black cock is –"

"Could you please stop saying the words 'big black cock'."

Lennox dropped back onto a stool, a pint of dark beer in his hand.

"Right, what are chatting about?"

Stephen's mouth hung open, unable to re-engage. Darren filled the gap.

"Ed was asking us if we'd like to see a big black cock."

"Mrs Churchill," said Ed. "You know her. Breeds poultry in her back yard."

"Oh, yeah," said Lennox, nodding. "It's huge."

Stephen stuttered. "You mean it's an actual... rooster?"

"Obvs," said Ed. "We were talking about birds. What? Did you think...?"

"You did that on purpose," said Stephen and sulkily drank his beer but spoiled it by smiling as he did so.

"I did wonder why you were so opposed to seeing a big black cock," said Ed archly.

"Has the man got something against big black cocks?" said Lennox innocently.

"Could you *both* please stop saying 'big black cock'! I'm pretty sure it's racist! I don't know how but I'm pretty sure you..." He stopped. Ed and Lennox had creased up with laughter. Darren's mind was elsewhere.

"So," he said, "you know that there's a ballcock in the toilet cistern?"

"No," said Stephen. "There are no ballhens."

Lennox raised his pint. "Just agreed with Florence. She's going to manage bar for the rest of the night. I'm going to join you guys for a couple and then I'm sure someone mentioned a kebab?"

"That's a plan and a half," said Ed.

126

The mention of night made Stephen look to the window. The sky was already darkening, and he'd done nothing to locate Rutspud.

"I had plans..." he said softly.

"Ah, we all had plans," said Lennox.

"Don't think I did," said Darren.

"Steve-o here was telling me that our worlds are as small as his poxy island," said Ed. "Me stuck in my shop. You in your pub."

"Practically a prisoner," said Lennox.

"And... and I don't even know what you do, Darren. Apart from a spot of Bible-bashing down at St Michael's, do you get out much?"

Darren pulled a face.

"So, basically none of us amounted to anything," said Lennox. "Is that the consensus?"

There were general mumbles of agreement.

"Those nights when we used to sit on the swings in Short Heath Park," said Lennox. "Didn't we talk about the future? Our plans?"

The four of them thought on it.

"No," said Darren. "We talked about fantasy novels and roleplaying and who would win in a fight between Batman and Judge Dredd."

"Batman, obviously," said Lennox.

"Judge Dredd!" said Ed.

"And we'd talk about all the girls we weren't having sex with," said Darren. "A lot."

Ed laughed suddenly. "Do you remember, we made a pact that when one of us lost our virginity that person who buy everyone a drink and we'd make it an annual thing?"

"Celebrate the anniversary of the first of us to actually have sex with a girl," smiled Stephen. "Oh, God. We did."

"Do we know who won?" said Lennox.

"So long ago," said Ed.

"Now, *that* has to be something you must miss out on your island?" said Lennox.

"What?" said Stephen.

"I take it that there's not a lot of action between the sheets, man."

Stephen tutted at the tedious comment. "No. You will be shocked to hear that there is very little monk-on-monk action on Bardsey."

"No sneaking across to the nuns' dormitories then?" said Ed.

"It's a monastery," said Stephen. "Monks. Just monks."

"Monk-cocks and monk-hens?" pondered Darren drunkenly.

"The nearest holy house of nuns is, I think, in Porthmadog. There's four of them and the youngest is in her seventies. So, no."

"Do you want to hear something truly sad?" said Ed.

"I think we're already scraping the sad barrel right now," said Stephen.

"I used to hate you, Steve-o. Really hate you."

"I got that. I mean it really hit me when you whacked a hamster ball off my forehead today."

"I plotted to get revenge on you."

"Actual plotting. Wow. Do I need to watch out for ticking parcels in the post?"

"I..." Ed stopped, hiccupped and took a swig of drink. "I decided to sleep with all your exes."

It was an unexpected statement. "Er, ok. Exes. As in...?"

"Any woman you slept with. I set out to find, seduce and bed them. In order."

"I'm a bit conflicted, mate," said Lennox, putting a hand on Ed's shoulder. "On the one hand that's a serious undertaking – I mean, the dedication involved... But on the other hand, sleeping with women only to get revenge on a man who wouldn't even know what you'd done. I can't work out if you're a genius or a psycho sex-fiend."

"Or that's just really, really sad," said Stephen.

"I did say," said Ed.

"There's a reason why I wasn't with some of them for very long. There was one who wanted to walk up and down on me in her high heels. I sometimes think I can still feel the bruising."

"Oh! Caitlin Franks."

"That's the one!"

"But what about Olivia Grinstead? She realised she was a lesbian."

"Yeah... you know, sometimes when a woman can't work out how to dump a guy..."

"I knew it!" said Stephen. "Actually, I didn't. Not a clue."

"So," said Darren cautiously. "How many...?"

Stephen tried to do a count on his fingers. The alcohol didn't help. He held up a number of fingers. Ed did likewise. They broadly matched.

"Even the last one?" said Stephen. "Nerys whatserthingy?"

"Nerys Thomas," nodded Ed. "That was a demanding woman with unrealistically high expectations. Had to promise to take her on an African safari holiday to even get her attention."

"You took a woman – a woman I knew for a grand total of five, six hours – you took her to Africa in order to score over my mark on the bedpost? Bloody hell."

"I said 'promise'. I didn't say I actually took her."

"Ooh, that's low, man," said Lennox.

"Hey, it ended worse for me than it did for her, trust me."

Stephen shook his head. "So, you with anyone at the moment?"

"Nah. Not for a year. You? Oh, right. The monk thing."

Stephen looked to Lennox.

"Hey, running a pub leaves zero time for romance."

Stephen turned to Darren.

"Puh-lease," said Darren. "What do you think?"

"I think you're a better guy and a deeper guy than you yourself think you are. No one?"

Darren lowered his gaze and shook his head.

"So, none of us have achieved anything of note and we're all sad lonely wankers," said Ed. "Brilliant. Thanks for coming over here and reminding us all, Steve." It could have been a damning comment, but Ed looked anything other than sad. He raised his pint. "The sad wankers, back together again."

Pints clinked. "Sad wankers!"

"Mine's empty," said Darren.

"My round!" declared Stephen. "And then it's kebab o'clock."

The scrape of crockery on concrete. Rutspud rolled over and opened his eyes.

"What's this?" he said.

"Ham, egg and chips, Lord Rutspud," said Mo. "Used to be my dad's favourite. Nothing for building up a growing lad like ham, egg and chips."

With aching fingers, Rutspud reached for a chip.

"Careful. They're hot," said Mo.

"You don't know the meaning of hot. You will." He shoved a chip in his mouth. It was a crunchy, copper-brown, sizzling on the outside and molten carbohydrate on the inside. "S'nice," he said and shoved another in before he'd finished the first. "Very nice."

Mo pushed the plate so it was fully inside the circle.

Rutspud grunted as he pushed himself into a sitting position.

"It hurts, doesn't it?" said Mo.

"Do you care?" he replied.

He ignored the cutlery on the plate, picked up a slice of ham, folded it over his finger and swallowed it whole. He looked toward Shafttoe's circle and Lackring's cage.

"No ham, egg and chips for the others?" he said.

"They're asleep," said Mo.

"Demons don't need sleep," said Rutspud. He thought. "Don't need food either." He shrugged, picked up the wobbly fried egg like it was a wriggling fish he was trying to land and tipped it into his gob before it could escape.

The egg was greasy and slick and felt good sliding down his throat.

"You should let me go," he said. It wasn't a threat of such. It was a piece of advice.

Mo gave a small, sad smile.

"We summoned you for a reason, Lord Rutspud."

"To make people more litter-conscious? To give squirrels a sense of civic duty?"

"We just want to make the world a better place."

He laughed or, more accurately, he croaked in a sort of laugh and then stopped when it hurt.

"The number of terrible things started by people who 'wanted to make the world a better place'... We should have a pit for them in Hell. Maybe we do, the pit of I Was Only Trying to Make Things Better."

"You believe we should let this world go to wrack and ruin?"

"Oh, I don't think you have much choice over that. To save this world? You'd need to decimate the population. Ha! Not even that. Cut it to a tenth of its current size. Turn all the nuclear missiles into potpourri. Turn all the oil and plastic in the sea back into the little creatures they once were, millions of years ago. Turn the coal back into trees while you're at it. And even then, I only give you a fifty-fifty chance of lasting another thousand years."

"We're doing what we can, in the ways we can," said Mo defensively.

"Yeah, that's how Merilyn sold it to you, right?" He used the last of the chips to wipe at the grease on the plate before eating them. "'Let's summon demons. Let's right a few wrongs.'"

Mo made an irritated noise.

"Shows what you know, mighty demon. In fact, this was all my idea."

"Oh."

"Oh? Why, 'Oh'?"

He licked his fingers. "You just don't seem the type."

"Am I too much of a sheep? A follower, not a leader? Poor, silly old Mo. Should stay at home and know her place. Spend her life living for others, not herself. Not the kind to pick up a book of arcane spells and rituals and think, *I could do that, I could achieve something with my life.* That?"

"Um. Yes?"

"We didn't have feminism in my day," she said. "Maybe they did somewhere, wherever Germaine Greer was hanging out but not in Sutton Coldfield. Men were the breadwinners and women were the housewives. We were never expected to make something of ourselves, for ourselves. But even the men…"

She reached over into the gap between Rutspud's circle and Lackring's and, as she did, Rutspud glimpsed that below the impressive black and gold robes Mo was wearing a pair of fluffy slippers and knitted socks with little demon faces on. Or they could be cat faces, maybe demon-cat faces. Mo pulled out some of the assorted pieces of electronic crap Rutspud had spilled when he removed Lackring's cover.

"My dad worked for Post Office Telecommunications," she said, holding aloft a piece of junk that might have conceivably been the innards of an old telephone. "The Post Office used to manage all the phone systems back then. Thirty years he worked for them, installing phone lines, helping to connect people to the world and then – bang."

"He exploded?"

"They privatised it. Sold it for a song on the stock market and he was 'strongly encouraged' to take early retirement which is another way for saying he had his job taken from him. Used and discarded. Just one of the little people."

She seemed to realise that she had been staring at the piece of telephonic junk for a long time.

"The silent majority rarely get their voices heard. We're cut off," she said and put the junk down. "But we want to be heard. We want to have our say. Rest now, Lord Rutspud. Build up your strength. We still have work to do."

She picked up his plate and went upstairs.

A crispy fleck of chip had wedged between Rutspud's teeth. He worried at it with his tongue.

"I'm in Sutton Coldfield," he said to himself. "I'm still in Sutton bloody Coldfield."

He retrieved the fishing rod from the back of his circle and used it to pull the telephone carcass over. Rutspud had a technical mind and clever fingers. A ruined old telephone was useless in itself, but if there were other odds and ends back there in the shadows…

"I'm in Sutton Coldfield," he grinned and set to work.

The journey from the Boldmere Oak pub to *McDoner's* kebab shop involved much wending and digression, both physical and mental. Ed, trying to read something on his phone, nearly collided with a phone box. Lennox pulled him back on track.

"Do you remember at school how they said we always had to have a plan for the future?" said Lennox.

Stephen nodded but kept his eyes on the drifting pieces of rubbish and takeaway papers rolling up the street. "Do your GCSEs, they said. Pick your A-levels. Go to university. The decisions you make, what we do in life, echoes in eternity."

"That's *Gladiator*," said Darren.

"Don't think he was our careers advisor," said Stephen. "I had no idea what I wanted to be."

"I wanted to be a rock guitarist," said Lennox.

"Could you play?"

Lennox wrinkled his nose.

"I always assumed I was going to work for the post office like my dad and my granddad," said Darren.

"Sex slave," said Ed.

"I don't think that's a job."

"At sixteen, I wanted to be a sex slave. Teacher told me it wasn't a proper job."

"Like I said," said Darren.

"Hah!" Ed declared. "Here it is!"

Stephen looked round. Ed was waving his phone. Stephen suspected it wasn't an online advert for the job of sex slave. He hoped it wasn't.

"What?" said Lennox.

"Wagon Wheels. They changed the ingredients which meant the British Wagon Wheel had a slightly thinner coating, so it became smaller."

"Not that much smaller," said Stephen.

"Here." Ed stopped to read, forcing the others to stop too.

Stephen watched a bundled chip wrapper roll past.

"The Australian Wagon Wheel is nine centimetres in diameter," read Ed, "which is one and half centimetres bigger than the British one."

"Australia here we come," said Lennox.

"But the British Wagon Wheel is four millimetres thicker, height-wise." He stopped and frowned. "So, which is bigger?"

"The Australian one," said Darren, holding his thumbs and forefingers in a circle.

"But it's about volume," said Lennox. "So that's the area of the circle times the height. What's the area of the circle?"

Ed muttered something about squaring and something to do with pi. Lennox agreed it had something to do with pi, but then looked up. "What are you staring at?" he asked Stephen.

Stephen pointed. "All the rubbish."

"And?" Lennox sniffed. "Welcome to the big city, where rubbish blows about in the wind."

"What wind?" said Stephen.

Lennox put his hand out. The night air was perfectly still.

"That's a little spooky."

Ed waved his hand about. "Freak weather? Wind you can't touch?"

Darren abruptly looked up. "Ah. We were here earlier today."

Stephen followed his gaze. They were passing the *Hallowed Grounds* coffee shop, now all dark and locked up for the night.

"How'd it go with Asmondius?" asked Ed.

"You mean Nigel Herring," said Darren.

"I thought I recognised that arsehole who was hassling you two," said Lennox. "He's the one who got kicked out of the Boys' Brigade –"

"Scouts," said Stephen.

"Right – for doing something unspeakable to a hamster."

"That's the one."

"What did you think of him?" said Ed.

Stephen thought on it.

"I think," he said after some consideration, "that he gave us a negative impression."

"You'd think nihilist Satanists would be a bit more happy-go-lucky."

"You would, wouldn't you?" said Darren.

McDoner's kebab shop was a steamy little takeaway, full of sizzles, meaty tangs and a haze of chilli sauce that caught in the back of the throat. Stephen found himself salivating as he gazed up at the photo menu above the counter.

"I will have a double chicken tikka doner on naan with salad, cheese, mint sauce and chilli," he said eventually.

"I'll have the same but hold the cheese," said Lennox. "Dairy intolerant," he told the others.

"That's one thing that's changed for the better," said Ed.

"Lennox has become dairy intolerant?"

"No. Times were, we'd only be outside, trying to scrape together enough change to get a tray of chips between us."

Stephen grunted in agreement and sat at a table by the window to wait for his order. The table was a nasty oval of hardened plastic. The seats were bolted to the floor. He realised his head felt woozy.

Ed dropped into the seat opposite.

"You all right, Steve-o?" he said, clearly worse for drink too.

"Hurt my head earlier," said Stephen rubbing it.

"It was only a hamster ball."

"No. Not that. Another one. Another injury. Not another hamster ball."

Darren squeezed in.

"You know what he did was unspeakable?"

"Nigel. The hamster. Yeah," said Ed.

"Does that mean 'unspeakable' as in no one can say or 'unspeakable' as in too horrible to say?"

"Someone would have to know what it was or else no one would have known to kick him out of the scouts," said Stephen reasonably.

"So, it's too horrible to relate?"

"Yeah."

Darren sat back reflectively. "I don't want to seem like a pervert –"

135

"Too late," said Lennox, coming over with a saveloy sausage wrapped in chip paper.

"– but I can't think of anything you can do to a hamster so horrible it is totally unspeakable."

"I just assumed that he'd stuffed it up his arse," said Ed casually.

"The classic Richard Gere," said Stephen.

"Did he actually do that?" said Lennox.

"Nigel or Richard?" said Darren.

"I think it was a gerbil," said Ed.

"No. That's apocryphal," said Stephen.

"What kind of animal is that?" said Darren.

"It was either that or Nigel stuffed himself up the hamster's arse," said Lennox and bit into his sausage.

There was a long moment of contemplation, finally (and perhaps fortunately) broken by the shop owner telling them their order was ready.

"Nigel mentioned a book with the Ukahdo ritual in it," said Darren.

Stephen had his chicken tikka kebab open in front of him and was simply savouring the piquant foetor of the thing. "The Krakow something or other."

"Krakovian *Livre des Esperitz*. Yeah, I used to own a copy."

"You didn't think to mention this earlier?"

"No. I sold it with my other occult stuff."

"To Ed?"

"Not to me," said Ed, round a mouthful of pitta and doner meat.

"It would have been to Ben at the second-hand bookshop," said Darren.

Stephen looked out the window, down the high street towards *Books 'n' Bobs*.

He frowned. A car was coming along the road. This was not noteworthy in and of itself, but it was a Trabant. It was his Trabant or, more accurately, it was Brother Manfred's Trabant. He stood awkwardly as the car pulled up to the kerb and hurried outside.

"What is it?" said Lennox.

"It's my car," he said, before stumbling onto the pavement.

The car door opened with a *squonk* and Stephen saw a team of squirrels on the driver's seat and in the footwell. There was a pair of squirrels on each of the pedals. There was another pair clinging to the steering wheel, hauling it into its final position by swinging the weight of their bodies, and there was another on tiptoes, managing the indicator stick. A squirrel who had been standing on the dashboard, presumably guiding the way ("guiding the way"? screamed a voice in Stephen's head. They're squirrels!) leapt down and bounded over to Stephen.

The lead squirrel held up the car keys to Stephen. He noted again the dots of red paint on its claw.

"Ah, Captain Redclaws!" said Stephen, teetering between drunken indifference and genuine madness. He accepted the car keys from the squirrel. "All fixed and repaired."

"Kwekwek!" said Captain Redclaws.

The squirrel gave him a cheery salute and then the whole gang of them scampered off into the dark.

Lennox was next to Stephen an instant later, still munching on his sausage.

"What was all that about?"

"Did you...?" said Stephen. "Did you just see a bunch of squirrels drive a car, hand me the keys and then run off into the night?"

Lennox peered with difficulty into the darkness. "Yes. I think so."

"Good. As long as it's not me," said Stephen.

His head really hurt.

137

Wednesday

The next morning, things did not feel any better.

First up and most obviously, Stephen had a hangover headache the likes of which he'd not experienced in years. They had plenty of beer on Bardsey but never in the strength and quantity he'd consumed the previous night. His mouth was dry, and his tongue coated with a mucus that was fifty percent chicken tikka, fifty percent dried saliva and one hundred percent wrong. He propped open the window (no squirrel on the sill today!) and let some cold fresh air in to dispel the beery funk of the room. Stephen cautiously made his way to the bathroom to clean his teeth and try to splash some life back into his face. He saw in the mirror that his head bump from yesterday had come up as a small but angry-looking bruise. This perversely made him feel a little better; at least he could now point to an outward sign of his inner pain.

However, it did nothing to alleviate the self-condemnation he felt for getting no closer to finding Rutspud. It was his second morning in Sutton Coldfield and he'd achieved nothing except find the possible location of a book that might have been used in the summoning.

The smell of greasy food rose up the staircase. Stephen wasn't sure whether to throw up or go eat his fill. A big fry-up after a night of beer was usually a case of kill or cure. Stephen was prepared to risk it.

He went downstairs and was mildly surprised to see Animal Ed next to Darren at the dinner table, tucking into a plate of sausage, black pudding and beans that had probably been meant for him.

"Don't you worry, Stephen," said Mrs Pottersmore, busying herself at the cooking hob. "I'll have yours cooked in a jiffy."

"Don't cook more on my account, please," he said.

"I've already put the black pudding on."

"Oh, okay then."

"I'll have to use up the last of the sausages and I don't go shopping again until Friday."

"Then please don't bother. I can manage without."

"No," she said firmly. "You've asked now so sit down and show a little patience."

"Yes. Yes, of course," said Stephen meekly, knowing he couldn't win and squeezed into the third chair at the small table.

"Looks like you had a rough night," said Ed, scooping up the last crumbs of black pudding on his plate.

Stephen cleared his throat and nodded. Darren pushed a cup of tea in his direction. Darren wore an eye-searing knitwear interpretation of the resurrection of Jesus Christ. The creator, Mrs Pottersmore presumably, had made the bold choice of rendering the tomb in pink yarn. The Son of God climbed out his tomb surrounded by rays of light in every colour of the spectrum. The sum impression was of Jesus not so much coming back from the dead as emerging from a disco-vagina.

"Painkillers?" said Ed and passed Stephen a blister pack.

Stephen popped two and washed them down with hot tea.

"They're meant to be for horses," said Ed, "but we're all mammals, right?"

Stephen stared at him.

"What are you doing here?" he said eventually.

"Ed's going to help us find the book," said Darren.

"Least I can do," said Ed.

After a mountainous breakfast of fat, protein and salt, Stephen's hangover was gone. Maybe it was the curious power of the British fry-up. Maybe it was Ed's dubious painkillers. Stephen stepped out onto the street feeling much better in himself but immediately and acutely aware that something was not quite right with the world.

It took him a few minutes and a hundred yards to pinpoint the cause: the street was clean. The suburban streets of Erdington had never been blighted by litter, but there had always been a loose piece of paper here or a crushed drinks can there. This morning, the pavements, verges and gutters were spotless, but piles of rubbish slumped against some houses' front doors. Many of the piles seemed to have thematic leanings. That one there was composed entirely of sweet wrappers. This one was a considerable hillock of cigarette dogends.

Stephen pointed it out.

"Council clean-up," said Ed with a disinterested shrug.

They turned onto the canal path that would take them towards Boldmere. Something equally weird had happened here. The banks and the towpath were marked with drying smears of canal bed silt as though, in the night, the contents of the canal had climbed up and out and slunk off elsewhere.

"Council clean-up," said Ed again.

A V-shaped ripple began to follow them in the water – a shallow wave, no bigger than the wake of a duck. But there was no duck. Perhaps it was an invisible duck, thought Stephen giddily.

"What's the biggest fish they have in the canals?" said Darren, who had also seen it.

"Dunno," said Ed. "Largest freshwater fish round here is the pike, but I don't think we have any in the canal."

Darren made an interested face. Ed looked round and saw the rippling bow wave.

"What the...?"

"Probably just a pike then," said Darren.

"Or an invisible duck," offered Stephen.

They walked on and spoke of it no further. Darren began, quietly at first, to hum the theme to *Jaws*. When he got to the fast 'dun-dun-dun-dun's, Ed punched him in the arm and put Darren between himself and the canal.

"Fucking thing can eat you first, baby seal."

There was squeaking noise and a panting sound behind them. Stephen turned. A young lad, not quite a teenager, was running towards them on the towpath. Ten feet behind but gaining slowly, a shopping trolley covered in duck weed and canal slime and bearing a plaque reading *Boldmere Ponies Street Polo Team* trundled after him, entirely unassisted by human hands.

The men stepped aside.

141

"It's trying to kill me!" gasped the boy as he sprinted past. "Kill me!"

The boy ran on. The trolley rolled merrily past in pursuit.

They watched boy and trolley disappear down the towpath, the trolley's little wheels spastically quivering and squeaking.

"Fucking poltergeists," breathed Ed.

"Demons," said Darren softly and looked at Stephen.

"Maybe we should just get back onto the regular road," said Stephen.

They each made an effort to look nonchalant as they walked to the nearest steps, but it all came apart as they fought to not be the last one up to street level.

When they entered *Books 'n' Bobs*, Ed closed the door firmly behind them and scanned the street through the window, perhaps fearful that a haunted trolley or canal shark might be following them.

The man at the counter, Ben, had a haunted look about him. Or, more likely, it was the pasty complexion of the near-ruined businessman who had neither money nor inclination to invest in either fruit, veg or sunshine. He stuck a fork in the pot noodle he was eating, wiped his fingers on his *Devil Preacher* rock T-shirt and smiled.

"Morning, Gentlemen. Darren, Ed..."

He frowned at Stephen as though his name had eluded him.

"I'm Stephen," said Stephen.

"Can't help but think we've met," said Ben.

"Doubt it," said Ed, leaving the door and wandering into the shop's erotic art section to steady his nerves. "He's been hiding on a tiny Welsh island for the last five years."

"It's the habit," said Stephen. "It makes all us monks look the same."

"Bardsey?" said Ben.

"That's right."

"I went to a wedding there."

"Whose wedding was that?" said Darren.

"Er, mine actually."

"And how is your good lady wife?" asked Stephen.

Ben turned to a pin board next to the counter and took down a postcard of some wildly ornate architecture. "She's spending another week in Yogyakarta and exploring the ruins of Ratu Boko. So, that's nice."

He carefully put the postcard back on the board, making sure the pin re-entered the hole it had previously occupied. There were many dozens of postcards on the board. From the images alone, it was clear that Ben's wife had already explored much of the Middle and Far East and, from the reverence with which Ben replaced the postcard, Stephen took it that the adage about absence and the variable fondness of the heart might have some truth to it.

"And what can I do for you today?" said Ben. He coughed loudly. "Ed, despite the fact that they are both full of books, do not confuse my shop for a public lending library."

"Weren't doing nothing," said Ed, putting a copy of Madonna's *Sex* book back on the shelf.

"It's all right really," Ben told Darren and Stephen conspiratorially. "He does bring them back. Mostly."

"The Krakovian *Livre des Esperitz*," said Darren.

"Gesundheit," said Ben and then smiled to show he understood. "One of your old books. You sold it to me."

"Do you still have it?"

"Not sure," said Ben. He took a set of keys from his pocket and turned to a wide, locked cabinet behind the counter. "Sell a lot of the rarer books on eBay and such," he explained as he fiddled with the padlock. "Make more money from them than peddling Catherine Cooksons and Nicci Frenches to the local biddies."

Inside the cabinet were a bundle of jiffy bags, an unstable stack of lever arch folders and two shelves of books – most with damaged covers. Some unexpected titles drew Stephen's eye.

"*Hello Kitty*?"

"The infamous *Hello Kitty* dictionary," said Ben, "includes a description of how to kill someone using a tyre filled with petrol. Misprint apparently. That's going to a buyer in Wisconsin."

Stephen started to ask how that could possibly be a misprint and why someone from Wisconsin might want to buy it, but Ben slapped down two folders on the counter.

"Photographs of books I've sold or am selling online," he said, pushing one aside. "Lists of sales," he said, opening the other.

Stephen opened the folder of photographs: children's books, cookery books, old autobiographies and...

"Wow. Do you specialise in selling books with racist titles?" he asked.

Ben gave an uneasy shrug. "There's a demand for such things."

"I knew about the Agatha Christie one, but this Joseph Conrad... I can't even say the name."

"I'd rather you didn't," said Ben, and returned to scouring his sales records.

Stephen thought it might be divine grace that his friend had a mild case of OCD. Ben's obsession with record keeping made him an exceptionally honest bookseller whose ads featured not only photographs of notable illustrations and the occasional fine binding but also close-ups of damaged pages. The eBay listing for the *Livre des Esperitz* had included at least a dozen hi-res images of foxed and mildewed pages with woodcut illustrations surrounded by text in both French and English.

He was drawn to an image of a demon with huge teeth and a flaming mane of hair. It stood at the centre of a pentagram within a circle and was cavorting round in either pain, dire need for the loo or (and it was an outside chance) an irresistible need to throw some shapes on the dancefloor. Was this what had happened to Rutspud? Was he trapped and in pain? A column of writing could be made out in a panel to the side, Stephen brought his face closer to read it.

"Ah, here," Ben said, consulting his notes. "Sale of *Livre des Esperitz*. Sixteen Finnemore Close."

"That's my address," said Darren.

"Right. That's from when you sold it to me. And sold to... Hmmm." Ben flipped the page and flipped back. "I haven't written anything else in."

Stephen finally deciphered the title at the top of the photographed page.

"This is the Ukahdo ritual," he said. "The actual ritual."

"Give us the details," said Ed, appearing at his shoulder.

"It's in French."

"*Merde!*"

"I can read French," said Stephen. "Badly. *D'abord, vous devez dessiner votre cercle.* So, draw your circle. *Inscris les runes de Salomon à la craie blanche.* You need a piece of chalk. *Vous aurez besoin d'une seule bougie d'église* – church candle – *d'une fiole d'huile d'acacia* – acacia oil? – *d'un collier en argent* – a silver collar?"

"Necklace," said Ben.

"I can source all of those," said Ed. "No worries. Satanic supplies, I'm your man."

"Right," said Stephen. "*– les os d'un chat –*"

"A cat?" said Darren.

"The bones – *et l'ingrédient le plus important est une plume prise d'un grand coq noir.* A feather."

"What kind of feather?" said Ed.

"One from *un grand coq noir.*"

"What's that?"

"A big black... rooster."

"Pardon?" said Ed, a grin growing on his face. "As in a big black cock?"

Stephen sighed. "Yes."

"You want a big black cock, I can sort you out."

"Please, stop – before I have to either petition the Oxford English Dictionary to rename male chickens or bludgeon you to death with *Volume III, Cham to Creeky.* "

On the walk from Ben's bookshop to the home of one Mrs Churchill, Stephen did his best to ignore the items of litter, mostly tiny, that were rolling under their own steam towards destinations unknown. The silence was punctuated by Darren's attempts to rebrand cockerels to spare Stephen's ire.

"He-hens?"

"Not bad," said Ed.

"Mr Hen?"

"That sounds like a fried chicken outlet."

"Chick daddy?"

"That sounds more than a little creepy. Over the road here."

Stephen fell into step beside Ed.

"Just to be clear," he said, "we don't want to actually buy the materials to perform the ritual."

"I can get them at a discount."

"We're more interested in who might have bought feathers in the past. If this Mrs Churchill is the preeminent purveyor of quality poultry, then we just need to ask who plucked her plume."

"People can be cagey about that sort of thing."

Ed led them up to an unassuming, mid-terrace house that looked no more like the premises of a premium poulterer than any of the other houses on the road. It was a very ordinary street indeed (if one ignored the man beside the white van further down, who was being affectionately mobbed by mattresses and off-cuts of wood and piping that looked very much like fly-tipping waste come home in search of their owner – sort of like *The Incredible Journey* but with soiled furnishings and building supplies instead of cats and dogs.) But how could one ignore him?

"That man is being attacked by mattresses," said Ed, in the matter-of-fact voice of a man who had no points of reference left to cling to.

"And bits of wood," pointed out Darren as though that somehow made it better. It didn't.

"That Rick's got a reputation for fly-tipping."

"Maybe this is how they punish fly-tippers these days," said Darren.

"By sending possessed rubbish to batter them to death?" said Stephen.

Ed seemed to give this some thought.

"Is it okay to be frightened at this moment? I feel frightened but maybe I've misunderstood."

"No," said Stephen slowly. "Frightened is probably about right."

"I think," said Ed, "I'm just going to pretend it isn't happening."

He stepped past the front door into an arched passageway between the house and its neighbour.

"Cooee, Mrs Churchill," he called.

"I'm in the garden!" answered a high, weak voice like that of a girl who had leapt straight from childhood into old age, bypassing the gravitas and maturity of adulthood.

The three men walked down the passageway and waited at a picket gate at the end of a narrow garden.

"It's just me, Mrs Churchill," said Ed. "I've brought some friends round."

At the rear of the house there was a strip of grass, a flower bed and a length of box hedging. At the far side of that conventional garden they saw a wire-fence-encircled morass of mud. It was like a small-scale recreation of the Battle of the Somme with chickens standing in for soldiers and a short woman in wellies as the British tank division. Mrs Churchill was squat, wide and slow-moving.

She put down a metal feeder, which the chickens hungrily flocked to, and brushed her hands on her blue and yellow floral apron.

"Come to pick out a bird for Christmas?" she said. "Bit early, mind, but I'd be thinking of that one." She pointed with a stubby finger at a fine and regal looking bird with sleek plumage that glistened like oil. "Blooming greedy-guts that one. He'll be plucked at the start of December."

"Doesn't even get to enjoy Advent," said Darren.

"Ah, you're little Darren Pottersmore," she said. "I'd recognise your mum's knitting anywhere. You're looking well."

"Thank you, Mrs Churchill."

"This is our friend, Stephen," said Ed.

Mrs Churchill gave him a big smile and, while the big smile stayed fixed, her eyes did a worried little dance up and down his habit.

"You look like one of them historical re-enactors," she said, nicely enough.

"I'm a monk," he said.

"Same thing, really," said Ed.

"Oi," said Stephen.

"I admire a man of the cloth," said Mrs Churchill. "Pillars of the community."

"We try," said Stephen, not sure what community the monks of Bardsey were upholding with their outlandish hobbies and near-constant biscuit-based squabbles.

Ed peered over the gate at Mrs Churchill's twenty-strong flock.

"Stephen here is doing some, er, research."

"Oh, yes?"

"Into local religious practices. A spot of cataloguing. Pins in maps."

"Well, I was born High Anglican but then went Methodist for the sake of my knees."

"He's actually trying to track down some, um..." Ed looked to Stephen.

"Occultists," said Stephen.

"Occultists?" said Mrs Churchill.

"Yes."

"I think there's some of them devil-worshipping types who like to congregate at that poncey café on the high street."

"Tried there," said Stephen.

"Not your thing? There's that vegan, pagan women's centre that that Millet-Walker woman opened on Penns Lane."

"Probably not what we're looking for."

"No. I don't hold with that kind of thing myself either. Soya milk and that vulgar *Tinker Bell Monologues* – not that they use the name Tinker Bell. Load of hippy nonsense."

"We're trying to find someone who has used the Ukahdo ritual," said Darren, in the manner of a man who wanted to be helpful and definitely wanted to get some distance from any *Tinker Bell Monologues*. "They would have used it to summon a demon from the sixth circle of Hell."

Mrs Churchill was entirely flummoxed by this. Several hens had clustered round her wellies and pecked at them on the off-chance they might be edible. Mrs Churchill shooed them away.

"I'm not sure I'd know anything about that kind of thing. Is this some sort of a game?"

Darren began to speak but Stephen got in before him.

"We think people might have come to you for one of your birds."

"Like I say, it's a bit early for Christmas," said Mrs Churchill.

"Just the feathers," said Ed. "From a black rooster, like matey-boy here."

"Only person who's ever asked me for those is you, Edward."

"Really?"

"You told me it was for making quills, but I knew you weren't telling me the whole truth."

"Oh."

"Quills, you need a bigger bird. Goose for preference. I just assumed you wanted it for something a bit, you know, *Fifty Shades of Grey...*"

"No one?" said Stephen.

"No one at all," said Mrs Churchill.

"Maybe someone sneaked in?" suggested Darren.

"The old fox has trouble enough getting in here and he's wilier than any thief," she said. "And that lad there would set up an awful racket if he did. And pulling feathers? No, if someone gave a tug on my cock, the whole neighbourhood would soon know about it."

"I'm sure they would," said Ed with a perfectly straight face.

Back on the pavement, Stephen tried to picture their current situation as any other than abject failure.

"So, we don't know who carried out the ritual and we don't know how to find them?" he said.

"Not yet," said Darren.

"I don't know what else we should do."

"Put up wanted posters?"

"What? 'Have you seen this demon?'"

Across the road, a band of squirrels were doing a spot of weeding along the grassy verge and nibbling any grass blades that had grown unacceptably high.

"His powers are being used to warp the world," said Stephen. "Everything's wrong. Subtly and horribly wrong."

"What do you reckon, Ed?" said Darren.

Ed, who Stephen suspected was not yet up to speed on the whole mission-to-rescue-a-demon thing, gave a hopeful smile.

"Pub?"

Hell was more pragmatic than Heaven. The Celestial City held itself up as a paragon of civic and cultural perfection which it assumed earth would aspire to emulate. Hell had much more of a 'I'll show you mine if you'll show me yours' attitude. Earth's innovations, especially technological ones, were embraced by Hell. When new inventions came along, Hell quickly explored ways to adapt them to local requirements. This exploration mostly involved inserting them into the damned and recording the noises that they made. If the noises proved interesting enough, the inventions were sent to Rutspud and his colleagues in Infernal Innovations (if they were lucky, some of the inventions were wiped down beforehand).

Rutspud held no preconceptions about what a piece of tech could or could not do – which in this situation was probably a good thing. A logical and rational human mind would know that a bunch of electronic junk from the previous century could not be used to create any kind of communication device, even if it had originally come from telecommunications equipment. Fortunately, Rutspud's was not a logical and rational human mind and with willpower, ingenuity, claws for screwdrivers and demon spit for glue, he constructed something that Alexander Graham Bell might have dreamt up after eating a sack of magic mushrooms.

Both Shafttoe and Lackring ignored him. Lackring was back under his covers, on the 'phone' to a distant relative who wouldn't let him get a word in edgewise. He produced nothing but a string of unfinished 'Uh-huh's and 'bu-'s and 'If I could j-'s. Shafttoe pretended to read his magazines, commenting loudly about so-and-so's beach-ready body or how what's-her-name had made an embarrassment of herself on a night out, and very occasionally muttering about Rutspud wasting his time with 'that filthy trash'.

When they heard the occultists on the stairs, Rutspud shoved his project into the shadows at the back of the circle. Shafttoe bounced off his chair and dropped naturally into what Rutspud recognised as Eager Servant pose #2: *'I'm washing my hands in stinky poo and I like it but one day I'll drown you in it.'* Rutspud adopted Basic Mephistophelean pose #7: *'I've hidden the remote control and I'm not telling you where.'*

There was no chanting this time, no sepulchral 'Mmmbops' from Winnie. Mo had the book open, but she was holding it like an actual book for once, rather than a ceremonial object, and flipping backwards and forwards between two pages. Merilyn crouched awkwardly at the edge of Rutspud's circle and touched fingertips to the outermost symbols. They were, Rutspud realised, worried.

"Greetings mighty ones," said Shafttoe theatrically, "what dark deeds bring y-"

"Quiet," said Merilyn without even looking round.

Shafttoe fell silent.

"The circle holds," said Merilyn. "Nothing spiritual can pass in or out without our say-so."

Merilyn's gaze rose to regard Rutspud. There wasn't much regard in that look.

Her head snapped round to look at Mo.

"Well? Is that right? Nothing can enter or leave? No magic, no... prayers, no messages?"

Mo made flustered burbling sounds as she flicked pages back and forth. "I suppose. It doesn't say. But we can reasonably assume... Can't we?"

Merilyn breathed deeply as though suppressing a terrible rage. She stood and turned to Winnie.

"He was a monk?" she said. Her voice was filled with glacial menace.

"That's what he said," replied Winnie nervously.

"Who sent him?"

Winnie looked to Mo. Mo looked to Winnie.

"I don't know," said Winnie. "All I got was that he was a monk."

"He's called Stephen," added Mo.

"Yes, he's called Stephen and he's come here to rescue a demon summoned from the sixth circle of Hell."

"Rescue," said Merilyn, tasting the word like a delicious morsel. "Do you have friends in holy places, Lord Rutspud?" she asked.

Rutspud shook his head slowly. He made a mask of his face because on the inside he was dancing for joy. He was in Sutton Coldfield! Stephen was in Sutton Coldfield! Stephen knew Rutspud was here and was looking for him! It made absolutely zero sense, but it was wonderful beyond all reckoning.

Behind Merilyn, Shafttoe was also struggling to keep a lid on his emotions. But he might as well have had the words 'WHAT THE FUCK?!' tattooed on his forehead.

"Are we in trouble?" said Mo.

"With who?" said Merilyn dismissively.

"With... the church?"

"The church. You think Reverend Purdey is on the prowl? You think he's going to come down from St Michael's and give us a ticket?"

"Maybe the church in Rome," suggested Winnie. "They've got those Swiss Army soldiers and I saw that Tom Hanks film – not *The Da Vinci Code*, the other one – where they've got their own version of the FBI and they have to stop all the priests getting murdered. I recorded it by accident on my Sky box. I was trying to do the *Dancing on Ice,* but it was a dead clever film, it was. I didn't understand a single word of it."

"Stop blathering, Winnie," said Merilyn. "The Catholics aren't interested. No one is. Not the church, not the police."

"Just Stephen," said Mo.

"It *feels* like we're in trouble," said Winnie. "Maybe we should stop. For a bit."

"Stop?" said Merilyn, her wrinkled brow shooting up incredulously. "Now? Have you not seen what's happened out there, what we can achieve with this demon?"

"Have we been of some service to you, mighty ones?" said Shafttoe obsequiously.

"*This* one has." Merilyn pointed at Rutspud. "What did you give us, Prince Shafttoe? Tricks with squirrels? Shooing away foxes?"

"I only do as I is asked," said Shafttoe.

152

"Using Rutspud as a channel for our will, we have litterbugs and mess-makers forced to face up to their own sins. We all saw who had mounds of rubbish outside their doors this morning, didn't we?"

"I'd always suspected that Rick Malarkey of fly-tipping," nodded Winnie.

"And now we know that Craig Fitton is a secret smoker," said Mo, "all those cigarette butts following him home."

"My Alvin was nearly suffocated by a mass of dog toilet bags," said Merilyn.

"Oh, really? That's terrible."

"Not at all," said Merilyn smugly. "That husband of mine has been lying to me for years, telling me he disposes of that dog's excretions in the appropriate manner! It was no less than he deserved. No, this is all quite, quite marvellous."

She wheeled to face Rutspud.

"With the power that this demon can give us, we are on the cusp of greatness!"

"Greatness?" said Winnie. "Golly."

Mo raised her hand timidly. "Is... is greatness a thing we are aiming for? I thought we were just generally sort of having a bit of tidy."

"Oh, Maureen," said Merilyn in what she probably thought was a gentle voice, "we can't be so selfish."

"No, no," agreed Mo. "I don't want to be selfish." She frowned. "Selfish how?"

"We're on the road to making great improvements to our local community, but we can't be parochial. The good we're doing, we need to extend to the wider world." The glee on her face was momentarily clouded. "But this Stephen individual is a concern. We will have to deal with him."

Rutspud's mask shattered. "You stay the fuck away from Stephen, buster," he snarled. "You lay one bastard finger on him and there truly will be Hell to pay."

Merilyn put her hand to her mouth.

"So, you do know him? How is this possible?"

"He's my friend, my best friend. Not that you'd know what that meant, you shrivelled up fucksack!"

Merilyn backed away, shaking her head.

"Enough with the vulgarities!" she moaned. "Really! It's unnecessary! What is it with young people today – and demons – that every other word has to be the F-word."

"You let me out of this circle and I might just drop the vulgarities!"

"My daddy flew in World War Two. We've still got all his medals and his old service revolver. He spent three years in Stalag Luft III."

"They were an electro-synth band, right?"

"As *a prisoner of war*," continued Merilyn forcefully, "he didn't let his situation bring him down. He didn't resort to barbarism and juvenile language."

"Ooh, we didn't do that kind of thing back then, did we?" said Winnie.

"Time was when we had respect for ourselves and for others."

"This used to be *Great* Britain," said Mo with a note of sadness in her voice as though she was realising this for the first time. "And things did use to be great. My dad..."

"He didn't fight in the war, did he?" said Merilyn.

"No," said Mo. "Protected occupation. He did important work for the post office. It was their computers – the world's first proper computers – that helped break the Enigma code."

"Oh, yes, like that film with Benedict Thingumabob," said Winnie. "He's dead good. Versatile. You want a posh weirdo in your film then he's your man."

"Your father built spitfires at Castle Bromwich, didn't he, Winnie?"

"He did," she said. "Him and his Birmingham screwdriver, making all those planes to fight off the Nazis."

We are a proud, island race," said Merilyn. "Good manners. Politeness. Grit. Ingenuity. Invention. These are the things that make us great."

"And Benedict Thingamabob."

"Quiet, Winnie."

"Right you are."

Merilyn turned squarely to Rutspud. "We are the nation of tool-makers and tool-users. You are the tool we need right now."

154

"Yeah?" he said. "You think I'm going to co-operate? After you've threatened my friend?"

"You think you can refuse, knowing what we'll do to your friend if you displease us?"

There was a moment of uncertainty, of panic, on Mo's face, but Merilyn didn't see it.

"You promise you won't hurt him?" said Rutspud.

Merilyn gave a cracked and puckered smile. "Help us and we'll make sure that you go home and see your friend again. We promise."

Rutspud gave her a sharp and calculating look. There were various thoughts and words bubbling up inside him. These occultists were idiots, harking back to an old war every other nation had learned to put aside, dreaming of a golden age of national pride that had probably never existed. And here he was, in a squalid little prison, offered promises that immediately rang hollow, and they had brought up the spectre of the Nazis and it would have been so easy to point out the parallels between old atrocities and what they were doing right now. But he kept his tongue. Use the Nazis in your argument and you sounded as loony as the people who wrote comments on YouTube.

"You will assist us," said Merilyn, softer suddenly, not in order to persuade but as though the argument was already won.

"To do what?" he said.

Merilyn glanced briefly at her confederates. "We need to see a return of decency and respect," she said.

"People should show good manners," agreed Mo.

"Ps and Qs," nodded Winnie vehemently.

"Courtesy."

"Chivalry, even."

"And people shouldn't be allowed to swear," said Merilyn. "There are other words one can use."

"I do this, and you promise to leave Stephen alone?" said Rutspud.

"Entirely unhurt," said Merilyn and raised her arms.

They chanted. Rutspud braced himself for the pain. When the sensation began, he yelled, knowing what would come next. It struck him – struck *through* him – like a volcanic geyser.

Blue light ripped into him. It didn't burn. 'Burn' was too nice a word.

When the power burst free and away, Rutspud had no breath left to scream. He fell. His bones felt as light and as brittle as dead twigs. He was surprised they didn't break beneath him.

Demon blood pounded in his ears, but he heard the occultists leave. Shafttoe creaked in his chair.

"You had to go and rile them again, didn't you?" he said.

Rutspud rolled onto his back and opened his eyes. The cobwebbed ceiling of the cellar was a blur of blacks and browns.

"Play the game," said Shafttoe. "Give and take. Else they'll destroy you and Shafttoe will have to... Well, I've got used to having you around."

Rutspud breathed deeply and focused on being able to produce proper words.

"They'll never let us go," he croaked.

"What's that?" said Shafttoe.

"Those evil *melon-farmers* will never let us go." He thought about what he'd just said and tried again. "Those... evil... mother... fu-*funsters*..." He gasped. His brain had definitely wanted to say something else. His tongue had definitely been given the message. "Oh, *sugar!*"

This was not good. He thought about what he'd just been complicit in and wondered how far the effects had spread. His vision cleared as he lay there, and he found himself looking at something he hadn't noticed properly before.

The ceiling was crossed with beams, beams on which fishing rods and bamboo canes had been stored. Flush against the underside of the ceiling were lengths of electrical wiring, held in place by plastic hoops. Rutspud realised now that not all the wires were power cables; a thinner, flat cable ran among them.

"That's a phone line," he said.

"I'd just lie back and rest now, mate," said Shafttoe, not particularly interested.

"That's a *blinking* phone line," said Rutspud.

Stephen stood at the bar of the Boldmere Oak and sipped his pint with a sense of déjà vu. Ed and Darren joined him in the lip-smacking communion of beer appreciation while Lennox polished glasses on the other side of the bar.

"I thought a rescue mission would be more straightforward than this, if I'm honest," said Stephen. "One, get to Birmingham. Two, locate Rutspud. Three, release him and send him home. I still haven't got beyond one and I'm out of ideas on how to locate him."

"Quests wouldn't be quests if they were easy," said Darren, a statement which sounded superficially wise but was no less unhelpful for that.

"We spent our entire teenage years doing quests," said Ed.

"Some of us did," said Lennox.

"Oh, yeah, that's right. Whereas some of us spent our teenage years doing quests and failing to get anywhere with girls."

"Are we seriously comparing my current problems with a roleplaying game?" said Stephen.

Darren took a frothy sip of beer. "We've reassembled the crack team here: Mr E Thief, Nox the Destroyer and Mirrorglim the Mage."

Ed laughed. "*Gosh*, I'd forgotten about all of that. Were we that nerdy?"

"The preferred term is geeky," said Darren.

"Nerdy *and* geeky."

"Aw, come on. You enjoyed it. Don't pretend you didn't. Rescuing princesses or raiding dungeons, we were a focussed team and every scenario we got results."

"That's my problem," said Stephen. "How can I be focused if I have no clue where I'm going?"

"Well, what would we do if we got stuck in a scenario?"

"As I recall," said Lennox with a nod at Stephen. "Games Master here would throw random encounters at us or get us involved in a tavern fight."

Stephen looked thoughtfully around.

"Oi! You're not our GM anymore and there will be no fights in this pub," said Lennox, wagging a finger across the bar for emphasis.

"If only life came with its own Games Master," said Stephen, miserably.

"What?" said Darren. "Isn't God the Games Master of your life?"

Stephen opened his mouth to reply but then bit down on his words. Ed was happy to fill the gap.

"*Fudge* me, Daz. That is the sappiest thing I've ever heard. You ought to get that printed on a T-shirt." He shook his head. "Don't tell me, you've got it knitted on a jumper."

"I might," said Darren primly. "We might not be able to see God's GM screen and the dice rolls might never go our way, but we know that if we stick it out we'll level up before the end."

"*Cheese and crackers.* Oi, oi. Random encounter. Orcs at three o'clock."

Two young men were entering the pub. Both wore baseball caps and candy-coloured hoodies (one pink and one yellow). As they crossed the threshold, a wind seemed to catch their caps and blow them back out into the foyer. The lads turned to pick them up.

"When did it become normal for men to wear that much colour?" asked Ed. "It used to be only kids and foreign exchange students who dared go further than safe sludgy colours – and denim, of course."

Darren gave a small cough.

"Point taken, Daz. Your mom's knitting is ground-breaking in more ways than one."

The young men put on their caps and headed back toward the pub, but as they crossed the threshold their caps flew away again. One skittered out the door.

"What the *flip* –"

158

"Course," said Lennox, "time was when every gentleman would take off his hat before going indoors."

The youth in the pink hoody approached his cap nervously, arms spread wide to block obvious paths of escape – looking very much as if he were trying to catch a chicken. He grabbed it and pulled it down on his head with a firm tug on the brim. A satisfied smile spread across his face as he stepped into the pub. Then a sudden wind ripped off his cap and hurled it out the door. Eventually, both men caught their caps and held them clamped under their arms as they approached the bar.

"And, er, what can I get you two gents?" asked Lennox.

"After you," said pink hoody.

"No, after you, good sir," said yellow hoody, inclining his head in the tiniest of bows.

Stephen looked up at the youths' faces. Their brows were creased in confusion, as if the words coming out of their mouths had no connection with the sentiments inside their heads.

The exchange continued in this way until Lennox interrupted. "Someone order a *blooming* drink. Or are you two not thirsty? I've got better things to do than listen to this *balderdash*."

Pink hoody managed an anguished nod, but after making a brief, strangled noise, he was only able to utter "no, after you," once more.

Yellow hoody closed his eyes in the manner of one concentrating on a very difficult problem. He swallowed hard, his Adam's apple bobbing, and eventually choked out a response: "Fine. A pint of bitter, but you must let me pay."

"No, no. I want to pay," said pink hoody. His hands immediately flew to his mouth as if he wasn't sure where the words had come from.

An older man who'd been sitting at a nearby table got up and approached the bar. "I couldn't help witnessing your distress and I wanted to help. Let me settle this once and for all and buy your drinks myself. I'll buy one for you gentlemen too," he said, gesturing over at Ed, Darren and Stephen. "Have one yourself barman."

Lennox grinned broadly, but the smile died on his face as the pub was filled with an almighty clamour of people wanting to buy a round for everybody else. Nobody was more surprised than Stephen when he discovered that one of the voices in the melee was his own.

"I insist on buying everyone a drink!"

"I think you'll find," said a man in a hideous smoking jacket, striding forward from a table further back, "that beer is not the most favourable choice for this time of the day. Lambrinis for everyone. It's the dog's *bongos*. It's on me, Lennox."

Stephen thought the man looked slightly familiar, but he really didn't want to hang around in the weirdness of the pub any more.

"Could this be your demon's work?" hissed Darren, leaning in.

"I don't understand it," said Stephen. "It's just random weirdness."

"I'm sure there's a reason behind it."

Stephen shook his head. "Guys, I've got to shoot off. Need to clear my head, maybe consult with the big Games Master in the sky."

Ed frowned. "Games Master in the... Oh. Sure. Never bought into that religious *sugar* myself, but whatever floats your boat."

"I'll see you back at the house," said Darren.

As Stephen left, he heard Lennox's voice. "Dog's *bongos*? What are you on about, Jeremy?"

"The dog's *bongos*. No! I mean the dog's *bongos*! *Fluff* it Lennox, why can't I swear? It's *blobby* annoying. Aargh!"

Stephen walked slowly up the road. If memory served, St Michael's church was only a short distance away. He often found that when he talked to God the talking itself was not the important part. If he could explain the situation and form the question that he wanted to ask, then he was much more likely to come away with answers.

"Good afternoon," he said, as he passed a man walking in the opposite direction.

He was mildly shocked with himself, as he hadn't registered the man's presence before speaking.

Moments later he did it again. He passed a woman and as he wished her a good afternoon he had an overwhelming urge to lift his hat – which was ridiculous as he wasn't wearing one.

Up ahead, there was a bus parked up at a bus stop. A man in a leather jacket stepped down, and then turned to place an arm around the woman behind him.

"Allow me to help you off the bus, madam," he said.

The woman shook him off in alarm. "Get off!" she said. "What do you think you're doing?"

"I'm so sorry to cause you distress, madam. Would you like to sit down for a moment and collect yourself?" he asked.

"What's wrong with you? You're being creepy and weird."

"It was far from my intention," said the man and he too seemed gripped by an urge to doff a hat he wasn't wearing.

"Don't make me call the police," said the woman.

"No, of course not. Perhaps you'd like me to call them for you?" said the man, his face horrified at his own words.

The woman pushed him away and strode down the road. Stephen saw that the man was about to go after her, so he coughed and asked a question.

"Excuse me, sir. Do you know what time it is, please?"

The man beamed and consulted his watch. "It's half past one," he said.

"Thank you," said Stephen, and walked on, satisfied that he had given the woman time to escape.

"Perhaps you'd like my watch if you haven't got one?" called the man. "Take it please, it would be my pleasure."

Stephen hurried away.

A short way up the street, a young man on a ladder cleaned the upstairs windows at one of the larger houses.

"Let me help you with that," he shouted to someone inside. "No, really, it's no trouble at all. It's just a matter of getting the zip past that cuddly middle section. If I just climb inside, we'll have you dressed in a jiffy. I really want to help."

Stephen paused in shock as the window cleaner levered open the window and climbed over the windowsill. It wasn't hard to imagine the conversation, even without the screams that filtered down to street level. Then the window cleaner toppled backwards over the windowsill and fell to the ground. Happily, a porch roof broke his fall, and when Stephen rushed up to see whether he was hurt, the young man was already on his feet, apologising for

161

disrupting Stephen's walk. The window above slammed shut and Stephen walked away, shaking his head.

"Okay," said Stephen. "This is some messed up *shinola*."

He made it to Saint Michaels without encountering any more crazed people, for which he was thankful. He passed through the lychgate and stopped when he saw the squirrels.

"Oh, no. Not you lot too!"

A squirrel with a pile of acorns was passing them out to other squirrels that waited politely in a long queue. Stephen saw a tiny grey head bow to its fluffy-red benefactor and heard a chattering of pleases and thank-yous. He stopped himself at that point. Did he seriously believe he could understand squirrel language? He noticed that one squirrel had fashioned a little bowler hat from the cup of an acorn and was tipping it at other squirrels as he strolled up and down, twirling a twig like a walking stick. Stephen sighed and hurried to the church door. It was locked.

"Lovely day isn't it, young man?" said a woman sitting on a bench by the church wall.

Stephen hadn't noticed her before, but she was clearly people-watching from her seat in the shade. Had she seen the squirrels?

"The weather?" asked Stephen. "Yes, quite sunny. For the moment."

Stephen was so accustomed to Bardsey's wild weather patterns that he still refused to trust that the weather might be stable for the entire day, as it so often was in the landlocked midlands.

"It's a lovely day for all sorts of reasons," said the woman. A certain coldness in her voice reminded him they'd met before, though it had been dark that first time and he'd had other things on his mind. Rees. That was the name.

"You don't have your little dog with you today," said Stephen.

Mrs Rees's generally-austere expression slipped with a flicker of amusement, a twinkle in her blue eyes like lightning across a clear sky. "My husband unaccountably found himself offering to take it out instead of me. I wasn't going to refuse such a polite offer."

"Yes," said Stephen sceptically. "There seems to be a lot of politeness about today."

"It makes a nice change to see people behaving themselves properly for once, don't you think? Almost restores your faith in humanity."

"Oh, I have lots of faith in humanity," smiled Stephen, indicating his habit.

"Surely, you have faith in rules. All those thou-shalts and thou-shalt-nots."

"I'm more of a New Testament guy."

She clearly found this distasteful. "That just doesn't work. Most people need to be told what to do," said Mrs Rees. "There are a great many people who are simply incapable of doing the right thing. Take the church. There was a time when all churches could leave their doors unlocked day and night."

"A position of trust in our fellow man," said Stephen, "and one that I very much support."

"Yes, but people just don't have the respect nowadays," said Mrs Rees. "They'd take the silver or use the altar as a urinal as soon as look at you."

"I'm not sure that's true," said Stephen, although a guilty memory of a band of starving monks taking St Cadfan's silver out on an ill-fated fishing trip in the hope that it would lure mackerel surfaced in his mind. He pushed it back down again.

"There's no respect," she continued, "because people can get away with wrongdoing. Where are the policemen on the streets? Where are the conductors on the buses? Parents aren't even supposed to slap their children any more. There are plenty of people who could do with an occasional slap to teach them right from wrong."

"As I said, I'm a bit more New Testament. Less of the smiting and more of the loving your neighbour."

She looked him up and down. "This isn't your neighbourhood though," she said. "You're a little out of your... jurisdiction."

"Jurisdiction?" What an odd word, he thought and wondered why this woman seemed to be immune to the politeness bug that had bitten everybody else.

"What are you doing here, Stephen?" said Mrs Rees.

163

"Here?" He looked at her, uncomprehending. He pointed at the locked church door. "Here?"

"I think you took a wrong turn," she said.

Stephen looked back over his shoulder.

"In life," she said.

"Oh, you'd know that, would you?" he said curtly.

"You know a man by the company he keeps."

"What the *heck* are you talking about...?"

A slurping noise made him glance down. He recoiled, even though he had no idea what he was looking at. It was the size of a medium dog and approached with such enthusiasm he half expected it to sniff his crotch. It was box-shaped, though, and dripped with stinking grey mud. It had left a thick trail of slime, so it was easy to see that it had come through the lychgate. The cuboid slug-monster was clearly intent on harassing him.

"Oh, dearie me," said the woman. "What's this? It looks to me as though someone's past is catching up with him."

Rutspud had loosened the phone wire from the ceiling and pulled it down with the fishing rod. Now he was splicing together his experimental gadget. Splicing in this instance involved mashing and twisting wires together while quietly imploring them not to come apart again.

"You want to spoil our little paradise with your half-baked electrics, can you at least keep the noise down?" complained Shafttoe, lolling in his armchair. "Trying to do a quiz here. Hmmm. I'm invited to a party, but having accepted, I get a better offer. Am I going to honour the original invitation, fake an illness and go to the second party, or go to bed and ignore them both?"

"What part of serving these idiots is paradise, exactly?" asked Rutspud.

"Fake an illness," said Shafttoe and circled an answer in his magazine.

"They will just chew us up and spit us out."

"Eh?" said Shafttoe.

Rutspud's hands were deep in a tangle of wires, so he jerked his head upwards to indicate the world above the cellar. "Merilyn, Mo, Winnie. When we're spent, they'll get themselves fresh demons. They'll never let us go."

"No! Oh, my goodness, no," said Shafttoe. "You serve your time, reap the rewards and head home. You must remember that this can be a mutually beneficial arrangement. There have been other demons before us – Scumplug, Pearsock and of course Shotbolt. Now then." He tapped his ballpoint pen against his huge teeth and read. "Last question. My best friend has had a disastrous haircut. Do I tell her it looks bad, lie to protect her feelings or avoid her company completely?"

"You do know you're a demon, don't you?" said Rutspud.

"Good. Yes, you're right. I'd tell her it looks bad," said Shafttoe, marking the answer in the magazine. "The ladies are careful to rest or retire demons who appear to be reaching their best before date. It's not in their interest to destroy us."

"They told you that, did they? Well, I'm seeing how that's worked out for Lackring, and I don't have a lot of faith." Rutspud turned his attention to the other demon in his cage. "How's your handset coming along, Lackring?"

Lackring tapped his dead rat and put it to his ear. He'd been adjusting it with an invisible screwdriver. "Just working on a loose connection. I'll be ready for testing in a minute or two," he said.

"Good work," said Rutspud.

"I've got an escape plan," said Lackring, still speaking into the rat. "In case this whole phoning a friend thing doesn't work out."

"Yeah?" said Rutspud.

"You've got me on speakerphone now."

"What?"

"I'm hearing a lot of echo. You'll need to pick up, so we're not overheard," said Lackring.

Rutspud sighed and picked up the handset. He held the end of the wire in his hand, so that Lackring wouldn't be able to see that he'd chopped off the cable that coupled it to the dead rat and reattached it to his device. "Better? So, what's the plan?"

"Plan?" said Lackring.

"The escape plan!"

"Oh, that. Dead simple. We'll disguise ourselves as a really big insect."

"Yes?"

"Clever, huh?"

Rutspud mentally rewound the last thirty seconds of conversation in case he had missed something. He hadn't.

"What?"

"It's clever, isn't it?" said Lackring.

"What is?"

"The giant insect plan."

"I don't get it."

Lackring tutted. "They'll be on the lookout for three two-legged creatures escaping, but if we escape as one six-legged creature, the element of surprise should buy us enough time to get clear."

"Wow," said Rutspud, "and the only thing stopping us is the fact that we don't have a giant insect costume? Oh, as well as the fact that there's literally *no such thing* as an insect the size of a pony?"

Lackring beamed with pride. "It's great, right?"

Shafttoe shook his head. "You two are wasting your time."

"We don't need your opinion," said Rutspud.

"Well, according to this quiz, I'm the sort of friend who believes in tough love. I calls it as it is."

"Is that so?" said Rutspud doubtfully.

"You can rest assured that I've always got your back," said Shafttoe. "Old Shafttoe will look out for you."

Stephen scanned the street as he arrived back at Darren's house in Finnemore Close. He'd taken a circuitous route and had moved as quickly as he was able to, which was not so much a flat-out run as a brief trot and then a walk followed by another brief trot. With fearful backward glances, he threw himself down behind his parked Trabant and peered over the bonnet. The close was quiet and, barring the gentle breeze through the rose bushes, everything was still.

There was a squeak next to him and Stephen almost wet himself with surprise.

"*Gee willikers!*" he exclaimed at the squirrel, Redclaws, who was crouched by the car wheel. "You nearly gave me a *fricking* heart attack!"

Redclaws squeaked questioningly.

"It's hard to explain," said Stephen and then realised he probably didn't need to explain with much clarity if his audience was a squirrel. "I'm being chased by a slithering mud-covered box-monster."

"Kwekwek?"

"That's what it looks like." He frowned at the squirrel's expression of disbelief. "I don't have to explain myself. It's a *melon-farming* box-monster, okay?"

He found himself wishing the muddy box would slither into view just to prove he wasn't mad. Although, if you were intent on proving your sanity to a squirrel, didn't that say something about the general level of your sanity?

There was no box-monster in sight, and he had nothing to prove to the squirrel. He stood, brushed himself down as though crouching behind cars was a perfectly fine thing for a grown man to be doing, and went up to the house.

He knocked on the door. There was no reply.

He opened the letterbox.

167

"Darren?" he called out. Still no reply.

He looked back along the suburban street. He didn't want to risk going back to the Boldmere Oak. He'd had enough of supernaturally polite people, impossibly chatty squirrels and filthy box-monsters for one day.

He tried the door handle. It was locked, naturally.

He looked under the plant pot near the front door in case there might be the clichéd spare key under there. There wasn't.

He considered forcing the garage door, but the bolts and padlocks looked far too sturdy.

"Got to be a way in."

He went to the side gate and wandered round the house.

"Can't find Rutspud," he muttered. "Can't get into the house. Couldn't even get into church for a bit of a pray."

Brother Manfred had often said, 'Failure is an event, never a person.. The man was a walking motivational poster sometimes, the human equivalent of a cute kitten and a trite saying, but he was generally right. Now, though, Stephen felt like the absolute physical embodiment of failure. What would Manfred say about this situation?

'Failure isn't falling down. Failure is refusing to get up again.'

'Failure is merely success in progress.'

'I'm just lucky. The harder I try, the luckier I get.'

'God doesn't close a door without opening a window.'

Stephen looked up. "Ah-ha!"

The window he had opened to air the spare bedroom was still ajar. It was on the first floor and there was a sturdy downpipe running up the wall to the bathroom, which was the next room along. Stephen didn't consider himself to be any kind of athlete, but Redclaws had had no trouble getting up there...

Thinking light and agile thoughts, Stephen hitched up his habit and launched himself at the wall.

Fifteen minutes later, he rolled over the window sill and landed heavily on the folding camp bed. Those fifteen minutes had included a lot of fearful whimpering, earnest self-recriminations for damaging the brickwork and downpipe, and a protracted five minutes of doing his best to swear his head off and getting only as far as 'Sock this for a game of *footing* soldiers. I've *flocking* had it up

168

to here with you *cussing aerosols*. If I'm going to die, I want to *funning* do it with a decent swearword on my lips. *Ships and ballast!'*

Once he had regained his breath and his temper, Stephen tramped downstairs to make himself a cup of tea. He called out for Darren and his mum, but it was clear that the house was empty.

He put the kettle on, dropped a Typhoo tea bag in a cup and numbly waited for the water to boil.

What brilliant advice would Manfred have offered this time? He'd certainly offer a different cup of tea – something herbal, possibly made with petals from an exotic flower or, more likely, a weed he had found in the monastery gardens. He'd probably suggest a spot of meditation and a bit of rejiggling one's chakras.

He could phone Manfred and ask for advice... There was no harm in that.

The telephone sat on an old-fashioned telephone table, between a broom cupboard and a shelf of crystal animals. Stephen smiled when he saw the personal address book next to the phone. It had a metal case with a spring-loaded lid that popped open when you pressed a button. As kids, he and Darren had used the flipping mechanism of this very phone list to launch small missiles and bits of paper. Stephen had once smuggled a similar address book out of his own home so they could go head-to-head in a game of Catapult Dodgeball with Darren's Star Wars action figures as targets.

Stephen dialled the monastery number – the only number he knew off by heart. The phone rang several times and then he heard Manfred's voice. It was the answerphone.

"You have reached the voicemail for St Cadfan's monastery. We all appreciate a little time and space in this world, so we will call you back, but perhaps not straightaway. Enjoy five minutes' quiet meditation after you've left your message and we can both go peacefully in the knowledge that you'll be more relaxed than when you picked up the phone."

Stephen smiled at Manfred's bizarrely endearing logic. "Manfred, it's Stephen. I'd love to talk to you if you can call me back on this number sometime today."

He left Darren's number and put down the phone. Then he brewed his cup of tea and returned to the living room. He settled

169

into a recliner armchair, sipped his drink and regarded the crystal animal ornaments that dominated the room. Some were lined up in front of books on a bookcase, but most were displayed on intricate, grid-shaped shelf units that were just the right size for a multitude of tiny ornaments. The room had lots of old-lady touches about it. The three-piece suite had antimacassars hanging down the backs and cushions galore. Stephen wasn't sure what a Macassar was or why antimacassars opposed them.

In fact, Stephen had never even seen antimacassars on sale anywhere, though he'd never looked. Presumably they were available from the same sort of retailer that sold the dinky shelf units and the wickerwork knitting basket that sat to the side of the armchair. Maybe there were specialist old lady shops...

Out of bored curiosity, Stephen lifted the lid of the knitting basket, wondering if another of Darren's sweaters was in progress. The basket shifted and he saw a book on the floor underneath it. It had an aged aspect to its thick cover and the bibliophile in Stephen automatically leaned over to retrieve it. He placed it upon his lap with a wry smile.

"Well, *burger* me," he said.

After the difficulties they'd had in tracking down Darren's copy of *Livre des Esperitz*, here it was. The daft man had never sold the book in the first place.

Stephen carefully opened the first dry pages. And then the telephone rang.

Rutspud clutched the handset anxiously.

"Who did you dial?" said Lackring.

"No one," said Rutspud. "I've linked it to the line and I can waggle a few wires..."

Rutspud had known all along that his plan had only the slimmest chance of success. Even if he could communicate with the outside world, he would have no way to direct his call. He was equipped only with a handset and a heap of electronics, so dialling was out of the question – not that he knew any numbers to dial...

But Rutspud was a great believer in solving one problem at a time, so he proceeded on that basis. "If I can just get a response," he said, "I might be able to reach an operator or telephone exchange. Hang on..." There was a crackle on the line and then a voice.

"Hello?"

"Hello?" said Rutspud.

"Manfred?"

Rutspud knew that voice. It was impossible, but he knew that voice.

"Stephen?"

It seemed so unlikely that by shouting into an unknown void (even with some homemade telephonic help) he would connect with the one human being who mattered the most...

"Stephen is that you?"

"Rutspud? Rutspud! Oh, my *gosh*! How is this possible? Where are you?"

"This is un-*fupping*-believable!" said the demon, grinning like an idiot and only a single crumb of joy away from whooping like an American. It really was Stephen! "I'm in a cellar, Stephen."

"A cellar?"

"Yeah."

Shafttoe looked up, his face filled with alarm and the realisation that Rutspud had actually made contact with the outside world and hadn't just slipped into the madness that had taken Lackring.

"Okay, okay," said Stephen with hurried, breathless excitement. "And this cellar. Where is it?"

"It's in Sutton Coldfield."

"You've really torn it now," growled Shafttoe. "Wait 'til they find out what you've done!"

Rutspud gestured angrily for him to shut up so that he could hear Stephen properly but his attempt to give Shafttoe the finger magically turned into a far less satisfying thumbs-up.

"Brilliant," said Stephen. "Sutton Coldfield. That's where I am. Right now. I've come to find you."

"You? How? Why?"

"Oh Rutspud, you've no idea how pleased I am to hear your voice. Tell me where you are. It's a cellar, in Sutton Coldfield, yeah?"

"So, this cellar. I don't know whereabouts it is. Made of bricks. I'm in here with two other demons, Shafttoe and Lackring." Rutspud ignored Shafttoe's increased grumbling when he heard his name mentioned. "There aren't any windows, only some steps. It smells of grease and oil in here, but that's probably Shafttoe."

"Okay. Not very useful information. What about the people who summoned you?"

"There's three of them," said Rutspud.

"Good. Good."

"Merilyn is seriously nasty."

"Merilyn?"

"Merilyn."

"Not a very common name. I can ask around."

"Merilyn's a complete *buzzard*. I can't wait until that one ends up downstairs. There will be torments aplenty for that *biscuit*."

"You said there were three of them," said Stephen.

"That's right. Merilyn, Winnie and Mo."

"They sound like women's names."

Rutspud clicked his fingers. "I knew it! I thought they might be women. I'm not very good at telling. My instincts said they were women and then I talked myself out of it." He shook his head. "Should have had more conviction. It was a fifty-fifty chance. Better than fifty-fifty."

"Describe them for me."

"Well, they all wear robes. Not like yours: these ones are black, and they have hoods that cover their heads. Mo has these fluffy slippers and socks with a weird design on them."

"Weird how?"

"Well I'm not sure if they are demon faces or cat faces. Weird, grinning cat-demon faces."

"Ri-ight. Not sure what I can do with that."

"I noticed the socks because Mo is the one I see the most of. Winnie and Merilyn come round for rituals, mostly."

"It sounds like you're in a house."

172

Rutspud looked around.

"It's a cellar. Like back at St Cadfan's."

"But you said it was brick-built."

"Yeah. Red brick."

"That's a house. Almost certainly a house. Can't be that many houses with cellars in Sutton."

"This is useful information, right?" said Rutspud and he couldn't help but notice the desperation in his own voice.

"This is great," said Stephen. He paused. "Have they... hurt you?"

Rutspud chuckled grimly. "They've threatened me with Enya," he said. Stephen laughed, but Rutspud shouldn't have said it; at the mention of Enya, Lackring began rocking back and forth on his rump, crooning piteously to himself.

"You've survived worse," said Stephen.

"The spells though..." said Rutspud. "The *wishes*..."

"I think I've seen them in action."

"Yes. The spells are agony, Stephen."

"Oh, mate."

"I'm not sure if I can last through many more of them."

"We need to get you out of there, buddy," said Stephen.

"There's one really important thing," said Rutspud. "They know you're here. I don't know how, but they've seen where you're staying, and they know you're here to rescue me. You need to –"

Rutspud saw a tiny movement in his peripheral vision and turned to look. At that moment, the line went dead.

"Stephen? Stephen?"

The call was lost.

Rutspud's claws rattled feverishly across the wires of his crazy contraption. He wasn't sure how he'd made it work in the first place, so it was difficult to repeat the miracle. He listened carefully to the handset and nudged each wire, hoping to restore the connection. Nothing! But as he checked everything for the third time, he heard a sound. It was Shafttoe clucking smugly at him from across the room. Rutspud looked up to see him shaking his head.

"Oh, dearie me, no. You've gone too far now. I wouldn't want to be in your shoes when they find out what you've done. No, no, no."

Still looking directly at Shafttoe, Rutspud lifted the handset. "Lackring? A call for Lackring." The other demon stopped rocking and scrabbled for his rodent.

"Yes? Who's calling please?"

"It's Rutspud."

"How did the test go?"

"It went well, Lackring, really well. Help is at hand."

"Hello? Hello?"

Stephen put the phone down and picked it up again, in case the call had magically reconnected.

He dialled 'last number called' but all he got was a robot telling him the number was withheld.

How had Rutspud managed to call him? Why was there a phone in a Sutton Coldfield cellar? And how did he know this number? These prudent and serious questions were shouted down by Stephen's cheers and giggles of joy at hearing from Rutspud.

Whatever worst-case scenario Rutspud might be facing here on earth – actual death was impossible for something that had never lived – it had not yet come to pass. And that was cause for celebration.

But it was disquieting to hear that this mysterious trio of occultists knew his mission. Someone he'd encountered must be connected with them. Stephen's thoughts turned immediately to Nigel Herring and his nihilistic Satanist friends. They certainly fell under the general category of people who wished him harm.

"Okay, Stephen," he told himself, "rational thought time. Lines of enquiry." He paced back into the living room. "Cellars. I could find out which houses have cellars. How the *hat* would I do that? Land registry? Local swingers' clubs?" He shook his head. "And who have we spoken to? The Satanists, Ed, Lennox, the guy in the bookshop..."

Books. He had just found Darren's old copy of the Krakovian *Livre des Esperitz*. He had other leads to follow, but fresh knowledge was never to be shunned. He sat himself down and forced himself to put his nervous excitement aside and treat the old tome gently. There was a large piece of folded paper inserted between two pages and the book fell open naturally to that section.

By chance, it was the Rite of Ukahdo, the same pages he'd seen in the photo at the bookshop. This wasn't just a fragment of the ritual; this was the whole thing. He flipped back a page and read the section on preparations. Something caught his attention.

Un autre démon est nécessaire pour compléter ce rituel. Ce démon est connu comme le traître.

"The ritual requires a second demon," he murmured. "A traitor."

Stephen looked at the accompanying picture. It was an ugly demon with a shock of hair like those gonks that everyone had back in the day and a set of huge teeth like piano keys. The text said it was known as the betrayer... Rutspud had mentioned two other demons, and one of them had helped the occultists capture him. This was interesting news. Belphegor hadn't mentioned another demon.

The folded sheet of paper that Darren had used as a bookmark had flecks of white paint on it and some neat but irregular holes cut out of it. Such a rough and paint-marked thing was hardly a decent or appropriate bookmark. Stephen took it out. It had been folded several times, but he only had to unfold it a couple of times to see the curved arrangement of the holes and see it for what it was.

"A summoning circle," he said. It was stencil for a summoning circle.

Stephen was comparing the stencil with the woodcut picture of the Ukahdo circle when he heard a muffled knock at the door.

Darren. Back at last.

Stephen put the stencil back in the book and hurried to the door. They had a lot to discuss.

It wasn't Darren. It wasn't his mum.

It was a mud-covered cuboid that moved as if alive. It reared up to its full three feet of height, balanced impossibly on its narrow end. It had no face, no limbs, no discernible motivation or mood, but it was the most terrifying thing Stephen had encountered in his life.

"Oh, my *funding gonk!*" he squealed and leapt back.

It flopped forward into the house, splattering muddy droplets across the hallway carpet and walls, and then slithered towards him on its belly.

"What in *golf*'s name do you want?" he howled, stumbling backwards into the living room. "Leave me alone!"

The box struggled with the sharp turn into the living room, shunting back and forth like a learner driver searching for the angle needed to fit through the door. Whimpering, Stephen looked about for a weapon with which to defend himself. There were, on reflection, very few weapons to be found in a living room. He grabbed a crystal mouse and a knitting needle and dithered over which would be best before concluding that neither would be of any use at all.

The box gave a final shunt against the doorframe, dislodging much of the muck that still clung to it, and slid towards him.

"Wait!" cried Stephen and then he saw the seam running round the box, the handle on its side. "Wait," he said, in a very different tone. "I... I know you, don't I?"

It was a suitcase, an old suitcase – tatty, ravaged and partially disintegrated, as though it had been dumped somewhere very wet a long time ago. It slid forward until it nudged against the tip of Stephen's toes.

"I know you," he said, suddenly no longer afraid. Very confused, as was only right, but no longer afraid.

He knelt, brushed the slime from its catches and tried to open it. They were rusted shut, solid lumps of crusty brown metal. He went to the kitchen to look for a knife with which to force it open. The suitcase spun around to follow him.

"Wait there," he told it. "I *am* coming back."

"What on earth has happened here?" said Mrs Pottersmore, standing at the open front door, a bulging carrier bag in each hand.

Darren's mum stared aghast at the splashes and smears of mud that marred her otherwise pristine hallway. The look of horror on the dear old woman's face yanked at Stephen's heart. He might as well have punched a puppy for all the uncomprehending shock he had inflicted on the house-proud Mrs Pottersmore.

"It's not what it looks like," he said, which was a lie. "It is what it looks like, but it's not my fault. I mean it is, because I threw it in the canal all those years ago, but if you'd just come in and take a look..."

He waved her forward, but Mrs Pottersmore wasn't going anywhere. She fixed Stephen with a hard and hurt look which he hadn't seen since he was a child.

"You come here," she said. "You stay over uninvited – not that I mind! – you don't wear any of the clothes I got out for you – not that it's any skin off my nose! – you eat all the sausages – and you're welcome to them! – and when I go out to replenish our supplies – two days early, mind! – I come back to find you've treated my hallway no better than a pig shed!"

"I really am sorry, Mrs Pottersmore," said Stephen, feeling wretched inside. "I can clean this up."

But she was shaking her head.

"Maybe it's just as well," she said. "There was a call for you earlier."

"A call?"

"From the monastery. Your superior, I think."

"Manfred called?" asked Stephen incredulous.

"Yes, that might very well have been his name. He said you need to go back. Something about you being needed urgently."

"Really?" Stephen tried to imagine what *urgent* would look like through the lens of Manfred's worldview. Perhaps the MOT was due on the Trabant in a month? No, that was ridiculous, there was no way the Trabant had an MOT.

He struggled to think of a reason that Manfred would ask him to return. Only the library was exclusively Stephen's domain. Had a demon manifested in his absence? Or worse, had Belphegor appeared and demanded to know what Stephen was doing?

"He sounded quite angry, if I'm honest," sniffed Mrs Pottersmore.

"Angry?" What had he done to make Manfred angry. That was an almost impossible feat to achieve.

"So, you'd just better go now," she said.

"Right," said Stephen.

He had no idea if he intended to go home to Bardsey. An urgent summons from Manfred was certainly not to be ignored... And yet, although he was far from locating Rutspud, he was suddenly closer than he had been before. Regardless, Mrs Pottersmore wanted him out of her house and he had no right to argue otherwise.

"I'll just get my things," he said, apologetically.

"No, I will fetch them," she said. "I don't want you causing any more mess or upheaval."

"I'm sure I can..."

She was already climbing the stairs. Stephen mooched back into the living room. The suitcase had done as instructed and was now a perfectly stationary, utterly normal suitcase, albeit one that had sat at the bottom of canal for over a decade and then magically returned to the person who had dumped it. Stephen was unsure whether to take it when he left. That would save Mrs P the unpleasantness of removing it herself. And it had sought him out, but the contents (assuming they'd survived) belonged to someone else. He could just tell Mrs Pottersmore to give it to Darren and let him deal with it.

His eyes fell on the copy of *Livre des Esperitz*. That *did* belong to Darren, but it could prove invaluable in the continuing search for Rutspud. And, he told himself, Darren was unaware he still owned it. Taking the book to the Boldmere Oak to show it to Darren could not be considered stealing.

"Yes," he said out loud, picking up the book. With a guilty glance upwards to wherever Mrs Pottersmore might be, he tucked it inside the front of his habit.

"These clothes of yours are in a right state," called Mrs Pottersmore.

"They are," he agreed, moving towards the stairs. "Slugs I think."

"Well, that's no excuse," she said.

Mrs Pottersmore descended the stairs slowly, carrying Stephen's rucksack not quite at arm's length but in a manner that suggested she wanted as little contact with the dusty thing as possible.

"It has all spent quite a number of years in the shed next to the Ship Hotel and I guess –"

The words caught in his throat when he saw her socks, level with his eyes on the stairs. They were hand-knitted and – like so many of Mrs Pottersmore's creations – adorned with a bright and unique design: a face which was an eye-watering fusion of cat and demon. Stephen recognised Grizznik, the winged cat-gargoyle that Darren's character, Mirrorglim, had kept as a sidekick. Darren had sketched it endlessly on the backs of character sheets and in his school books. And his mum had turned it into a pair of socks.

These were the socks that Rutspud had described.

"Guess what?" said Mrs Pottersmore.

Stephen's brain raced through the evidence: the *Livre des Esperitz*, here; the address in Ben's sales ledger; the telephone call which had connected to this house for no good reason at all.

"Mo," he said.

Maureen Pottersmore held the rucksack out to him. "Come on, Stephen. Let's get you on the road before dark. I'll say goodbye to Darren for you."

He didn't take the rucksack. His eyes darted to the door to the cupboard under the stairs and a second later his legs were darting too. He flung the door open. There were coats, a hoover, and a surprisingly-extensive array of mops and brooms, but there was also a second door. He opened it, swatted the light switch and all but ran down the narrow stairs into the cellar.

Directly in front of him was a mess of dust sheets partially draped over an old dog cage. Inside the cage was a creature that looked a bit like a shaved bulldog, a bit like a melted waxwork of the Buddha, and a lot like a demon. Off to the right, the cellar floor was dominated by two circles. Stephen saw demons in both of them, one lounging in a recliner chair, the other being Rutspud.

The demon in the recliner leapt to his feet.

"Mortals," he intoned, "once more you come to my domain, and – Who the *dickens* are you?"

"Stephen!" gasped Rutspud in wonder.

"Rutspud!"

Stephen dashed to his friend and clasped his hands.

"You found me!"

"Nearer than I could ever imagine. I'm sorry it took so long."

Rutspud was hardly a fastidious demon. He did work in Hell after all, a place with the hygiene standards of a toxic waste dump, but it wrenched Stephen's heart to see him here in such a dank and unregarded place.

"So sorry," he said.

"You're here now," said Rutspud and gave him an enlivening punch on the shoulder.

"Let's go," said Stephen and tried to lead Rutspud away. Rutspud's hand forcefully slid from his as he pulled.

"The circle," said Rutspud, gesturing downward. "I can't get out."

"What?"

"And we can't go without Lackring and Shafttoe." Rutspud pointed one hand at the sorry thing in the cage and the other at the demon with the comfy chair.

One of Rutspud's fellow prisoners had a panicked look on his face (and not because he was eager to be off). He was, Stephen realised, surprisingly familiar with that hair and those teeth...

"Hey, you look just like the picture in –"

Stephen didn't get to say what the demon looked like, as something clonked him then on the back of his head with sufficient force to drive all words, thoughts and general consciousness straight out of him.

Mo put the frying pan down and went forward to check Stephen's pulse. She felt around on his neck for far too long and Rutspud ached with a wretched concern of the kind no demon should ever feel, particularly not for a mere human.

"He's alive," she said and turned her head to Rutspud. "Don't look at me like that."

"Like what?" said Rutspud, furious on the inside, coldly quiet on the outside.

"I couldn't let him go, knowing what there was down here."

She touched the back of his head. Her fingertips came away tipped with blood.

"I'll have to put some Germolene on that," she tutted.

With clear difficulty, Mo hauled Stephen to the wall between Rutspud's and Shafttoe's circles and leaned him up against the brickwork. She went to the corner under the cellar stairs and threw back a dust sheet to reveal a tall tool chest. Mo went straight to the third drawer down – like a woman who knew exactly where she kept things – and took out a fat roll of silver duct tape and a scoring knife.

Rutspud looked to Stephen. His friend was very still and very pale.

"Is he breathing?" he said. "He doesn't look like he's breathing."

"Does it matter?" said Shafttoe. "Coming down 'ere to our inner sanctum and givin' us all the shock of us lives."

Mo came back to Stephen.

"He's breathing," she said and bound his hands and then his ankles together with the sticky tape.

"What are you planning to do with him?"

"Now, don't go questioning the masters," said Shafttoe, his manner all diplomatic and reconciliatory.

"I don't know what I'm going to do with him," said Mo and Rutspud saw that her hands were shaking, violently. She was afraid.

"You're an evil woman," said Rutspud.

She fumbled the tape and ended up with a twisted strip, all useless and stuck to itself. She made a self-pitying squeak and hacked at the twisted end with the knife.

"Have you never heard that the end justifies the means?" she said. It was a strangled form of speech, on the verge of tears.

"I hear it all the time," said Rutspud. "In Hell, you can't walk ten steps without hearing someone say it. Or scream it."

She didn't meet his eye as she put the tape and knife away, but he eyeballed her furiously all the same.

"And what end?" he said. "Keeping Sutton tidy? Making sure the local wildlife contributes to society? That's worth his life, is it?"

"Be quiet!" she spluttered, her voice a frail tremor. "Just be quiet! You don't understand!"

"Oh, I do," said Rutspud. "Ends and means. It's for the greater good. You have to be cruel to be kind, don't you, Mo?"

She all but ran for the stairs.

"I tell you what, Mo," he shouted after. "We can be kind in Hell! We're very, very kind!"

A door slammed, and she was gone. The sudden silence that followed echoed even louder.

It was Shafttoe who broke the silence.

"Well, that was a fine to-do and no mistake," he said. "In all my years of being summoned, I don't think I've known anything like it."

"Shut the *front door*, Shafttoe," said Rutspud.

"It was all very *Eastenders*, wasn't it? Like that time Mick Carter threw Kat out of the Queen Vic." He picked through his pile of magazines apparently in search of an *Eastender*, whatever that was.

"Just shut up," said Rutspud softly.

Stephen was breathing but he was out cold. Rutspud couldn't be sure if having Stephen here and unconscious was better or worse than Stephen being out there, hopelessly searching. For the first time, Rutspud found himself thinking Stephen would have been

182

better off having never come to find him. But this wasn't the time for moping or defeatist thinking.

"Call for Lackring. Call for Lackring."

The demon, who had sat obliviously through the excitement, put his dead rat to his ear.

"Rutspud, is that you?"

"Yes."

"Is help on its way?"

Rutspud massaged his brow with thumb and forefinger.

"Sort of," he said. "It came. It..." He cleared his throat. "I think we're going to have to help ourselves. We need to escape. And we're taking Stephen with us."

"Who's Stephen?"

"He's my friend."

"Friend?" scoffed Shafttoe.

Rutspud gave him a vicious look. Shafttoe wisely buried his head in his magazine and read up on his *Eastenders*.

"Are we doing Operation Succubus?" asked Lackring.

"I'm afraid we still don't have a sexy dress or two half-coconuts."

"What about Operation Kitten Surprise, in which we escape disguised as cats wearing costumes we've knitted ourselves."

"Okay," said Rutspud slowly. "Can you give me any details?"

Lackring hunkered down and pressed the rat even more closely to his ear. "Well, in Operation Kitten Surprise, what we do is we escape disguised as cats. And we do that by putting on costumes that we've knitted ourselves."

Rutspud waited in case there was more.

"I think," he said eventually, "we might go for something a bit more straightforward."

He picked up the fishing rod from the place in the shadows where he'd stored it. It was as long as a man and gave him considerable reach but not as much as he needed.

"There's a tool box-cabinet-thing in the corner under the stairs. It might contain something that could help us."

"Cat costumes."

"Or something else. It's on wheels. Can you see it?"

Lackring leaned to the edge of his cage and looked out.

"Goodness me there is. And you can see it from where you are?" He looked around at the upper corners of the room. "Is there CCTV in here?"

"Um, yes. Why not? I can't reach it but you're nearer to the stairs. If I pass you the fishing rod, do you think you could snag it?"

Lackring laughed. "Well, that's all good and well but how are you going to get a fishing rod to me. I mean I'm in here and you're all the way –"

Rutspud jabbed him in the side of the head with the fat end of the fishing rod.

"Parcel for Lackring."

"Ooh," said the demon, thrilled. "Some people complain about the modern world. To hear Mo and her friends talk, you'd think the world was going to wrack and ruin – have you met them? Lovely people. And when I say lovely I suppose I really mean they're *foxing* evil *cults*. But when they criticise the modern world they forget some of the simple advances there have been. Like same day delivery."

"Quite," said Rutspud.

Lackring pulled the rod much of the way into his cage and admired it like a new toy.

"And it's often free delivery too. How do they do that? Economies of scale, I suppose."

"Can you reach the tool chest, Lackring?"

"Hang on. Let me put you on speakerphone." He put his rat down, prodded its belly and provided his own beep sound effect. "There. Can you still hear me?"

"Yes."

"Good."

Lackring swung the rod around with little regard for (or awareness of) anyone who might be in a nearby circle and angled it towards the stairs. The very tip was able to reach past the lower stairs but was a good arm's length short of the tool chest.

"*Bunnies*," said Rutspud with feeling.

"It's not long enough," said Lackring. "Fortunately..."

He lifted it back, loosed several lengths of fishing line from the reel and began to swing it back and forth – a tricky act in the confines of the cellar.

"In Hell, I was on the maintenance crew at the pool of Yan Ryuleh Sloggoth," said Lackring. "Used to go fishing with oil company bosses."

"Fishing *with* oil company bosses?"

"Absolutely. If you want to catch a demon squid, there's no better bait than an oil company man. Many demons will tell you a BP man is best, but I always favoured an Exxon Valdez. Call me sentimental."

"Yes, yes. The tool box..."

"Casting a line with a fat oil exec on the end is tricky. They can be very unbalancing. But it's all in a flick of the... wrist!"

Lackring whipped the rod forward and the line shot out in a beautiful flat arc that resulted in a length of line and the barbed hook wrapped solidly around the tall box.

"I got it," said Lackring. "I don't know if you can see it on your _"

"I see it! I see it!" said Rutspud, excited despite himself. "Pull it in!"

Lackring turned the reel. There was some initial resistance and Rutspud momentarily feared the line would snap, but then the chest shifted jerkily, the wheels aligned and it trundled forward.

"Yes!"

"Now, let's not have any silliness, lads," said Shafttoe testily, putting down his magazine. "Mo will not be happy if we're seen messing around with her things."

"*Fup* Mo," said Rutspud.

Too late, Shafttoe tried to intervene. He propelled himself out of his chair and tried to grab the chest as it passed, but his hands stopped, seemingly of their own volition, at the edge of his circle. He grabbed the cushion off his armchair and flung it at the chest. It was a big cushion and the toolbox was hard to miss. The tall unit teetered and fell with a cascade of clatters. The fishing wire snapped and Lackring fell back in his cage. The chest came down with the lip of its top edge mere millimetres inside Rutspud's circle.

"*Dance* you, Shafttoe!" said Rutspud. "What are you doing?"

"I'm not having you screw up this cushy little number."

"Cushy?" Rutspud crawled to the edge of the circle and tried to get purchase on the corner of the chest. "This cushy little number is madness. They've nearly killed Stephen."

"He's a monk, mate! He's one of the enemy!"

The very tips of Rutspud's claws touched the metal corner. If he could just pull back with sufficient pressure on the surface...

"He's my friend," said Stephen, "and normal people don't go around killing other people."

"You can't question the masters," said Shafttoe. "You can't understand them because they've got *vision*."

"You mean they're really short-sighted, yeah?" said Rutspud. He grunted, and the chest came forward. He scrabbled for a few more millimetres and then pulled again. It shifted enough for him to hook a finger into the top drawer and haul it almost completely into his circle. "Yes!"

Quickly, he hauled it upright and ransacked the drawers. Mo was clearly a woman with a tidy mind and had packed it well. The chest was filled with tools and materials of all sorts, many of which might be used to effect an escape if Rutspud had time to think of how to use them. He pulled out pots of white emulsion paint, sheets of sandpaper, a power drill, an electric torch, wood glue, screwdrivers and hammers, white spirits, tiling grout, a palette knife, a chisel, a spirit level and a little plastic tub filled with all manner of screws, nails, hooks, rawlplugs and those little identifiable odds and ends you always have left over after assembling a piece of flat-pack furniture.

Rutspud went for an obvious option. He cracked open the white spirits, poured it liberally over a section of his imprisoning circle and then attacked the paint with a chisel and a palette knife.

"What are you doing?" demanded Shafttoe loudly.

"Shhh," said Lackring. "I think I can hear him. He's definitely up to something."

"Leave that alone. That took me ages to paint."

Rutspud was scraping the paint with such fury it took a good few seconds for the words to trickle through to his brain. He looked at Shafttoe.

"*You* painted it?"

The expression on Shafttoe's face was an odd one. It wasn't fear or anger or contempt. He looked at Rutspud with a new blankness, a lack of expression, as though Rutspud had suddenly ceased to exist, that he was no longer a player in whatever game Shafttoe was playing.

Shafttoe leapt onto the arm of his chair, picked up his lamp and used the base of it to bash at the ceiling above.

"Help! Help! They're trying to escape! He's breaking the circle!"

Rutspud attacked the painted symbols with renewed energy.

Stephen woke with the sound of shouting in his ears, a chemical stink in his nostrils and a pounding pain in the back of his head. He gasped and grunted and sat upright. He couldn't move his hands and then saw that they had been taped together, from wrists down to fingers, with heavy duct tape.

To his right, Rutspud was scraping violently at the edge of his circle with a flat blade. To his left, the other demon was whacking at the ceiling with the now-broken base of a standard lamp. It was like watching two caveman discovering music and it wasn't good music.

"What's going on?" said Stephen thickly, his tongue a leaden weight in his mouth.

Rutspud stopped.

"You're awake!"

"And regretting it."

"Shafttoe's on their side!" said Rutspud, pointing at the other demon.

"I know," said Stephen.

"Me?" shouted Shafttoe. "I'm just playing the game. You're the one who's sided with the enemy! I don't know what they teach you in the sixth circle but I'm definitely reporting you when I get home."

Rutspud threw a hammer at Shafttoe. Shafttoe dodged it but lost his footing and fell heavily on his chair.

There was the thump of hurried footsteps on the stairs and three women descended.

"He's trying to break free!" shouted Shafttoe.

"Get the broom, Winnie," said Mo Pottersmore.

The short and dumpy Mrs Churchill, owner of the finest big black cocks in town, grabbed the sweeping brush near the base of the stairs and used the base of it to bodily force Rutspud away from his attempts at vandalism. Mo Pottersmore nipped forward and dragged the scraping tools and the bottle of spirits out of the circle and out of Rutspud's reach.

The third woman watched, all the while contemptuously shaking her head. Stephen had met her on two occasions; once in the street on his first night in Sutton Coldfield, a second time in the churchyard of St Michael's. Mrs Rees. And based on what little Rutspud had said, this flinty-eyed and joyless woman was clearly Merilyn. Merilyn Rees.

He groaned inwardly. He had met them all before. He had let slip his plans and what little he'd known to them. They'd always been one step ahead of him. In truth, that probably hadn't been much of a challenge for them. He had been out-played by three old women. Was it ageist and sexist of him to beat himself up for that fact? Probably, and yet he was annoyed by the ridiculousness of it all, three women, dressed in black and gold robes like understudies for a pantomime villain, three women who should surely be enjoying their golden years doing cross-stitch and gardening and... bingo? and... what did old women spend their time doing?

All of this turmoil, confusion and upset came out as a single syllable.

"Why?" he said.

"Why?" said Mo.

"Well, because he was going to ruin that circle," said Winnie. "Shafttoe spent an age painting it and did a lovely neat job of it too."

"You is too kind," said Shafttoe sycophantically.

"It's so hard to get tradesmen to make good these days. Do you remember when 'making good' was part of the job?"

"No," Stephen told her, grunting as he tried to sit upright.

"He means, why this?" said Merilyn. She was almost amused. Almost. It was hard to tell. The woman didn't exactly ooze emotion. "He means, why are we doing this at all? Why are three sweet old dears summoning devils? Why aren't we sitting at home, listening to *The Archers* and baking cakes for our darling grandchildren?"

Ah, yes, thought Stephen, a little woozily. Baking. That was something old women did.

"It's your Darren's fault, isn't it?" said Winnie.

"Not his fault exactly," said Mo. "But he certainly got me into it." She looked at Stephen. "You know what he was like. It was devil this and Satan that. I think all young men get obsessed with their hobbies. That's a man thing, isn't it? Hobbies."

"I have hobbies," said Winnie. "I've got my birds."

"But you're not bird mad, are you? Men, it's... He had me knitting protective covers for his books, making Satanic seat covers. I did a lovely crocheted blanket with Baphomet, the goat of Mendes on it. Lovely, it was. And then he gave it all up, threw a lot of stuff out. I tried to give some to charity, but the Heart Foundation wouldn't take it and the RSPCA said it wasn't their sort of thing. I ended up reading some of the books."

"And you brought that one to the Wednesday book club," said Winnie. "The one with the racy pictures."

"Those spells and rituals are dangerous," said Rutspud.

"Are you telling us what we can and can't do?" said Merilyn. "Even in the afterlife, are we to expect to be told that we're not capable, not able? That we should know our place? Men!"

"Who are you calling a man? That's slander!"

"The books are a means to an end," said Merilyn. "The world has no regard for us and wants nothing more from us than to sit by the fireside, knitting or reading *Take a Break* magazine, watching the world our ancestors built crumble in ruin and chaos."

"And what is this achieving?" said Stephen. He would have gestured to the trapped demons, but his hands were bound together so the action looked like he was doing 'grind coffee' from *Agadoo*.

"Achievements?" said Merilyn and looked archly to her two co-conspirators.

"The town is looking much neater," said Mo. "The pavements have never looked tidier."

"And the young people are better behaved," agreed Winnie. "Three men fought each other to open a door for me this morning." She laughed. "I wasn't even going that way."

"And they're certainly not loitering around the place as much, I notice," said Mo. "None of them hanging about on street corners or clogging up the aisles in Tesco."

"They're probably terrified of what's happening," said Stephen.

"A little fear of authority isn't a bad thing," said Merilyn. "Time was when people had a bit more respect. For the police. For the government."

"Back when people swallowed the lies they were told?" said Stephen.

"Back when people trusted their elders and betters."

"When everything made sense," said Winnie.

"When you could leave your door unlocked without fear," said Mo.

"Because people respected what was yours and you respected what was theirs."

"And people weren't whizzing all over the world expecting hand-outs."

"And getting their hands on what we'd worked for."

"And building on our greenbelt with their ugly little houses."

"Ruining our respectable little town."

"With their burger bars."

"And that place that only sells chicken. Only chicken!"

"And their Virgin trains."

"And that excuse that passes for the Royal Mail these days."

Stephen's gaze met Rutspud's.

"Mate," said the demon, "trust me, I've had to put up with this for days."

"This has to stop now," said Stephen. "People are being hurt."

"Who?" said Merilyn.

"Well... well, me." He looked to Mo and Winnie, suspecting, hoping they were the weakest links in the chain. "You can see this is going too far."

Mo pursed her lips.

"I didn't want to be ignored anymore. I wanted things to be right. As they should be."

"And that's what we're doing," said Merilyn firmly.

"I wanted things to make sense again," added Winnie. "It's all so confusing. I can't even get my Sky box to record the *Bake Off*. I think I was happier when there were only the five TV channels."

"Four," said Mo.

"Three."

"Two."

"Or just the one. We were never allowed to watch ITV in our house," said Winnie. "My dad said it was all just silly nonsense and violence."

"Nonsense and violence? Have you looked outside recently?" said Stephen.

Mo and Winnie exchange glances.

"We don't have to stop," suggested Mo timidly. "Not 'stop' stop."

"But we could give it a rest for a bit," agreed Winnie.

"A bit of a breather never did no one any harm," chimed in Shafttoe.

Merilyn nodded. For a foolishly optimistic instant Stephen thought she was agreeing with the others but he saw that she was nodding because she knew this moment was coming. Merilyn had a canvas tote bag over her shoulder. She slipped it off and pulled out an intricately engraved and bulbous bottle that Stephen had seen before on a desk in the upstairs office of a coffee shop. And then she pulled out a gun.

Stephen wasn't a gun expert. It was a revolver, he knew that much. It looked old. There was a well-oiled sheen to it. From the rich grey-brown burnish of the metal, he reckoned that it was only oil and elbow grease holding it together. Mo stepped away at the sight of the gun and clung to Winnie. Winnie was certainty stout enough to stop a bullet although she was too short to provide much actual cover.

"The courage of their convictions," said Merilyn. "That's what people lack today."

"Put that away now," said Mo fearfully, "before you hurt someone."

"That is its purpose, Mo." She lowered it to aim at Stephen.

"Don't you *fumbling* dare!" snarled Rutspud.

"You don't know if it still works," said Winnie.

"My dad cleaned and polished it every other Sunday. Religiously," said Merilyn. "I still keep it in my bedside drawer. He knew the responsibility that came with power such as this."

"Your dad was Spiderman?" said Stephen without thinking and would later blame it on concussion.

"That thing's older than any of us," said Winnie. "Put it down at once, Merilyn. I insist."

"Insist?" Merilyn gave a dry, fractionally hysterical laugh. "You know, you fat fool of a woman, I wish that, for once, people would just do as they're told and not question everything." She was still for a moment and then turned, smiling, to Rutspud. "You heard me," she said. "I wish people would just do as they are told."

Rutspud glared at her. "You want to do the ritual now, *britches*?"

She raised the pistol to aim at Stephen again. He could see straight down the barrel. He thought he might see the shiny point of the bullet inside, but there was only a circle of empty blackness.

"I believe we can dispense with the ritual."

"You've got to do the ritual. You've got to say the words!"

Merilyn pulled back the hammer with a thumb that was almost too weak to complete the task. He wondered: if she slipped and the hammer fell forward by accident, would he hear the bang before it killed him? The hammer clicked into place.

"I'll give you the final phrase," she said. "I remember that much."

"Fine. Fine. Just don't hurt him."

"Very good," said Merilyn and then uttered a string of tongue-throttling syllables. The room was illuminated with a flash of blue light that left spinning pixels of colour in Stephen's vision. In his circle, Rutspud had collapsed, rasping for breath, limbs robbed of energy.

"What did she wish for this time?" said Winnie.

"Be quiet," said Merilyn.

Winnie's lips moved but no sound came out.

"Superb," said Merilyn. "Now, since everyone else has developed a somewhat yellow streak, I will be taking these demons with me to continue our good works and no one is going to stop me."

Mo's arms fell to her sides.

Merilyn jiggled the bottle at Shafttoe.

"You still wish to serve me, don't you, demon?"

"I only lives to serve, mistress," scraped Shafttoe. "In so much as a demon lord such as myself can be said to –"

"*Shakti!*"

The yellow-haired demon vanished from his circle and, with a glutinous *glunk,* something appeared inside the bottle.

"I bought this jinn bottle from an interesting young businessman on the high street," said Merilyn. She looked sharply at Winnie even though Winnie had said nothing and was incapable of uttering a word. "No, not that kind of jinn, Winnie. They say King Solomon made items such as this. The young man assured me it was as secure as any circle. Lackring?"

The pathetic-looking demon in the cage stared up into the air.

"Mother? Is that you?"

"Hardly. *Shakti!*"

The bottle rocked. There were now two *somethings* inside.

She turned to Rutspud. He pushed himself up with evident difficulty and glowered at her.

"There's no *mullet-fuzzing* way I'm going with you, you power crazy *brisket cake!*"

"You don't have a choice," she said. "This poor excuse for a monk has failed in his mission. There is no victory here for you. You are an abomination. And this 'friendship' is a perversion of all that is decent and right."

"Hey!" said Stephen.

She looked down on him. "You disgust me," she said simply and shot him in the heart.

Stephen was knocked back against the wall and fell still, a ragged hole blasted in his chest.

Mo screamed. Rutspud bellowed in wordless shock.

Hands and body moving ahead of thought, Rutspud snatched up a tin of white paint. A smash against the concrete floor and the lid sprang free. A sweeping throw and the paint splashed down over the edge of his circle, obliterating it. He bounded forward through the gap and launched himself at Merilyn.

He could have tried to disarm her, but he had only murder on his mind. Rutspud had spent an eternity (or something indistinguishable from an eternity) torturing damned souls, but he had never actually killed anyone. Killing wasn't in a demon's nature, but today he was willing to give it a go.

Merilyn shouted – more in annoyance than fear – and batted at the child-size demon with her gun hand. Rutspud powered through her blows and clawed at her face. Then he reached for her neck.

"*Shakti!*"

Without any sense of transition, he was elsewhere. His body was folded up, squeezed into a tiny space that was both hard and soft, neither warm nor cold. Through warped glass,

195

he could see Merilyn above him, holding the neck of the bottle.

Rutspud screamed and thrashed.

"Keep it down, mate," said Shafttoe, who was pressed up against him in undefinably intimate ways. "You're not the only one in 'ere."

"I expected more legroom in first class," said Lackring, definitely but imprecisely close by, "but the service is impeccable. Free glass of champagne? That would be lovely, thank you."

"What have you done?" sobbed Mo.

"Silence," said Merilyn and the woman was silent.

Merilyn stepped forward and kicked Stephen's foot. It flopped and was still.

"You *banjo!*" screamed Rutspud. "You *bunting banjo!*"

Merilyn could hear none of this. Or didn't care if she did.

"Mo, Winnie," she said. "You will dispose of Stephen's corpse and then, if you are willing to serve, you can join me at my house." She wiggled the bottle. Rutspud's compressed form rolled against the others. "I have all I need here," she said and turned toward the stairs.

Rutspud tried to look back at his dead friend, but moving inside a bottle of compressed demons was like trying to swim in sausages.

Merilyn carried the bottle up the stairs, through a cupboard and into the hallway of a house. Rutspud looked out at floral carpets, patterned wallpaper, cute crystal ornaments and thickly upholstered furniture – all dusted and cleaned to the point of obsession. He had been held prisoner, not in the grim lair of a depraved occultist, but in the basement of a dull and ordinary human being. He shouldn't have been surprised, he thought hollowly. Evil was banal, and the most terrible evil grew in the hearts of ordinary people, where it had room to sprawl and fester unencumbered.

196

Outside, Merilyn walked briskly through residential streets. The sun shone down from a blue sky. Rutspud had always hated the sun, but he hated it more now. The sun didn't deserve to shine on this world. Stephen was dead and, if there was any justice in the cosmos, he was now in the Celestial City where Rutspud would never see him again.

"Excuse me, madam," said a young man, stopping in front of her. He didn't look the type to use the word 'madam' willingly and by the surprise on his face, he wasn't using it willingly at all. "May I inquire, is that a real gun?"

"It is."

"I beg your pardon."

She pointed it at him. The young man, wisely, ran.

"Stop," she called.

The man froze in his tracks. He whimpered and attempted to curse his uncooperative legs.

"Come here," she said.

The man's legs turned and carried him back. He was clearly not happy about this.

"Young man, you are to go to the high street in Boldmere. There is a coffee shop there called *Hallowed Grounds*, which is a preposterous name for a coffee shop but there you go. You will find the proprietor, who goes by the name of Asmondius – which is an equally preposterous name – and tell him to bring his demon-worshipping cronies to my address at four Birlings Close. Do you understand?"

"Yes."

"Then go. And make no mention to anyone of the gun."

The young man marched off. Merilyn continued on her way. It took Rutspud a while to realise that she was humming quietly to herself, a merry little tune.

"Course," said Shafttoe, "when I was summoned by them there Swiss back in seventy-six they had a diabolists' lodge high up in the Alps. On a good day, you could see Mont Blanc. Nothing gets you in the mood for demonic works like them

197

cool, crisp mountains. They has a beautiful bleakness, if you get me. Whereas this place, it's all right but –"

"Stop talking," said Rutspud. "Stephen is dead, and you helped them."

"Oh, is your friend dead?" asked Lackring. "That's sad. What happened?"

"They're holding us here against our will, Shafttoe, and you helped them," said Rutspud. "Stephen knew."

"Cos, he knew how the game works. We've all got our roles, en't we?"

"What happened to the other demons, the ones who came before you? Scumplug, Pearsock, Shotbolt..."

Lackring moaned, "Poor Shotbolt. Poor, poor Shotbolt."

"They weren't here before you, were they?" said Rutspud. "You've outlasted the lot of them. It's always been you."

"Spent," muttered Lackring. "Used up. Nought but dust and bones."

"When I return to Hell," said Rutspud, "you are coming with me, Shafttoe."

"It would be nice to see the old gaff again," agreed Shafttoe with false cheeriness.

"I'll show you how we do things in the sixth circle."

"Always open to new experiences."

"Oh, yes," said Rutspud with a viciousness that was not part of his nature but which he clung to now because he had nothing else to cling to. "There will be lots of new experiences for you. Lots and lots."

Shafttoe was silent for a time but he couldn't keep silent for long.

"I think you've got to understand where I'm coming from," he said, and there was a tremor of fear in his voice. "I was only playing the game, Rutspud, me old mucker."

"The game, hmmm."

"You see... you see..." Shafttoe struggled to latch onto whatever he wanted Rutspud to see. "You see, it's like this... Have you ever heard the story of the frog and the scorpion? It's a good 'un. You see the scorpion wanted to cross the river but couldn't swim so he asked the frog for a ride but the frog was worried, as you would be, that the scorpion would sting him but the scorpion pointed out that –"

"I'll stop you there," said Rutspud. "In the end, does it turn out that the scorpion is an absolute *mustard* who is going to get the *chips* kicked out of him for the next thousand years?"

"Um, well..."

"Thought as much," said Rutspud.

Merilyn walked up the driveway of a house that looked much like Mo's, and let herself in. A tiny creature bounced up to her in the hallway, yipping and sniffing. It had a face like an ugly human child – Rutspud had in fact seen more handsome demons – but he was forced to concede it was probably a dog – a snack-sized dog, the sort you could eat between meals without ruining your appetite.

A man in a knitted tank top came bustling into the hallway.

"Ah, there you are, dear," he said. "Do you know anything about that mess on the kitchen floor?"

"If you are referring to the circle of Ogdu Jahai, then I painted it," said Merilyn.

"I don't know what *bally* reason you did that for," he said. "But it will be a *ding-dong* to clear up, dear."

Merilyn ignored him and walked past into the kitchen. Dining table and chairs had been pushed to one side and three wide summoning circles had been painstakingly executed in the middle of the linoleum floor.

Shafttoe whistled. "Look at the girths on them, eh? A demon could be happy in a circle like that."

Rutspud didn't believe Merilyn could hear them through the glass, but she lifted the bottle up so it was level with her frosty blue eyes. "Do you want to come out, Shafttoe? Do you want to assist me in great works?"

"I only lives to serve, master."

"*Bektu!*"

Shafttoe's presence beside Rutspud was abruptly gone and the big-toothed demon now squatted in the centre of a summoning circle.

"My *goodness!*" exclaimed the man. "Wh-what is that?"

"Stop interfering and go do something useful," said Merilyn.

"Like what?" said the man, his feet already taking him out of the kitchen.

"Sorting and pairing the socks," said Merilyn. "You're a grown man. I'm tired of having to do it for you."

"Yes, dear," he said and was gone.

Shafttoe paced his circle, not nervously or excitedly. He paced it like a demon measuring out his new home and planning what furniture he would buy from IKEA.

"Will Mo and Winnie be joining us?" he asked.

"I don't know," said Merilyn. "I hope not. I think I have, as they say, outgrown them. We don't need to effect many more changes to bring order and civility back to the world. A tweak here, a tweak there. I don't want much, Shafttoe."

"You has always been very humble," bowed the demon. "I is always telling people that."

"I just want my corner of the world to be perfectly lovely. It's not much to ask, is it?"

"No, it ain't."

Merilyn crossed to the counter and looked out the window at the gardens. "This was my parents' home before it was mine. It's my name on the deeds, not Alvin's. My daddy wasn't interested in dying in a corner of some foreign field. He fought on through and came back to claim his own plot, make his own castle." She looked about wistfully. "High strong walls to keep the rest of the world out."

"Yeah, yeah," agreed Shafttoe readily. "Gotta have high strong walls."

She turned, gasping. "That is what I want."

"Walls?" said Shafttoe.

"This is my home, my castle, and that's what it should be. Shafttoe, I wish this to be my castle."

"Right-o," said the demon. "Shall we crack out one of the other lads and get them to do it for you?"

"I don't think we need to bother with them just yet, do you?"

"I is more a facilitator, yeah? I think we'd both be happier if –"

"Shafttoe. I wasn't offering a choice."

"I see. Well, in that case then..."

"Time for you to lead by example."

Stephen awoke with a painful gasp.

Mo screamed and dropped the shovel she was holding. Winnie mugged silently and flapped her arms like a woman who wished she had the option to scream but couldn't.

Stephen grabbed the back of his head with one hand and his chest with the other. There was a big lump forming on one and hole in his habit on the other. He sat up, questions forming on his lips, but these were brushed aside when he saw what was in front of him.

"Were you going to bury me?"

"No," said Mo and tried to step in front of the shovel.

They were in the Pottersmores' back garden. The two women had dug a long but not particularly deep hole in the middle of the lawn.

"You were going to bury me!"

Winnie flapped and pointed and looked like she was about to wet herself.

"What is it?" he demanded, irritably. Being clonked on the head and shot had brought out the worst in him, it seemed. "Just spit it out and tell us."

"But he was dead and he now he's alive and that can't be!" blurted Winnie, as though someone had just turned her volume up. "We all saw it! She shot him!"

Stephen groaned and patted his chest. He reached into his habit and pulled out the Krakovian *Livre des Esperitz*. There was a crater in the front cover that descended through several dozen pages but, thankfully, not all the way through.

"God bless thick books," he whispered. His feet were dangling in the hole. "*Gok Wan* it, Mrs P! You were going to bury me?"

"We had no choice!" said Winnie, brushing dirt from her wringing hands.

"That's no defence, Mrs Churchill," he admonished.

"It's true," said Mo. "She said, and we were compelled. I think we've stopped because... well, because you're not dead so there's no corpse to dispose of. We're sorry."

"Yes, really sorry," said Winnie.

Stephen got up, checked himself over and pulled away the last of the duct tape that clung to his wrists.

"Where's Rutspud?"

"Merilyn took the demons," said Winnie.

"Back to her house. Birlings Close," said Mo. "I think she's gone a bit, um, power mad."

"You think?" he said.

"Like that Amber Rudd or Mary Berry?" said Winnie.

"Perhaps we should call the police," said Mo.

"You should call the police," said Stephen. "Tell them everything. You have to pay for what you've done."

The women turned and, together, returned to the house to phone the police and confess their sins. Stephen had no intention of waiting around for the police. He nipped round the side of the house, magic book still in hand, and went straight to the Trabant.

The engine turned over on the first try. It didn't scream like a kicked dog as it had when he'd first driven it but, instead, purred like a big cat (or, at least, a small cat dreaming of being a big cat). Perhaps the squirrels had given the engine the once-over before they returned it to him.

Stephen reviewed that thought the moment it popped into his head and knew he needed to put a stop to this madness now.

He drove to the Boldmere Oak as fast as the little car could manage and ran inside. Two of his friends were propping up the bar and a third was working on the other side.

"You're still here!" he said.

"We were wondering where you'd got to," said Ed.

"You found *Livre des Esperitz*," said Darren, seeing the book.

"I did," said Stephen.

"Why the *bell* are you covered in mud?" said Lennox.

"Because Mrs Pottersmore clonked me on the head with a frying pan, Mrs Rees shot me with her dad's old service pistol, and Mrs P and Mrs Churchill tried to bury me in the back garden because they thought I was dead."

"My back garden?" said Darren, agog.

"Yeah. They weren't doing that good a job of it."

He tutted. "I laid that turf myself. Spent ages rolling it."

Stephen gently place his hands on his oldest and largest friend's woolly arms.

"It was your mum," he said gently. "Your mum and her two friends. They're the occultists."

"Are you confusing occultists with a book club?" said Darren.

"They had the demons. They had my friend."

"But why?"

Stephen had already given this some thought. "A bit of a midlife crisis. A little bit enjoying their second childhood. A lot of confusion and anger. Oh, and that Mrs Rees is a *blooming* psycho *bench*."

Darren nodded. "I can see that."

"I need to rescue my friend. Your mum is calling the police, but I doubt they're going to believe her story."

"Have they been outside recently?" said Lennox. "The world's gone cuckoo."

"That's why we're hiding in here, if we're honest," said Ed. He offered his empty glass to Lennox. "Would you be so good as to pour me another, barman?"

"But I need you," said Stephen. "I need the gang back together. It's like Darren said before, we've reassembled the crack team – Mr E Thief, Nox the Destroyer and Mirrorglim the Mage."

He passed the old spell book to Darren. "I'm sorry there's a bullet hole in it. But as the mage of the party, you should have it."

Darren took it reverently.

"We're really doing this, huh?" said Ed, went to drain his glass, realised he had already emptied it and put it down on the bar.

Lennox reached under the bar and pulled out a sword. It was a samurai blade, almost certainly a cheap knock-off. There were four inches of blade missing from the end where the previous owner had broken it trying to get it off his wall.

"Florence! I'm off out!" he called.

"Where are you going?" said his niece, midway through pouring a pint further down the bar.

"We're off to do a quest."

"You are such a nerd."

Outside, Stephen waved them toward the Trabant. "Jump in."

"That's a two-seater," said Ed.

"No, it isn't. It's got back seats."

"That's just a parcel shelf for parcels that like to ride in style."

"We'll all fit. Trust me."

They trusted him. Three minutes later, Darren was filling the front seat and Ed and Lennox weren't so much sitting in the back as locked in an awkward, limb-bending embrace like a rejected illustration for *The Joy of Sex*.

The car groaned alarmingly as they accelerated, confirming that the manufacturers hadn't expected anyone to actually ride in the back seats.

As they left the main road, they all turned to look at the railings outside the old folks' flats. They'd been in need of painting for a while, but now two groups of people were busily painting them. For reasons that were not clear, one group were using white paint and the other group were using black paint. The two groups were clearly eyeing each other up, exchanging wide, beaming smiles interspersed with unhappy scowls. As the Brabant drove past, team white yelled something at team black and a tin of paint arced through the air, bouncing messily off the railings and covering the people, the pavement and several passing cars with white paint.

"Good grief. Birlings Close, here we come," said Stephen, more as an incentive to the car than anything.

Stephen knew where Birlings Close was – at least he thought he did. However, the interwar residential streets of Sutton Coldfield were confusing, curved loops of near-identical semis and frightfully neat front gardens.

"It's down there," said Ed, pointing with his one free arm. "To the right."

"No," said Darren. "It's up a bit, left along Kamchatka Drive and *then* right."

"I'm sure it was just along from the soup kitchen place," said Stephen.

"We passed that already," said Lennox.

"Did we?"

"You didn't see the crowd of people fighting?"

"My eyes were on the road."

"Is the soup that good?" said Ed.

"It wasn't the homeless people," said Darren. "I think it was people fighting over the opportunity to show kindness to the needy."

"There! There!" shouted Lennox. He had a big voice and it was right in Stephen's ear and he nearly crashed the car for the second time in a week. Stephen slammed on the brakes, fought the car for possession of the reverse gear and turned round in the road, a task which wasn't easy when one's rear view mirror was full of Ed and Lennox.

"Now, where?" he said as they continued.

"It's left ahead," said Ed.

"Right then left," said Lennox.

"Um, does anyone else think it might be that enormous castle?" said Darren.

Stephen leaned forward to look up through the small windscreen. A castle that had definitely not been there in Stephen's youth now loomed over this corner of suburbia. It was a monument of gleaming white stone. Towers with pointed roofs crowded the upper levels like saplings competing for the sun. Turrets sprouted wherever there was room, hoping for a piece of the glory. Lush, well-behaved ivy wound itself around the stonework. As a functioning defensive castle, it looked more than a little impractical, but it was undoubtedly imposing.

The little Trabant stalled and stopped. Stephen stepped out. Then, Ed and Lennox fought their way out of the back seat – over-sized twins struggling to free themselves from their East German mother's mechanical womb. Ed picked himself up off the pavement and looked up at the castle.

"That's where we're going, huh?" said Ed.

"I think it is," said Stephen.

"Well, at least we tried."

Stephen turned and looked back at him. "We can't give up before we start."

"It's usually the best time. It's a *sopping* castle, Steve-o."

"It's just like the Dread Castle of P'tang," said Darren.

"The what?" said Lennox.

"The *Infernal Adventures* campaign, one of our last great adventures."

"This is slightly different," said Ed.

"Is it?" said Darren. "The land had fallen under an evil curse. Strange beings terrorised the enchanted locals. And we were hired to fix it by rescuing a woman from a monstrous demon." He thought. "Okay, scratch that last bit and reverse it."

"But I'm not equipped," said Ed.

"In what way?" said Stephen.

"Nox – Lennox has got his sword. Darren's got his book of spells. You. You've been dressed in cosplay all week."

"This is my monk's habit."

"See? You've been keeping in character for years! What am I? Mr E Thief. And apart from being the cleverest pun ever invented, what else have I got?"

"What did Mr E ever need?" said Stephen. "You've got your wits, a ready lie and I bet if we found a hair grip or something you could turn it into a set of lock picks."

"Actually, I've already got some lock picks," he said and patted his pocket. "Purely for, ahem, entertainment and recreational purposes."

"Well, there you go," said Stephen. He pointed at the car. "Would it help if I showed you a motivational picture of a moose saying it believes in you?"

"Probably not."

"That's the spirit," said Lennox, clapping his friends on the shoulders. "Let's go."

The four of them entered Birlings Close. Some of the local residents were in their driveways and gardens, peering over hedges and fences at the medieval monstrosity that had taken up position in their cul-de-sac. Many more were peeking fearfully from behind twitching curtains.

A moat cut across where the front garden of number four had once been and a drawbridge lay in place of the driveway. Three men armed with stout clubs guarded the portcullis archway. They were bearded and tattooed surly men with well-practised brooding looks and a penchant for black clothes. Stephen hadn't met these ones before, but he recognised the type.

"Nihilist Satanists," he said aside to the others.

"There's only three of them," said Darren.

"Count the muscle mass," said Ed. "They outnumber us."

"Does anyone remember how we managed to sneak into the Dread Castle of P'tang?" whispered Lennox.

"We pretended we were escorting prisoners to be fed to the Unspeakable Thing in the dungeon and blagged our way in," said Darren.

They were now sufficiently close that the guards had seen them. They could either continue and try to get directly past the guards or turn tail and immediately draw suspicion.

"I don't think Mrs Rees owns an Unspeakable Thing," said Stephen.

"She has a little pug dog," said Darren.

"Not quite the same thing. Plan, guys?"

"Halt! Who goes there?" said one of the guards.

208

The middle one looked at him. "Seriously, dude? 'Halt, who goes there?'"

The first one flexed his muscles. "It goes with the territory. How many situations do you get to legitimately say that in?"

"Well, if you're gonna go whole-hog," said the third guard, "you might as well add, 'Friend or foe?'"

The first guard shrugged and called out, "Friend or foe?"

Stephen felt panic rise in him, panic and urgency. His instinct was to run at the men screaming, windmilling his arms and hoping for the best. He squashed that instinct as hard as he could.

"Friends, definitely," said Ed, stepping ahead. "We're here to see Count Lizbet Pepperman the Third."

"Who?" said the guard.

"The dog," said Ed as though it was the most obvious thing in the world. "Mrs Rees' darling pug."

"Oh," said one.

"The dog's name is Teddy," said another.

"That's its common name. But its pedigree name is Count Lizbet Pepperman the Third, a purebred wonder. We're here for some light pampering and grooming."

There was suddenly a business card in Ed's hand which he was presenting graciously to the guard.

"Ed's Pet Supplies," he read.

"Pet Supplies and grooming," Ed assured him.

A guard looked past him at his companions. "Why's he got a sword?"

"It's a jungle out there at the moment. This man is my personal bodyguard. This man in the holy robes is my spiritual advisor. And this man in the gaudy gear is the canine fashion designer BowWow Rimmington."

"Ah dress ze dogs," said Darren in the worst French accent Stephen had ever heard.

The guard scrutinised the business card closely as though it would yield the truth of the matter.

"You expect us to believe this bull *shine* nonsense?" said clearly the cleverest guard.

"Yes, I do," said Ed confidently. "You should let us pass, not bother us with any other questions and direct us to where we can find Mrs Rees and her dear pooch before you all get into serious trouble."

Stephen clenched his fists and readied himself to fight, which was a bit of a tall order since he'd not had anything resembling a proper fight in decades. Nonetheless, violence was about to erupt, and he wasn't going to go down willingly.

The guard handed the business card back to Ed.

"Very well, sirs. Go straight inside through the courtyard. You want to head up the grand staircase, keep bearing left and you'll find them in the throne room on the right."

Ed was momentarily thrown. Even he hadn't expected it to work.

"Um, okay. Thanks. Straight inside, up the stairs, bear right –"

"Left."

"Left. And it's the throne room on the right."

Lennox was already prodding him and shepherding them forward, rightly fearful that the guards might change their minds at any moment. Once they were through the archway and walking across the sun-trap of a courtyard, Ed gave a nervous giggle.

"That was amazing," said Lennox.

"You maxed out on your charisma roll there," agreed Darren.

"That was too easy," said Stephen.

"Pessimist," said Ed.

"No, I don't think so..." said Stephen. "There's something else going on."

They passed into the main building of the castle. The entrance hall and sweeping staircase were huge and imposing. Either several nearby houses had been obliterated to make room for this palace or Merilyn Rees's wishes had done something unhealthy to local space-time.

As they walked forward, a man leapt out of the shadows and tackled Darren.

"Orc attack!" squeaked the mage of the party.

Lennox whirled round with his sword. He swung it about in an impressive manner although, Stephen noted, he didn't look particularly inclined to physically poke anyone with it. Or, perhaps, he had judged the assailant to be no threat, given that he was an older man who seemed only intent on removing Darren's shoes.

"He's going for my feet!" cried Darren.

"It's Alvin, isn't it?" said Ed.

"What are you doing, man?" said Lennox.

"Must... pair... the socks," the frantic man panted.

"It tickles!" said Darren.

"Just stop it, the both of you," said Stephen, casting about in case anyone might be watching because there was no way the dog-groomers-for-hire ruse was going to work twice.

Alvin Rees gave up the fight and sat sprawled on the floor, wheezing and weeping.

"What was all that about?" said Lennox.

"Man's a creepy-*asp* sock-fetishist," said Ed.

"No, he's not," said Stephen. "Merilyn's controlling him." He held out a hand to help Alvin up. "Is your wife in the throne room upstairs?"

Alvin nodded, shamefaced and mortified.

"Are the demons with her?"

Another nod. "She's got these three circles painted on the floor. Made a right mess of the lino."

Stephen turned to Darren. "Do you know how to free them from the circles?"

"Destroying any section of the circle will break it," said Darren. "I think there's also a spell of unbinding in here."

"Then get reading."

Rutspud was consumed. His brain (and it was a considerable brain) was a vessel weighed down by huge boulders of anger and grief. But massive though these boulders were, there were gaps in between which a pebble of thought might drop. One such pebble was the thought-memory that you could tell a lot about a person based on their dream home. In Hell he had listened to despot after tyrant after warlord sob wistfully for the grand residence they had once owned, their pleasure pavilion, their eagle's nest, their mansion on the bayou. And there were others in Hell's depths who craved only the creature comforts they had been denied. Rutspud had tortured an Englishwoman for a century by providing her with everything she needed for a perfect pot of tea except... sometimes the tea-strainer was missing, sometimes there were no saucers, sometimes the tea caddy was empty but for a dusty cobweb.

Merilyn had wished herself a castle but, at the heart of it, her throne room was nothing other than a larger and more orderly version of her old kitchen diner – every surface lemon-fresh, every sparkling glass aligned with perfect precision in the cabinet, every hermetically-sealed jar correctly alphabetised in the spice rack.

If someone wanted a picture of the future Merilyn had planned for the world, they need only imagine a bottomless bottle of disinfectant spray that would drown everything new and wipe clean all that had changed. It would be a world preserved in a perfect and uninhabitable showroom moment – forever.

She had decanted Rutspud and Lackring into their new circles. Lackring was padding his fleshy feet on the cream linoleum, seemingly torn between disgust and fascination. Shafttoe hunched in his circle, drained by this last considerable bout of wish-granting and probably mourning the loss of his recliner chair and stack of vacuous entertainment magazines – the only features of his own private dream home. Rutspud glared at Merilyn. She stood in discussion with a bald and bearded fellow called Asmondius who looked like a cross between a stage hypnotist and a Mediterranean waiter and was, Rutspud suspected, neither. A bundle of other beardy types slouched nearby, sipping tiny coffees and doing their best to look cool.

"Psst," said Lackring.

Rutspud looked at Lackring. "Hang on, you're not phoning me."

"Of course not," said the demon. "You're right there, silly."

"Uh, yes. I am."

Lackring smiled. It was a weak smile, a fragile thing. "I've got an escape plan."

"I'm not sure I'm in the mood," said Rutspud. "I've kind of decided to devote my entire existence to the vengeance business."

"It's a good plan though. And the only thing we need is a blade."

"What's the plan?" said Rutspud despite himself.

"We walk out of here," said Lackring.

"Yes?"

Lackring nodded, an eager puppy-like gesture.

"And what else?" said Rutspud. "How do we get out of these circles?"

"That's the clever part," said Lackring. "We don't."

Rutspud held his breath and counted to ten. It would be easy to spit and swear at Lackring for yet another moronic plan – damn it, it wasn't even a plan – and it would feel good to vent his emotions at someone, let it all pour forth, but Lackring wasn't the right target for his fury. His enemy was the foul old woman standing over there. The things he would do to her when he finally had her in his pit in Hell... Dante could write a sequel to *Inferno* just about her.

The double doors of Merilyn's dream kitchen flew open and four men ran into the room. The first one charging through swinging a long blade about his head and Rutspud was surprised that he actually recognised the man. It was Lennox, the barman from the Boldmere Oak, one of the few humans he had got to know on his previous mission to earth. But if that surprised Rutspud, the second man stupefied him.

"*Funk*-a-doodle-doo! Stephen!" he yelled, his chest swelling with whatever demons felt instead of love. "Stephen!"

"Stop them!" commanded Merilyn and the beardies ran to intercept the intruders.

This was just like the old table-top roleplaying days of their youth. Not in terms of their actual abilities in a fight because they didn't have any, which was one of the reasons why they had enjoyed living vicariously through fantasyland warriors, rogues and wizards. No, this was just like the old roleplaying days because they simply ran in with no plan and hoped that the dice fell in their favour.

Nature had given Lennox a fighter's frame. Years of chucking-out at the Boldmere Oak had given him the practice. He was the wedge in their attack, swinging his sword back and forth, knocking clubs and knives aside to get him close enough to plant a fist or a knee in the vulnerable points of these hipster devil-worshippers.

Ed charged in, targeting the ones Lennox had already cast aside.

"Get to the circle," Stephen said tersely to Darren. "Free them!"

A heavy figure barrelled into Stephen, knocking the breath out from him. The much-pierced nihilist, Cain – ears, nose, cheek, eyelid and – what was he'd said? Testicle? – pummelled Stephen's stomach with punch after punch. Stephen fought as best he could, which meant giving girly slaps to Cain's head and trying to push him away.

Cain laughed at Stephen's weak blows. That hurt. Obviously not as much as the punches to the gut but, in a different way, it definitely hurt.

Stephen was contemplating rolling up into a ball and playing dead, but Cain was having too much fun.

"Up you come, bruv," he grinned, hauling him up. "You wantta die on your feet like a man."

"I'd rather not die at all," Stephen panted.

Cain came at him again, pounding Stephen like a novelty, monk-shaped punchbag. Stephen clutched at Baal's face, wishing he had longer nails.

There was a loud cry. Darren was on the floor, creased into a foetal position and faring no better than Stephen. Asmondius was sticking the boot in and enjoying every moment.

Stephen forgot his own problems in that moment of anger. He whirled and pointed at Asmondius.

"Oi! Nigel! Leave him alone!"

Asmondius stopped kicking Darren, stepped back and, with a look of considerable bewilderment on his face, ran to join a different part of the melee.

Stephen realised that Cain was no longer punching him. He looked back. The Satanist was staggering around, clutching his eye while blood poured through his fingers and down his cheek. He was squealing in a high-pitched voice, almost beyond hearing.

There was something snagged in the rough weave of Stephen's habit sleeve: a silver piercing ring and the tiniest fragment of Cain's eyelid.

"Nasty," said Stephen and, despite his religious love for all people, smiled. He ran to assist Darren.

Lennox was walloping the men that clustered around him. He had discarded the sword for a pair of clubs. Stephen hadn't seen whether this was out of necessity or choice, but Lennox observably found blunt instruments morally freeing and was dealing out bruises, cracked ribs and crunched knees to all that dared get too close.

Asmondius had either decided that his men didn't need any help or that he didn't fancy any of what Lennox was offering. Instead, he charged at Ed with a messy tackle.

Darren found his feet and coughed in pain.

"The circles," said Stephen, helping him forward. "The spell of unbinding."

Ahead, Rutspud, Lackring and Shafttoe watched the shambles of a rescue attempt from the confines of their magic circles. Merilyn Rees might as well have been in a magic circle herself. She stood stock still, watching the carnage in haughty disgust.

"How the *hex* are you alive?" Rutspud called the Stephen.

"Never underestimate the power of books," Stephen replied.

Darren was riffling hurriedly through the bullet-holed book. He saw Stephen looking at him. "It's here somewhere..." he insisted.

Lennox was tiring. The men baiting him looked like they would be spending the next few days regretting their life choices but, right now, Lennox was struggling to keep up the onslaught. Elsewhere, Ed and Asmondius rolled on the floor, evenly matched.

"Behind you!" said Lackring.

Stephen looked.

One of the nihilist Satanists had broken away and was coming up behind Darren. There was a gleaming and jagged knife in his hand, more movie-prop than weapon but deadly nonetheless.

Stephen's automatic reaction was to shout that knives were unfair and someone could get hurt. It would have been a stupid thing to shout but he never got a chance to shout it.

"Everyone stop what you're doing!" shouted Merilyn.

216

And the fight ended like that. The wounded thugs stepped back from Lennox. Ed and Asmondius rolled apart. Without any intervention from his brain, Stephen stood and waited.

"Drop your weapons!" said Merilyn.

Weapons fell to the floor. Lennox dropped his clubs. The man behind Darren dropped his dramatic knife. It landed on the floor, impaled point first in the lino.

Merilyn quivered with restrained rage.

"I cannot believe that you would dare invade my home like common thieves. Brawling like drunkards! And would someone give that man a hanky? He's bleeding all over my floor."

"Release the demons and we'll go," said Stephen.

"Release...?" Wrinkles shifted and twitched in amusement. "Hardly. One has barely started."

"One what?" said Darren.

"She means her," said Stephen. "Her herself."

"She's gone bonkers," said Ed.

She waved an imperious hand. "Asmondius, hit him."

"Wait!" said Ed and then was on the floor, clutching his face.

"You three, friends with this idiot monk, you will surrender and make no attempt to escape or resist. Asmondius, you and your men are to take them prisoner."

The nihilist Satanists (those not trying to make an eyepatch out of a blood-soaked handkerchief) took hold of Ed, Lennox and Darren. Darren grunted in pain as Baal hauled his arm up behind his back.

Stephen pointed at Merilyn.

"Don't you hurt them!"

Merilyn twitched as though a fly had just landed on her nose. "Don't you tell me what to do," she retorted. "Don't you *ever* tell me what to do!"

It was impossible to feel the absence of something that was not yet there, but Stephen felt a moment of sensation and the knowledge that he wouldn't be able to command Merilyn to do anything again. That wish of hers, that everyone would do what they were told; she hadn't been specific enough. Everyone would do what anyone told them. Anyone.

"Baal, let go of Darren," he said.

The Satanist immediately released his arm.

"Stand on one leg."

Baal did so.

Stephen took a breath and turned to address them all.

"Not another command from you!" cut in Merilyn. "Not a single instruction to anyone!"

Stephen's words died in his mouth.

"Put your foot down, Baal," said Merilyn.

"It was like he was doing a Jedi mind trick on me," said the mortified nihilist. "Can all monks do that?"

Merilyn approached Stephen slowly.

"You are a very rude man. You stick your nose in where it is not wanted. You don't have the decency to die when someone kills you. You never give up, even when you are clearly beaten." She frowned, pretending to be confused. "It's as though you don't know your place in the order of things."

"He just cares for his friends," said Rutspud. "I don't think a cold and heartless *ditch* like you would ever understand that."

"He needs to pick better friends." She looked to her underlings. "Hurt them!"

Fists fell, boots kicked and clubs pounded. Stephen leapt to help but a curt, "Freeze!" from Merilyn held him in place.

Darren gasped and winced. Lennox went down on his knees, magically barred from fending off the attacks.

"By the way," said Merilyn, happily. "*I'm* not hurting them. I'm just getting someone else to do it."

Ed's legs had gone from underneath him but Asmondius had him by the scruff of the neck and was propping him up to deliver one last punch to his bloodied face. And then another and another...

"Hey. This takes me back, Ed! Large Mike's. All those years ago." Asmondius grinned. "You started on me and my mates and we soon put you in your place then. Remember? Good times." He looked at Stephen. "Oh, my *gonk*. And you were there, weren't you? I'd totally forgotten. Admittedly, I only saw the back of your head, so..."

Merilyn raised a questioning eyebrow.

218

Asmondius gave her a servile nod. "Back in the day, Mrs Rees. These two were giving it large in the local chippy. They started on me and my mates but the Jesus-freak here" – he waved a bloody-knuckled hand at Stephen – "ran at the first sign of trouble."

"Is this true?" Merilyn said. "Be honest."

"It's true," said Stephen, unable to lie.

Ed spat blood and wheezed. "He did it to... to... help me. To protect me."

Merilyn studied Stephen's face.

"But that's not true, is it?" she said.

"No," said Stephen.

"Why did you run away?"

Stephen looked Ed in the eye, the one that hadn't already closed over with a bloated purple bruise.

"I ran away because I was afraid. I was frightened I would get into trouble. I was thinking only of myself."

Ed's one good eye blinked. Stephen couldn't read his friend's face.

"I left Ed alone with Nigel and his friends."

"My name is Asmondius!" shouted the Satanist.

"And Ed went to prison for assaulting a policeman."

Merilyn clapped her hands like an excited child. "This is delicious. What were you saying, Rutspud? 'He cares for his friends'? You appear to be very much mistaken. Stephen here is the type who will abandon his friends and run away."

She moved in closer to Stephen.

"Run away," she said. "Run away, now, like you did back then. Abandon your friends and never stop running."

His legs moved of their own accord and were building to a sprint before he was halfway to the door.

"And know it will end very badly for them all!" Merilyn shouted after him.

"Ed..." called Stephen but he didn't have the breath to produce more than a whisper and he was through the door and running for the stairs.

Stephen ran. He had a stitch in his side before he even reached the drawbridge, but his legs would not stop. Merilyn had

219

told him to run and to never stop. He wondered miserably if his legs would stop if he collapsed with exhaustion or would he keep running until he had a heart attack, died of thirst or ran into the sea and drowned.

As he huffed and puffed through the streets of Sutton, he realised he had a modicum of control over his actions. He was not compelled to run in a straight line. Merilyn had ordered him to run away, and he soon discovered that he could veer right or left when he liked, as long as he kept moving farther away.

Great, he thought bitterly, he could run in an ever-expanding spiral until he died. Meanwhile, his friends were suffering at Merilyn's hands because of him. There was nothing he could do about that.

Stephen mentally kicked himself for such defeatist thinking. Maybe there was something he could do. There was always something to be done. He wanted to shout at the locals on the streets (many of whom were stopping to watch the running monk – and probably assuming it was something for charity) but pleas for help or calls to stop him and pin him down got magically stuck in his throat.

He needed help, but he couldn't ask for it, couldn't demand it.

There had been a doggy poop bag full of nuts and seeds in his pocket. He patted himself down to check it was still there. He took it out. His fingers were numb and clumsy, their energy reserves called away to other parts of the body that were experiencing unusually high levels of demand, but it didn't take much energy to tear a plastic bag.

Nuts scattered on the pavement and, instantly, they rolled to follow him.

Rutspud stewed in his own thoughts at the centre of his circle.

Stephen had been alive, then he'd been dead, then he'd been alive again and now he was apparently doomed to run until his last breath. Rutspud couldn't work out whether they were currently ahead or behind on their graph of personal success.

Stephen's three friends were standing against a far wall bound firmly together with nothing but words. Merilyn had instructed them to stand still and silent and make no attempt to escape and they had no choice but to obey. Blood dripped from the split lip of the one called Ed and he could do nothing to treat his own injury.

Merilyn and Asmondius sat at the world's largest kitchen table and pored over the *Livre des Esperitz*. The fact that a bullet had carved its way through half the pages did little to spoil their enjoyment.

"What about this one?" said Merilyn, pointing to a page.

"Treyvaw the demon hunter," nodded Asmondius thoughtfully. "Could be worth a go, Mrs Rees. If we use Shafttoe there to snare us Treyvaw then, in turn, we can use Treyvaw to bag us some truly powerful demon lords."

"Yes."

"Build up your collection until you have all the power you need. It's like the Pokémon."

"Pokémon?" she said, nonplussed.

"Gotta catch 'em all."

"I have sincerely no idea what you are talking about, young man."

"Sorry, Mrs Rees."

A scraping sound made Rutspud look round. Lackring was outstretched at the limit of his circle and had pulled free the impractically wicked knife one of the goons had dropped there.

"And how are we going to escape with just a knife?" whispered Rutspud.

"We're going to walk out of here," replied Lackring.

"Without leaving our circles?"

"Exactly."

Lackring adjusted his grip and then stabbed the knife into the lino at the outermost point of the circle he could reach. He hauled the blade round in an imprecise circle, slicing through the smooth floor covering. The cut edge flapped loose. There was nothing fixing it to the stonework underneath.

"*Santa's bells!*" whispered Rutspud in amazement. "You're a genius!"

He glanced round to check they weren't being watched. Merilyn and Asmondius were too engrossed in their discussions. The beardy occultists were by the door, comparing tattoos and telling the injured Cain that his ripped eyelid didn't look too bad and that chicks dug eyepatches. Shafttoe was the one most likely to raise the alarm but he was still bushed from magicking up this castle and was looking at nothing but his own pudgy belly.

Lackring had finished his circle and now cut out two further circles: one around his left foot and one around his right.

"Absolute genius," said Rutspud.

"Parcel for Rutspud," said Lackring and tossed the knife into Rutspud's circle.

There were squirrels pursuing Stephen. Several of them clutched clawfuls of nuts but it's hard for a rodent to run without both front legs. Some bounded ahead to try to draw Stephen's attention to his deplorable littering habits. One, wearing an acorn bowler hat, waved its twig walking stick at Stephen in a most disgruntled manner. Another latched onto his habit and ran up to his shoulder.

"Redclaws!" he said, recognising the pillar-box red nails. "I can't stop. I've been commanded to run for ever and ever. I can only stop if – *gng-nng urg.*"

His own voice box strangled the words as he came dangerously close to asking for something. Redclaws squeaked forcefully at the other squirrels and Stephen saw several run off.

"Maybe if you just try and trip me up and tie me down. At least I'll be able to get my breath back."

Redclaws tugged on Stephen's ear and pointed down a side road.

"Down there?"

Redclaws tugged harder.

"Okay, okay."

At the next junction, Redclaws nudged his head and pushed him the other way.

"Up here? Got it."

There seemed no reasoning to this course and when Stephen saw a line of squirrels across the road at the junction ahead, he didn't initially see their purpose. The line stepped forward to the 'STOP' instruction painted on the road and performed what Stephen could only describe as a combination of disco-pointing and jazz hands. A couple of squirrels hung from the STOP sign at the corner of the road and did their own pointing dances.

"You want me to stop," said Stephen and was, at once, able to do so. He staggered in exhaustion and nearly fell.

Seconds later, the last of the uncollected nuts and seeds bumped up against his feet. He wearily picked them up and stuffed them in his pocket.

"Thanks, guys. You're the best."

Several of the squirrels bowed. The squirrels looked at him expectantly.

"My friends are trapped in Merilyn's castle," he said and chalked that up as another sentence he really hadn't expected to say today. "I need to rescue them. I need help."

He looked back the way he had come. He felt like he had run a dozen miles, but it had probably been less than two. As the crow flies, he was no more than a mile from Merilyn's house. In fact... He looked up and realized he was just round the corner from Darren's.

"I need a lift," he said to himself.

Redclaws chittered.

"No, I'm not asking you to carry me," he said. "This way."

He forced his aching legs to carry him down the road to the Pottersmore house. He rapped on the door loudly.

Mo Pottersmore answered it.

"You're back," she said, surprised and worried.

"I need your car."

"I don't have a car."

"*Burger*." He put a hand on the door frame and thought exhausted and sweaty thoughts.

"What's happened?" said Winnie, coming up the hallway. "You look like you could do with a cup of tea." She saw the squirrels clustered round Stephen's feet. "Would they like a cup of tea too?"

Bowler hat began to chitter a polite and definitely agreeable reply, but Stephen cut across him.

"She has Darren prisoner," he said.

"Merilyn?" said Mo. "But why?"

"Because he was trying to do the right thing." It was true, but it was a self-serving answer. "Because he followed me," he added.

He looked at the garage and the heavy lock on it.

"You have keys for that door?"

Mo nodded and went to fetch them. Stephen felt horribly unprepared.

"I don't know how to defeat Merilyn," he told the squirrels. "She can command anyone and anything with a word. People hear her, and they have to obey. God help us if she gets on TV or radio."

Redclaws scampered into the house. There was small shriek somewhere from Winnie and then Redclaws was outside again, struggling under the weight of a block of Cheddar cheese.

"I don't think cheese is her Kryptonite," said Stephen kindly.

Redclaws broke off a crumb and stuffed it in his own ear and made a 'you see?' gesture at Stephen.

"That is really clever, Redclaws!"

Redclaws offered a fat chunk to Stephen and the other squirrels gathered round to claim their own dairy-product earplugs.

"Hang on," said Stephen. "Before we all make ourselves deaf, let's come up with a plan."

"Here are the keys," said Mo, stepping outside. "Has she hurt Darren?" she asked as she put them in his hand. There was a look of terrible dismay and fear on the old woman's face.

"I commanded her to not harm him or the others," he said, which was both true and deeply untruthful at the same time.

He unlocked the garage and pulled the doors wide open. Between the rows of filing cabinets stood a once-red post office bicycle with a tray basket on the front.

Stephen rolled it backward toward the door. As he passed the cabinet with the old stack of board and roleplaying games on it, his eyes latched onto the small box of *Truths and Dares*.

"Ooh," he said, thoughtfully. "I have an idea."

Lackring's escape plan might have been genius-level lateral thinking but it wasn't easy to execute. The demons had to gather up one side of their lino circle and then the other and then hold it all together around their chests, so their legs could poke through the holes in the bottom. Rutspud felt an unexpected sympathy for any nineteenth century lady who had ever needed to hitch up her massive skirts and run. He suspected however that the two of them looked less like nineteenth-century ladies and more like burglar's swag bags that had grown legs and decided to steal themselves.

The second obstacle to their escape was sneaking out past the Satanist guards.

"This would be a lot easier if we had knitted ourselves some cat costumes," said Lackring.

"Obviously," said Rutspud. "We will need to create a distraction."

A distraction appeared all by itself. A beardy at the door gave a shout and pointed as a squirrel ran into the room. It was soon followed by second and a third.

"Rat!" squealed Asmondius and leapt hurriedly onto the table.

"What are you doing, young man?" demanded Merilyn.

But a fresh scream of "rat!" was the only answer the terrified Asmondius would give.

The squirrels ran to the three prisoners. To Rutspud's keen eyes, they each appeared to be carrying small lumps of cheese in their claws. That made extraordinarily little sense but as the guards ran to intercept the rodents, Rutspud decided this wasn't the moment to be questioning such things.

"Let's go," he said and led the way round via the opposite wall towards the door.

Shafttoe gave a shout when he belatedly realised they were escaping, but the big-toothed demon's cries were only one shout among many.

A servant woman (some local impressed into Merilyn's service, Rutspud guessed) shrieked and dropped her laundry as the two demons ran past.

"Nothing to see here," Rutspud told her cheerily. "Just two demons out for a jog!"

They charged down the stairs and Rutspud had to skid to a stop when he saw Stephen running up the other way.

"Rutspud!"

"Stephen! I thought you'd been told to run away."

"I came to rescue you," said Stephen in a peculiarly loud voice.

"We were able to get away," said Rutspud, "but your friends are still up there."

"Are my friends still up there?"

"That's what I said. How do you intend to rescue them?"

Stephen's expression was grim. "I have to rescue them."

"That's what – have you stuffed cheese in your ear?" asked Rutspud.

"So much of this is my fault."

"You can't hear a word I'm saying, can you?" Rutspud shouted.

"Yes," Stephen agreed loudly. "The squirrels are helping me."

"We're not going to be able to communicate if – Do you have a plan?"

"I've put cheese in my ears, so I can't hear her."

"I'm not sure if that's helping right now."

"Thank you. We've got to stop this chaos."

Rutspud sighed. "Are you just going to blunder in like last time and assume that goodness will prevail?"

"I think they are already bad."

Rutspud turned to Lackring. "This is worse than talking to you."

"The more the merrier," said Stephen. "The squirrels should be in position now and I've got these."

He held out a three-inch-high pile of black cards then peeled off half an inch each for Rutspud and Lackring.

"What are these?" said Rutspud.

"Clever, huh?" said Stephen. "Come on."

Stephen ran up the stairs. Rutspud looked at the top card. It said, 'Dance a jig'. The next one said, 'Try to pickpocket something from a friend'.

Rutspud followed Stephen with his ungainly lino skirt flopping around him.

"Are we going back already?" said Lackring. "That was a short holiday."

"Don't worry," said Rutspud. "We'll be leaving soon. I think I understand his plan."

"I bet it's not as good as my giant insect plan."

"Well," said Rutspud charitably, "it would be impossible to compare it to your plans."

Lackring beamed.

There were still shouts aplenty coming from the throne room-kitchen (and the high-pitched screams of the rodent-phobic Asmondius).

Stephen stopped in the shadow of the door.

"Ready, mate?" he said to Rutspud.

"Ready for what?" said Rutspud.

"Of course, you are," grinned Stephen and dashed in.

The Satanic thug closest to the door turned to Stephen, who presented him with a card. The man looked at it and began to perform what Rutspud supposed was meant to be a sexy striptease dance. Stephen was already handing out cards to others. One closed his eyes and recited 'Peter Piper picked a peck of pickled peppers' as fast as could. One started to parade around the room clucking and strutting like a cockerel. Another dropped his trousers and slapped his butt cheeks, playing an unidentified song.

"What's going on?" said Merilyn, seeing the expanding commotion.

Over by the wall, squirrels shoved deafening lumps of cheese in the three captives' ears and then presented each of them with a jagged-edge scrap of paper. From the men's immediate actions, Rutspud could guess what was written on them. They unfroze from their positions and ran straight for the door. A beardy tried to bar their way but Lennox felled him with a clothes line blow as he dashed past.

"Stop!" shouted Merilyn. "Stop! Come here!"

"Don't think they're listening to you anymore," Rutspud called back to her.

"And you come back here too, demon!"

Rutspud looked down at his feet. They didn't seem inclined to automatically obey her.

"Guess that last wish only applied to humans," he said. "Hey, Asmondius," he said to the Satanist trying to creep round behind him. "Go pick a fight with yourself."

Asmondius punched himself in the face and fell over in surprise.

"Ah, but it seems we can *give* commands," said Rutspud. "Slap yourself, Merilyn."

Merilyn's hands stayed disappointingly by her side.

"My wish, *Prince* Rutspud," she sneered. "It doesn't apply to me. You lot!" she shouted at the Satanists, all currently prancing, miming, dancing and making fools of themselves. "Stop what you're doing and get that monk out of here!"

Stephen, deaf to Merilyn's shouts, saw the change in the men. He held up a card to one, but the man covered his eyes and ran at him.

"Leave him alone!" shouted Rutspud.

The men veered away from Stephen or just stopped.

"Get him!" shouted Merilyn.

"Stick your fingers in your ears, sing loudly and run away!" shouted Lackring.

228

The men obeyed. Merilyn shouted at them. She screamed. None of them heard. None of them turned. The last to depart was Asmondius, his nose bloody, his beard partly ripped out and singing *He's Got the Whole World in His Hands* at the top of his lungs. The singing echoed and receded through the castle corridors.

An exhausted silence came over the room, empty now but for Merilyn, Stephen and the three demons.

"It's over, Merilyn," said Rutspud.

"It's over, Merilyn," said Stephen a second later.

"Ignore him, he's deaf."

"Over?" said Merilyn. She placed her hands lightly on the magical tome on the table. "I hold all the cards." She pointed to the jinn bottles on the kitchen counter. "With a word, you are back in there again."

A squirrel pushed one bottle off the edge to smash on the floor. Merilyn made to grab the other but not before it followed the first. She made a bitter growl in her throat and lashed out at the squirrel. It danced out of the way. On the floor, two squirrels, operating a dustpan and brush between them, swept up the shattered glass.

"And we can break more stuff if we have to," said Stephen, deafly.

Merilyn's ice-blue glare now had a swivel-eyed lunatic glint about it.

"I still have the power," she pointed viciously at Shafttoe in his circle. The demon, pale and drained by previous exertions, attempted to straighten up into Mephistophelean Pose #15 ('I've got ten sticky fingers and I'm looking for someone to wipe them on').

"If it's all the same with you, oh, mighty one, I might just want to lie down for a bit."

"I have one final wish I want from you and then you can rest."

Shafttoe's face ticked and shifted uneasily. "Well, if it's just the one. I'm tired."

"I'm tired too," she said. "Tired of this nonsense. I'm tired of meddling outsiders. I don't want strangers coming into my house. I don't want the wrong kind of people cluttering up my town and destroying all we've striven to create."

"Couldn't agree more," said Shafttoe.

"I want everyone and everything to go back to where it came from."

"Right, and when you say that, what you mean is –"

"*Everyone* and *everything*, back to where they came from, Shafttoe."

"But –"

"Things to be exactly as they were in the first place."

"Yes, I can see the general point you're aiming at, but I wonder if –"

"Shafttoe! Undo all of this now."

He gave a weary and scraping bow. "I exists only to serve."

Rutspud shook his head. "You don't have to do this, Shafttoe. You can refuse."

The demon gave him a look both pitying and pitiful.

"You still don't understand, mate. You've got to play the game, en't ya?"

Rutspud ran forward and deaf Stephen, realising there was something afoot, ran too, but Merilyn only had to intone the key syllables and Shafttoe's circle became a brilliant column of light that sent them reeling back. The light lasted perhaps no more than a second but left spinning after-images on the retina that would take far longer to clear.

"Ooh, fairies!" said Lackring, gazing round.

"Think I've gone blind," said Stephen. "I'm deaf and blind. Anyone?"

In the circle, Shafttoe swayed, still upright for now. His eyes stared at Rutspud – no, through Rutspud and at something far, far away. A light breeze played over Shafttoe, pulling broad flakes of skin from his arms, like dead leaves. Then he fell apart, as though he had been constructed of nothing but chicken bones and ancient papier-mâché.

Blinking, Stephen looked at Shafttoe and then looked around.

"Did she do something?" he said.

Shafttoe's final wish appeared to have done nothing, apart from bring an end to Shafttoe himself. The breeze peeled away layers of dried demon flesh, exposing his pathetic bones.

"Where is that breeze coming from?" said Rutspud, to no one in particular because his one friend had cheese in his ears and the other had cheese for brains.

The wind grew in strength. Broken glass flew from the dustpan and the glittering shards skittered and bounced towards the door. Squirrels ran to tidy them up and those that didn't found they were being blown in that direction anyway.

Merilyn must have seen the shock blooming on Rutspud's face and mistaken his dismay for her victory.

"Everything and everyone back to where it came from," she said. "Bye-bye grey squirrels! Back to America with you!"

Wooden chairs slid along the floor.

"Goodbye chairs," she said, a little less certainly. "Back to... the shop?"

Rutspud watched them go. To the shop? To the factory? To the trees? To the seeds? If everything went back to where it came from, where would everything end up?

"Soon, everything will be perfect again!" declared Merilyn but with more hope than certainty.

Rutspud could have argued with her but there was no time to waste on someone who was already beyond listening.

He tugged at Stephen's habit. "Time to go, Stephen!"

Stephen was gawping at the cuff of his habit. Individual threads were standing to attention, like hairs under static electricity, tugging and twisting, desperate to unthread themselves.

"I think it's time to go," he said.

"Took the words right out of my mouth," said Rutspud and pulled him towards the door, hauling the oblivious Lackring with his other hand.

Rutspud ducked a flying cutlery tray, nearly dropping his lino skirt in the process, and ran through the hurricane bottleneck at the door. There was a tide of objects bouncing down the stairs that threatened to knock them over or whip their feet away from under them. For a few seconds, Lackring rode a polished coffee table that bucked and kicked its way to the grand entrance hall and deposited him with a *thump*.

There were no people visible in Merilyn's castle. Rutspud supposed they had either run away or been blown away. The contents of the place were all making a bid to escape through whichever door or window they could reach. On the drawbridge, the three of them were almost mown down by a high-speed sideboard and Stephen was very nearly given the Aladdin treatment by a flying rug.

"This way!" yelled Stephen. Along the cul-de-sac, a red bicycle battled fiercely with the hedge it had become stuck in. It bucked and butted at the hedge but only came free when Stephen took hold of it by the handlebars.

Paving slabs bucked underneath the wheels, straining to wrench free of the pavement.

"Hop in!"

Lackring needed no encouragement and scrambled readily into the broad basket at the front. Rutspud was, however, momentarily distracted by the hedge itself. The leaves were shrinking. They were becoming thinner, darker, rolling themselves up into balls, into buds.

"Holy moly!"

He jumped up onto the bike and then, much to his friend's surprise, grabbed Stephen's face in both hands and studied him furiously. It was hard to see but it was there. The lines on his brow, in the corners of his eyes, were filling in, fleshing out and vanishing. Stephen was getting younger.

"This is very, very bad!" shouted Rutspud.

"I love you too, man!" Stephen shouted back.

Rutspud reached out a claw and tenderly scooped the cheese from Stephen's left ear.

"Ow!" said Stephen and said it again when Rutspud did the other ear.

"We have really got to get out of here!" said Rutspud.

"No need to shout," said Stephen, walked the bike into the road and, with a little run-push, swung his leg over the crossbar and pedalled hard.

Stephen knew where he wanted to go but the bike had its own ideas. It didn't fight him, but it definitely tried to influence his choice of direction like a nagging back-seat driver.

"Towels!" shouted Lackring as a small flock of towels whipped by.

"The bike really wants to go that way," he said, raising his voice against the wind.

"And what is that way?" said Rutspud.

Stephen thought. "Birmingham? Erdington? Darren's house?"

"And it's his bike, right?"

"Yeah. Do you – woah!"

He had to swerve, gripping the handlebars tight as a shallow sea of colourful gravel poured out of a driveway and across the road. The bike slewed across the escaping pebbles with an accompanying machine-gun racket as they pinged against the wheels.

"Kettle!" shouted Lackring as a white plastic thing flew overhead.

"Everything is going back to where it came from!" said Rutspud.

"Where it originally came from?"

Rutspud's face, ever expressive, was a picture of grim possibilities.

"Cuddly toy!" shouted Lackring.

"Once we're out of this wind, we need to come up with a plan," said Stephen.

"I don't think there's any getting out of this wind!" said Rutspud.

At that, a gust caught Lackring's portable circle and blew it up into the air, Lackring held onto it for a second and then fell out. Strangely, he didn't fall far. As the lino circle took to the wind like a sail, Lackring was suspended beneath it by an unseen force, unable to break away. The demon spun away upwards, a parachutist on invisible strings.

"Your friend..." said Stephen.

"The road!" yelled Rutspud.

A wheelbarrow skittered and turned in front of them (the flowers in the pots within, Stephen noticed, seemingly racing to shrink back into the soil). Stephen leaned sharply, popped a kerb and pulled an entirely unwanted wheelie for several yards before slamming down hard onto two wheels again.

"I am not enjoying this," growled Rutspud.

Lackring had gone from sight. There would be time to look for him later. Or maybe no time at all.

"Nearly there," said Stephen, as they skidded around a corner leading towards Boldmere high street and then switched the other way down a side street leading to the Boldmere Oak. A drain in front of them erupted like a geyser, spewing mud, water and unimaginable detritus. Stephen swerved to avoid it, but there was no getting away from its appalling stink.

"We're going to the pub?" said Rutspud as they slid to a stop.

Stephen held the bike while Rutspud hopped out and then tried to lean it against the wall. It immediately righted itself and rolled in the direction of Erdington.

Stephen frowned and patted his belly. "I think I'm losing weight. I know cycling is good for you but..."

The wind snagged rudely at Stephen's unravelling habit and he decided to file away any body-shape concerns for future review. He pushed on the door to the pub. It didn't open. He hammered with his fist.

"Drink is not the answer at a time like this," said Rutspud.

There was the scrape of dragging furniture and the door opened. Lennox looked out and hurriedly ushered them in.

He barricaded the door after them and, for a moment, it seemed to Stephen they were away and free from the storm of chaos rampaging through the streets. The bar was virtually empty, the wind rattled at the windows but there was a degree of calm in here.

Lennox waggled a finger in his ear. "I've still got cheese in there somewhere. You knew I was dairy intolerant."

234

"I don't think it affects you if you take it aurally," said Stephen.

"We ran here as the paper commanded," said Darren, almost keeping from his voice the indignation of having to run anywhere. "What's the plan?"

"Batten down the hatches and wait it out?" said Stephen but immediately knew that wouldn't do.

He could see the herd of tables nudging against the door, clicking and knocking against each other. He saw Ed draw himself a pint and attempt to drink it, only for the beer to force its way out of his mouth back into the glass and then leap into the tap. Stephen then saw their faces, properly saw them.

Age was a peculiar thing. From childhood to adulthood, the signs of aging, of growing up, were measured in inches and in pounds, in the bloom of facial acne and the appearance of hair in all the usual but nonetheless unexpected places. Beyond that, one's own advancing age was an immeasurably small process. A line here, fewer hairs there, a growing tiredness to the face that had nothing to do with actual fatigue. It was invisible to the constant observer, and only noticeable after a long separation or, indeed as in this case, if everyone had jumped back approximately...

"You all look ten years younger," said Stephen.

"We thought five or six," said Darren, "but thanks."

Darren had always had boyishly youthful looks, but he'd definitely regained an inch or two of hairline. Lennox's face had traded some of that senatorial authority for youthful vitality. Ed... Ed...

Stephen remembered the words Merilyn had forced from him.

"Ed, I need to apologise," he said. "About what I said. About that night at Large Mike's. It was true. I ran. I just ran. I'm the worst friend in the world and you were right to hate me all those years."

Ed came round the bar and approached him solemnly.

"Steve-O. I could listen to you ramble on about what a *funky* liar you are and about what kind of *winker* you were as a teenager. If I could travel back in time and slap the seventeen-year-old you silly for being such a *crab* friend, I might. But, given that if we don't do something about this situation, and fast, we're all going to find ourselves shrunk down into our teenage bodies –"

"And beyond," said Lennox.

"*Jingle Crisps!*" said Darren horrified.

"– I think we've got more important things to worry about," said Ed. "So, let's put our differences aside for the moment."

Stephen nodded.

"So, when do we expect this magical effect to stop?" said Lennox.

"When everything and everyone has gone back to where they came from," said Rutspud. "Right back, to where they *originally* came from?"

"And where's that?" said Ed.

"That, dear human, depends entirely on your views on creation. If you guys not only keep de-aging but begin devolving into hairy tree-dwelling apes, then we might eventually get to see the Big Bang up close and in reverse."

"That would be bad," said Stephen.

"Or we might see the Almighty unflood the earth, Adam and Eve get kicked back into Eden, Eve transformed into one of Adam's ribs and the Almighty roll the whole thing up before turning out the lights."

"Also, bad."

"So, what do we do about it?" said Ed.

"Kill the demon who granted the wish?" suggested Lennox.

"Already destroyed," said Rutspud.

"Kill Mrs Rees?" said Ed.

"The wish is granted. It's beyond her control now."

"Then what?" said Darren, flinging his arms wide, the wool of his self-unknitting jumper dangling like Elvis tassels. "Tell us, Stephen! You're our priest!"

"You're the mage of the party, *darn* it! Why don't you tell us?"

There was a rap at the window. Redclaws the squirrel fought against the wind to hold himself in place, his eyes wide with fright. Then a gust caught him and he was gone – dragged into the maelstrom of the world unmaking itself.

Stephen let out a heartfelt sigh. "Listen, I'm sorry, Darren. Didn't mean to snap. I don't have an answer."

236

Darren gripped his bottom lip pensively. "I mean," he said, slowly as though excavating the thought carefully, "if this was a magic spell – like, from a game – then we would just need a counter-spell."

"A counter-wish," said Rutspud.

"Exactly."

The demon walked to the centre of the group of friends and dropped his lino skirt. It unfurled with a slap onto the barroom floor.

"I even come with my own portable magic circle."

"Wait," said Stephen. "We can't just wish for you to undo everything Merilyn's done."

"We can," said Darren, kneeling beside the circle. "This is a Paracelsus ring, isn't it?" he asked Rutspud.

"Don't ask me. I just work here," said Rutspud.

"I mean you can't do this," said Stephen. "That last wish destroyed Shafttoe. If you try to reverse the same spell, won't it do the same to you?"

"I'm stronger than he was."

"Bull*shoes*," said Stephen.

"I think I know the ritual that will open up a power path to Hell," said Darren. "From back in the day."

"So, we can do it?" said Rutspud.

"This will kill you," said Stephen.

"Never lived."

"But you'll be gone."

Rutspud huffed. "You have risked your life for me, Stephen. You very nearly died for me in that cellar."

"And you think that laying your li–, your existence down for me is the right thing to do?"

"No! Of course, it *blobby* isn't but I think it's a bit hypocritical of you to try to dissuade me!"

"Greater love hath no man than he who would lay down his life for a friend," said Darren.

"That's right!" snapped Rutspud. "Make it worse, why don't you?"

Something – a car perhaps or even a tree – crunched heavily into the side of the pub, throwing spirits of bottles off their optics stands and freeing the vodkas and whiskeys and gins to go off to wherever vodkas and whiskeys and gins considered to be their natural homes.

Stephen looked at his hands. They were pale and unblemished, youthful. He looked at his friends. What were they down to? Their mid-twenties? Earlier?

"What do we need for this ritual?" he said, sick inside.

"Just ourselves," said Darren.

"What? Like we just stand round the circle, holding hands?" said Lennox.

"We don't have to hold hands," said Darren.

"But we could?" said Ed. "That is, if we're a bit scared?"

"And if we want to," said Lennox, taking Ed's offered hand. Stephen took Ed's other hand and then also joined hands with Darren.

"All this human camaraderie and love is making me have second thoughts, guys," joked Rutspud. "Now, be careful what you're wishing for."

"We should wish that all the wishes be undone," said Ed.

"*All* wishes?"

"All wishes granted for Mrs Rees, Mrs Churchill and my mum," said Darren.

"Everything they achieved through the summoning of demons," said Stephen. "Undone and put back as it was."

"Instantly," said Ed.

"That should pretty much cover it," said Lennox.

"Very good," said Rutspud and did a few limbering up exercises. "Ready when you are."

"The circle's in place," said Darren, "the demon already bound. I just need to recite the magic words."

"And us?" said Ed. "What do we do?"

Darren shrugged. "Just look, you know, mystical." He sniffed and cleared his throat.

Stephen looked down at the demon.

"Hey," said Rutspud. "It's going to be okay."

"Is it?"

Rutspud grinned but Stephen could see he was fooling no one.

Darren spoke larynx-tangling guttural syllables. Light flared. Even when the brightness forced Stephen to close his eyes, he could still see Rutspud's form at the heart of it.

Lennox put a glass of lemonade down on the table in front of Stephen.

"Thank you."

The words came out of his mouth automatically, with no input from his conscious mind. Stephen's mind was barely conscious at all. It was numb, frozen and didn't want to be anything else.

The bar of the Boldmere Oak was back to its original almost-tidy self. Smashed glasses had been magically un-smashed. Spirit optics were back on the wall, their contents behaving themselves again. The herd of tables had returned to their homes and were now still. Stephen's hands were once again those of a man who was not yet middle-aged but had certainly filled out the necessary paperwork.

Lennox crouched to roll up the circle of lino.

"Don't touch him," said Stephen.

Lennox stopped. He put his hands on his knees and looked at Stephen.

"There's nothing left of him. Not even... not even anything."

He was right. There was dust on the floorboards, but it could have easily been regular pub floor dust. There was nothing left of Rutspud.

Stephen closed his eyes and wondered why he wasn't crying.

"Just... leave him, Lennox. Please."

Lackring the demon sat on the bar, the handset of the pub telephone against his ear.

"Hello? Hello?"

He saw Stephen looking, waved and gave him a smile. It was a weak smile, a fragile thing, but Lackring was giving it a bit of exercise, building it up.

"Hello? Police? Yes, I'd like to report a woman who has been threatening people with a gun. Yep. Number four Birlings Close. She keeps it in the beside drawer. Be careful. She's dangerous, that one. Name? Merilyn Rees. Oh, you want my name? Well, you can't have it. I'm using it."

Lackring hung up and gave Stephen another smile, a better one.

"Do you want to go home?" said Stephen.

"Home?" said Lackring.

"Hell. I can give you a lift."

Lackring jumped down from the bar which was a 'yes' of sorts.

As they stepped outside, a man clearly in need of a drink barged past them and into the pub.

"Lambrini me, Lennox, my man!" he declared loudly and then the door swung shut.

The sky above Stephen and Lackring was clear and the sun was shining.

"This world needs a roof over it," said Lackring. "Can't trust a place that doesn't have a ceiling."

"That's what Rutspud said to me," said Stephen. "I once made the mistake of telling him how far away the sun really is."

"How far away is it?"

"What kind of answer wouldn't freak you out?"

"A hundred feet. Two hundred."

"Yeah, that's about right," said Stephen.

Ed and Darren came up to them, the latter's Jesus-emerges-from-the-disco-vagina jumper restored to its old hideous glory.

"Guess what?" said Ed. "Sutton tornado is trending on Twitter."

"Some have even suggested it's the reason animals have been behaving oddly of late," said Darren.

A squirrel watched them from an overhanging tree. Stephen waved at it. The squirrel didn't wave back. Of course, it didn't; it was just a squirrel.

"And the rubbish chasing after people?" said Stephen. "The magic ban on swearing? Were they caused by the tornado?"

"No one's said that yet," said Ed, "but give 'em time."

Stephen looked at Ed. There was still unfinished business between them. It would have to be addressed eventually. A thought struck Stephen.

"Ooh!" he declared. "I've got something for you!"

"A good thing?" said Ed.

"The best. We need to get my car first. It's still outside Merilyn's, unless it took itself somewhere else. Up for a walk?"

"I can call us a cab," said Lackring, produced a desiccated rat corpse and prodded it expectantly. "Battery's dead," he tutted.

They walked.

They passed two police cars going the other way as they entered Birlings Close. Outside number four (which was a perfectly innocuous suburban house and not a massive castle at all) was a Trabant car and a confused Alvin Rees holding a pug dog.

"They arrested her," he said.

"Yes," said Stephen.

"It was the oddest thing. I was pairing socks and..."

He stared into the middle-distance, bewildered. Lackring poked the pug dog. The pug yipped at him.

"Mr Rees," said Darren, "my mum left a book round here earlier. She asked me to come collect it."

"A book?"

"Probably on the kitchen table," suggested Ed.

Alvin Rees nodded absently, still staring.

Darren collected the Krakovian *Livre des Esperitz*. Three men and a demon squeezed into the unaccommodating East German car and Stephen drove them back to Darren's house.

Mo Pottersmore and Winnie Churchill were in the kitchen, looking for all the world like two naughty children who knew they had done wrong and had been told the dreaded words: 'wait 'til your father gets home.' Seeing Stephen, they stammered and stuttered and tripped over their own apologies.

"It's not me you have to say sorry to," said Stephen, putting a hand on Lackring's shoulder.

Their apologies to the demon were profuse and babbling. Winnie even got down on her knees. Darren looked at his mum with a mixture of pity and condemnation. Unfinished business there too, thought Stephen.

"Just remember," said Stephen in a stern voice that did not come naturally to a mild-mannered man, "I have friends upstairs. And down."

He went through to the living room, prepared to make his gift to Ed and saw that the case wasn't there.

"It's not here," he said.

"What's not?" said Ed.

"Damn it," said Stephen. "The wish was undone."

"What wish?"

He clicked his fingers. "To the canal!"

The others hurried to keep up.

A kick in the shins and suddenly he had legs.

A stomp on the belly and, at once, he had a body, a torso, arms.

A bigger hoof-strike to the head and he had a face. He had a mouth and eyes. He had a brain.

He opened his eyes.

Jeremy Clovenhoof looked down at him like he was something he had just scraped from the bottom of his hoofs. He *was* something he had just scraped from the bottom of his hoofs.

"Get up, Rutspud. You've got work to do," said Clovenhoof and drained the last of a glass of what looked like fizzy piss.

Rutspud sat up on the floor of the Boldmere Oak in his freshly-reformed body.

"Work?"

"Yeah. You distract Lennox while I nip behind the bar and steal a bottle of sweet, sweet Lambo."

"Don't you dare," said Lennox, coming round the bar and slipping on his coat. He stared at Rutspud. "Where did you come from?"

"I have no idea," said Rutspud honestly. "Where's Stephen?"

"Down by the canal. Got the text from Darren. He reckons Stephen's having a mental breakdown or something. Come on."

Rutspud followed Lennox across town. Lennox had long legs and Rutspud had to run to keep up. Not that he minded. He'd only recently been in a state of having no legs at all (or arms or body or anything) and that put him in the mood for a good run.

Lennox stopped suddenly on a bridge and looked over the iron parapet. Rutspud had to haul himself up to see over.

Darren and Ed stood on the towpath. Stephen was in the swirling brown water, up to his chest. A little way along the bank, Lackring sat with his feet in the water and a fishing rod fashioned from a dead branch in his hands. There was no line on the fishing rod but that didn't seem to bother Lackring.

"Nearly got it that time," Stephen said. "One more tug and..."

He threw himself under and there was nothing but ripples for several seconds. A curious duck drifted over and then flapped away when Stephen surfaced, gasping and weighed down by a filth-encrusted box.

"Here! Here!" he said, struggling to propel the case to the bank. Darren leaned over and took it from him. The weight nearly pulled the big man in, but Ed grabbed his belt and helped him back from the brink.

"What is this?" said Ed.

"Suitcase," panted Stephen and, like a fish trying to get a head-start up the evolutionary ladder, flopped onto dry land.

"We can see it's a suitcase," said Darren. "How did you know it was down there?"

"Because I put it there. I dropped it there."

Ed gave him a startled look and fumbled at the catches. They wouldn't open. A moment later he had some suspicious-looking tools in his hands and was working the rusted catches and forcing them open. The rotting lid flew back. Inside, there was a big square package, wrapped and double-wrapped in waterproof cellophane. Rutspud could make out colourful printing through the opaque surface.

"This..." said Ed. His hands were shaking.

"Mana Clash cards," said Stephen.

"The *Dimensions* expansion cards?" said Darren.

"Each card worth up to two grand, wasn't it?" said Stephen.

Ed was speechless.

"They are yours, Ed," said Stephen. "It's not enough of an apology I know but –"

Ed hugged him tightly, squeezing brown water from his soggy habit. "It's a bloody start, Steve-O. It's a bloody start." He pulled away. "You're sopping wet, mate."

"And you look stupid," Rutspud called down.

Stephen brushed mud away from his eyes.

"But you died!"

"Never lived."

The idiot grin blossoming on Stephen's face made him look even stupider.

"I told you it was going to be okay," said Rutspud.

Stephen laughed. "Get down here."

"No way," said Rutspud. "Not unless you promise not to hug me. Or dry off first."

"Or?" said Stephen.

Rutspud shrugged. "Or."

The Authors

Heide Goody and Iain Grant are married, but not to each other. Heide lives in North Warwickshire with her husband and children. Iain lives in south Birmingham with his wife and children.

CPSIA information can be obtained
at www.ICGtesting.com
Printed in the USA
LVHW111536030120
642458LV00001B/188/P